HeartshoT

Steven F. Havill

HeartshoT

Happy Birthday,
Chris.
Best wishes,
Steven Havill
10/24/92

A · THOMAS · DUNNE · BOOK

St. Martin's Press
New York

Design by Dawn Niles

Library of Congress Cataloging-in-Publication Data

Havill, Steven.
    Heartshot / Steven F. Havill.
        p.   cm.
    "A Thomas Dunne book."
    ISBN 0-312-05442-4
    I. Title.
PS3558.A785H4   1991
813'.54—dc20   90-15554
                                            CIP

First Edition: March 1991
10 9 8 7 6 5 4 3 2 1

For Kathleen,
Who put up with all the late hours in good humor,
and offered encouragement when it was most needed.

ACKNOWLEDGMENTS

Several people were generous in assisting with technical information that I used in this novel. I would like to thank the Yates County Sheriff's Department of Yates County, New York, and Chief Beverly Aragon of the Ramah, New Mexico, Police Department. Special thanks to pilots Tom Humphries, Charles K. Gunderson, John Mabry, and David Stewart, and particularly to Stewart Brothers Drilling Co. for the time spent in their Cessna T-210.

1

The sheriff leaned against the doorjamb of my office without saying a word, lounging there until I finally decided to notice him. I grunted what could have been a greeting, and that broke my chain of concentration. I punched the wrong goddamn key, swore, wound the platen up, and began to smear the mess on the paper some more with that miserable white correction fluid that flakes all over everything when it dries.

"Thirty-five thousand dollars' worth of computers, and you still pound that thing," Sheriff Martin Holman said. I glanced at him without much interest. He blew across a full cup of coffee as if the stuff was hot. If it came out of the vending machine down the hall, it wasn't.

"Us antiques got to stick together," I said. I wound the paper back down to retype over the blotch, groping in my shirt pocket for a cigarette with my other hand.

"Did anyone show you that on a computer you can make corrections on the screen, and when it prints out, it's a perfect copy?"

"No shit."

"I mean, you don't have to go through all that." He waved a hand at my typewriter, and I took a minute to light the cigarette. I leaned back in my chair until its springs squawled, and looked at Holman. He'd just been elected, and we were stuck with him for at least four years. A goddamned used-car salesman. He spent a lot of time trying to figure out who was on his side.

"Did you need something in particular?" I asked.

"Uh, no. You want some coffee?"

"No, thanks." He did want something . . . I could see it wiggling around inside that skull of his every time he shifted his baby-blue eyes.

"You know," Holman said, and pushed himself away from the jamb, "I'm working up sort of a department profile for the newspaper . . . nothing formal, but you know, all the publicity we can get helps. And I was looking in your folder, and wanted to check all those years."

"Those years?"

"Right." He cleared his throat. "How long were you in the service, anyway? Twenty years?" I nodded and waited. "Twenty years. Damn. You went in right after the war?"

"In 1946."

He shook his head in wonder. "That's what I thought . . . I figured twenty in the service, and twenty for this department." He grinned at the wonder of his mathematics, and I began to get the uneasy feeling that the son of a bitch was trying for more than historical accuracy in a press release. "And you must have been about twenty when you went into the service . . . eighteen, twenty, about that."

He was about to say something else when the radio just behind him came to life. "PCS, three-oh-six." Holman turned and looked at the radio. The dispatcher wasn't in his room, which adjoined my office, but Holman made no move. "PCS, three-oh-six," cracked again, and this time Holman took two steps, reached out and pushed the transmit bar of the microphone stand.

"Go ahead, three-oh-six," And while he waited, he asked me, "That's Baker, isn't it?"

"Yeah." I returned my attention to the paperwork in my typewriter, only half-hearing Deputy Baker say that he would be at home for a while. Holman acknowledged and keyed off. He reappeared in my doorway. "When's his baby due?"

"Anytime." These days, Baker checked in at home at least twenty times during each shift as his wife podded out with their first kid.

Holman sipped the coffee again. "And so," he continued, "you served from '46 to '66. And you got to see Korea?"

"Twice. Not much to see either time."

"Just them oriental beauties, eh?" Holman leered with a fake Oakie accent, and I just offered a little sniff of amusement as I penned corrections on my paper. "What rank did you retire with?"

I turned my head and gazed at him for a minute, wondering what the hell he was after, then decided I wasn't going to play games. "Gunnery sergeant."

Holman nodded, as if weighing rank against years and concluding something profound. "Damn, that means you joined this department in 1966."

"That's right. Eduardo Salcido was sheriff then." Salcido was probably the most popular sheriff ever elected in Posadas County, and I got a twinge of pleasure out of reminding Holman about Salcido's good sense in hiring me. And yes, it had been a long twenty years. Now, I was just finishing up twelve years as undersheriff. I didn't need to be reminded that, since I didn't have civil service protection, this newly minted politico could tell me to take a walk, anytime.

The dispatcher, just returning from a trip to the can, plopped down in front of the radio, and Holman turned to greet him. I was glad for the interruption, even though I thought less of J. J. Murton than I did of Holman. Murton, a runty, tangle-tongued illiterate whom I had nicknamed "Miracle," fawned enough over the

3

sheriff to earn himself membership in a goddamned kennel club.

"Well, I need to go," Holman announced. "Bill, see you this afternoon."

"Yeah," I said. I folded the report into a manila envelope, walked into the dispatch room, and chucked the envelope into Detective Estelle Reyes's mailbox. Miracle Murton watched a little nervously. Sweat beaded on his bald spot.

"Are you workin' the parade, Mr. Gastner?" he asked.

"Why?"

Murton looked flustered. "I was just tryin' to get straight in my mind who was workin' when."

I pointed at the laminate board that was screwed to the wall just above the radio. The various deputies' names, printed neatly on magnetic blocks, were arranged in the usual weekly schedule. "You might ask yourself why we bother to put that there," I said, and Miracle cringed . . . who knows why, except he was scared to death of me. That was all right. It kept him from being a total screw-up as a part-time, days-only dispatcher. In days gone by, Sheriff Salcido wouldn't have tolerated Murton's incompetence for fifteen seconds. I had a suspicion that the son of a bitch was distantly related to one of the county legislators. That would appeal to Holman, too. I reached up and took a set of keys off the board.

"I'm taking three-ten," I said. "The trustees did wash it, didn't they?"

"They sure did. Waxed it, too."

"Wonderful. I love parades, don't you?" I didn't wait for Murton to figure out an answer.

And the parade was all right as parades go. The weather on that July Fourth was hot and clear, with a hint of the afternoon thunderheads that would bloom along the horizon above the jagged San Cristobal moun-

4

tains separating us from Mexico. I had no intention of being in the parade that plodded up the wide, dusty street of Posadas, but I enjoyed watching the color. Posadas needed all the color it could get, since it wasn't much more than a scruffy wide spot, a watering hole for tourists hurrying to get somewhere else. July Fourth was a big shindig, with the parade officially opening the holiday arts and crafts fair in the small town square. For two days, the law turned its back on alcoholic beverages in public places, and the aroma of Indian fry bread became so thick it blanked out even the red dust. I parked at a cross street, blocking traffic with 310 while I stood out in the sun with the crowd. By the time the thirtieth unit of the parade passed, I had cleared the office politics out of my head and started to enjoy the scenery.

The high school pom-pom team rode by, sitting pretty on hay bales piled on a flatbed. I waved at one of them whom I'd known since she was born, and then my good mood was ruined. The cheerleaders were throwing penny candy out to the crowds along the street, and just to my right was a fat little kid, maybe four years old, busy scrambling for the goodies. He came up with a piece of pink bubble gum and saw me. His eyes took in all the bright, shining hardware on my belt, the colorful patches on the uniform shirt, and the tan Stetson. He kept looking at me as he backed uncertainly toward his mother's legs. When he was firmly nestled there, he looked up at her and said, "How come he's so fat, Mommy?"

I guess I was standing far enough away that the mother, blond and fat herself, thought I hadn't heard. She bent down and patted the little brute's stomach and murmured, "Watch the parade, Jerry. He's just old, that's all."

I turned so I could ignore them both, and after five minutes gave up on sucking in my gut. Hell, 210 pounds for five feet eight inches wasn't that bad. It's just that the extra pounds tended to collect immediately behind the Sam Browne belt. I crossed my arms and stood comfortably, leaning against the gleaming white fender of the county patrol car. In a minute, I felt a hand on my elbow.

I turned and saw Benny Fernandez, a blocky man shorter than me by a foot. "You ought to get some business out of all this," I said. Benny owned a fast-food joint down the street that would be mobbed after the parade broke up.

"Hey, maybe," he said. "How you doin', Bill?"

"All right."

He joined me in leaning against the car. "How's that boy of yours?"

"Which one?"

Benny looked puzzled. "Don't you have a boy who's out on the Coast or something?"

I laughed. "I got one on the West Coast, and one down in Corpus. And a daughter in Flint, Michigan, and another one in New Britain, Connecticut."

"Hey, that's something," Benny said, having already forgotten what I'd said. "I got relatives all over this state, man, and when we all get together . . ." He rolled his eyes heavenward. "Hey, and talkin' about parties . . ."

"Were we?" I lifted a hand in casual salute as two New Mexico State Police units rolled by, their grille lights pulsing.

"You know what I heard?"

"What did you hear?" I smiled and waved at the Eastern Star ladies, one of whom was particularly attractive, even if silver-haired. She was perched on a hay bale in the back of a new pickup truck, lending moral support to someone pretending to be the Statue of Liberty. I caught her eye, and she threw a handful of penny candy my way. I reached up a finger and tipped my Stetson . . . and ignored the candy.

"I keep hearin' about a party tonight."

6

"So what?" I remembered then that Benny's boy had been nailed a month or so ago by the state cops for driving while intoxicated, and that had just about turned Benny's nice little conservative, parochial world inside out. Somehow it was all right to sneak the twenty miles south, cross the border to raise all kinds of hell in a little cantina somewhere, and return home without disturbing the old folks in Posadas. "It's summer. A kegger or two goes with the territory."

"Well, maybe," he continued lamely, "I just thought I'd mention it to you, you know? I mean, the kids at the restaurant, they were talkin', you know. I thought I'd just mention it."

"We'll keep an eye out, Benny. We'll check up at the lake." Our "lake" was just a seepage-filled mining pit up on the mesa, adjoining the National Forest. The water there was clear, cold, attractive, and dangerous as hell.

"I'm still worried about the boy, you know? Ricky, he's pretty headstrong."

And DWI-prone, I thought. Keep the little bastard home, then. I said, "Tell you what, Benny. I'm going to be out and around tonight. I'll pass the word to the other deputies, too. If I see Ricky, I'll throw him in jail for you until morning."

"Hey, now, you don't have to do that, Bill," Benny protested, grinning. "He's not a bad kid, I mean. But I thought maybe I should talk to you. Then I saw you here, and I just thought . . ." He fluttered his hands. Nothing like convenience when a man has a problem.

I straightened my shoulders and hitched up my gun belt as I painted on my best public servant's face. "Tell the kid to keep 'er slow." Benny sidled away with a half-hearted wave of his hand, eager to be back in his restaurant slinging burgers.

I could see the last unit of the parade, the antique fire engine owned by the Posadas Volunteers, and figured it was time to beat the crowds out. I started 310, and as I waited for the fire engine, saw the fat little kid who'd tweaked my mood with the comment about my gut. When I pulled 310 out onto Bustos Avenue, I glowered at him, waved an index finger, and said, "Eight points." The patrol car's window was up, but I think he understood me. He jumped back up onto the curb, seeking Mama.

2

By dusk, I'd had enough of parades, crowds, and noise. I drove up the smooth macadam of County Road 43, away from Posadas. The crowds would be gathering in the village park for the July Fourth fireworks display. The peace and quiet of the mesa top would be a good place to watch the rockets . . . not that I was in the mood for fireworks.

The road wound through the foothills that hid Consolidated Ore's abandoned mine from casual view, and then passed within a quarter mile of the lake, one of the county's most popular party spots. I turned off onto the dirt road and kept it slow and easy, windows down, radio turned low. There wasn't much to listen to except the crunch of the big LTD's radials on gravel.

The lake covered about three acres, and its attraction was obvious. Sheer rocks formed most of the perimeter, leaving only a hundred yards of semi-smooth, approachable shoreline. If you don't think it was fun to stand on those sheer palisades on a hot summer night and dive off into the deep, cold water, then you ain't never been a kid, as they say. Consolidated Ore had fenced the lake off and posted threatening signs every fifty feet. The Forest Service, whose land abutted Consolidated's, had fenced it from their side. Most of the fences still stood, wires gleaming. The posted signs that remained here and there still carried portions of their original messages. The fences and signs served no useful purpose. Kids just parked outside the wire and slipped through. Or they cut it to make gates. Or just drove through it with four-by-fours until the wire was a useless snarl.

Along the short stretch of shoreline, dark smudges marked previous campfires. A favorite spot was over where the south palisade started, under a rock outcrop that protected the fire from winds and casual view. The rock was smoke-smudged from years of kids watching the embers pop while they worked up courage to do more entertaining things. Part of the attraction, I guess, was to see if you could get plastered before someone came along and told you to scram. Not many kids had drowned in the lake . . . there was enough of an aura about it that they were careful, even when drunk.

From where I parked, I could see that the shoreline and palisades were deserted. I figured that if I checked back around ten that night, I'd nail any party in the early stages. I headed away from the lake and the mine and spent an hour or so cruising the back roads. I left the busy state highways and county roads to the other two deputies . . . they were thirty-five years younger than me, and eager. Had it not been for Baker's pregnant wife, I wouldn't even have been working. Todd Baker was a nervous Nellie. I had offered to sit his shift for him, and he'd jumped at the chance. It was no sacrifice on my part. We rarely had three deputies working anyway . . . just on a few busy holidays. The extra coverage almost always turned out to be a waste. I figured to catch up on paperwork later on.

Deputy Bob Torrez jabbered away on the radio, passing license plate numbers to our dispatcher. He was working radar hard, keeping the tourists honest on the state highway. The other deputy, big, slow-talking

Howard Bishop, kept quiet. He hated paperwork more than any man I knew, and wrote fewer traffic tickets than I did. If it had been up to him, our combined county files—enforcement, assessor, clerk, highway, everything—would have totaled about two papers. I was constantly on his tail, but it didn't do any good. Bishop had aspirations toward the FBI, but he wasn't going to make it, not with his allergy to pencilwork.

A couple of minutes after nine, I stopped at one of the big chain motels that had sprung up near the interstate interchange southeast of Posadas. They had a coffee shop and, with one exception, miserable food. Their iced tea, though, was rich and dark and delectable. I strolled inside. A guy in electric-blue Bermudas was at the register paying his bill, and he looked me up and down with interest.

He nodded a greeting and then, as I started to step by, asked, "Much hassle getting over the border and back?"

"Depends what you're trying to smuggle across," I said. I didn't crack a smile, and he blanched, then tried a weak laugh. I fumbled for a cigarette, and when he saw that it wasn't cuffs I was reaching for, he decided I was kidding.

"Me and the missus are going over tomorrow, unless it's a hassle; then to hell with it, you know what I mean?"

"It's no hassle," I said, and lit the cigarette. "Just follow the rules. Stick with the limits. No problems at all. Very pleasant people."

"Oh, yeah?" He sounded relieved.

"Yes." I fed him the usual customs line. "Just remember that our laws are not their laws." If he read the little Border Patrol pamphlet they'd hand him eighteen miles south at the port of entry, he'd see it in print.

Joe Tourist looked a little more interested. "You lived in these parts for some time?"

11

"Twenty years."

"Much drug running?"

I shrugged. "Same as anywhere along the border. Probably not as much as in Cleveland." One of his eyebrows shot up, so I must have been close. "Have a pleasant trip." I took a seat by the window. The lights outside illuminated the interchange, and I watched the traffic for a little while, sipping the tea. If the village was popping off fireworks, the displays were out of view, behind the motel. I enjoyed two minutes of peace and quiet before Tina, the waitress, came to my table to tell me I was wanted on the telephone.

The dispatcher that night, Gayle Sedillos, was efficient. She knew my hangouts, and was as astute as Miracle Murton was stupid. I said, "Gastner," and she said, "Bob Torrez wants your help with a motor vehicle accident. He called for two ambulances already. County Road 43, one mile south of the lake."

"I'm on my way." I left the coffee shop without paying and seconds later 310 spun parking lot gravel and then chirped onto pavement, engine bellowing. Not more than ten seconds later, Torrez was on the radio.

"Three-ten, three-oh-seven. Ten-twenty?"

"Three-ten ETA in six minutes." That was optimistic, since the lake was twelve miles away. But most of it was open road, and the Ford could sit fat and comfortable at a hundred.

Torrez acknowledged, then added, "Strawberry jam." He'd been a deputy for five years, and in that time had acquired his share of the graveyard humor that kept us all sane. And I knew what he meant, as did anyone else who knew him even a little and was listening to the scanner. I cussed and backed off a little as I flashed through an intersection, then punched 310 hard up the hill.

The wrecked car had been heading downhill when it shot off the outside of a gradual sweeping curve. As I

pulled to a stop, I could see in the glare of my headlights where the tires had first scattered the loose cin-
ders of the shoulder. It was a Firebird, maybe six or
seven years old, the kind with the big decal on the hood.
One of the emergency units had arrived, but the scanner
ghouls hadn't, so there were no spectators underfoot yet.
I heard the wail of other sirens as I scrambled down the
bank, my way illuminated by the spotlights from above.
The car had been airborne for the better part of 160
feet. Then it hit a rock outcrop and stopped dead,
pounded into shapeless junk. The rescue crew was working with the gas-powered jaws and a half dozen wrecking bars. Torrez's face was pale.

"They ran," he said to me between breaths. He was
working to tear a mangled door ajar. His bare hands and
the wrecking bar weren't going to do the job. "They
were up at the lake, and I rolled in. I pulled up behind
'em just to check, you know, and they lit out. I stayed
well back, 'cause I didn't want this to happen."

"You're going to have to go in from the other side,"
I said, and looked back up the bank.

"They were doin' at least a hundred, sir. Had to
have been."

I could hear the hot, twisted metal pinging gently
as it cooled. "How many?" I asked. The car was partially
on its side, nosed into the rock like a big missile. From
mangled plastic in front to the tip of its cooling ex-
hausts, the wreck was now no more than ten feet long.

"We're not sure yet," Torrez said. "Can't see
nothin'."

"Christ," I muttered. I scrambled over rocks and
through weeds to where one of the emergency medical
technicians worked the power jaws.

"I can reach one here," he shouted, and other hands
took the jaws. He almost had to lie down to see. "A
touch more," he shouted, and the jaws groaned metal a
fraction of an inch. "I can see most of it now. Shit."

There was a moment of silence, punctuated only by the idling motor of the jaws. We saw him twist a little, and then I caught a glimpse of light from his flashlight through a small crack.

"How many?" I shouted to him.

"Five," he replied. "At least I think it's five." He wormed his way back out, looking sick. "You'll have to peel the lid off, Bart," he yelled. The car had hit so hard that it had folded in the middle. The roof had crumpled in, and I guessed that the top of the fire wall was no more than three feet from the back deck.

The EMTs continued to struggle, and I worked my way back up the bank. Gayle Sedillos had already called Emerson Clark, the coroner, and Detective Estelle Reyes. I made sure one of the deputies was available to help old man Clark down to the wreck scene when he arrived, and then I met Estelle Reyes as her car rolled to a stop. If she was apprehensive, she didn't show it.

"You need a hand with anything?" I asked as she hauled a briefcase and a small suitcase out of the county car's trunk. She was a small, slender girl, but it wasn't her physical strength that I was worried about.

"No," she said, already looking for the best route down the hill. I let her go, and corralled Howard Bishop into managing traffic and the growing ring of spectators. The scanner ghouls were out in force now. In another ten minutes, there would be no place to park along the shoulder of the road. Most of the curious stood back where we told them, quiet and shocked. Some wanted to know who was in the car, some just wanted to look at mangled flesh.

As the EMTs took the car apart, Estelle Reyes's electronic flash ripped harsh light into the car again and again. Eventually enough metal was can-openered loose so that we could make some progress. Clark arrived. He was a semi-retired orthopedic surgeon, and a damn good coroner. He stood grimly by, and as the victims were reached, he stepped forward and pronounced them, one after the other, dead. Reyes took more pictures. I could see that figuring out where each one had been sitting before the impact wasn't going to be easy. In this case, the only obvious one was the driver himself. Not content with the original, he'd bought a new steering wheel at one of those discount houses. The spokes were cheap spring steel. They hadn't broken, but the spokes had folded forward as the heavy engine drove the column back. It was difficult to pull the kid off the steering column, since the fancy hub of the steering wheel had tangled in the remains of his seat back after crushing through his chest. The EMTs were still working to remove him when I heard shouts up on the road. I glanced up and saw Bishop, illuminated in the headlights, physically restraining Benny Fernandez. I scrambled up the bank.

"Benny," I shouted over his babbling, "we're not going to let you go down there."

"Ricky," he sobbed, and lunged toward the bank. Bishop hugged him still.

"We'll do all we can, Benny," I said, and helped Bishop carry the man away from the shoulder of the road, guiding him toward my car.

Someone came up and started talking to Fernandez, and I snapped, "Get out of here." I held Benny's arm. "Get in the car, Benny."

"They called me at the store," he said. "They said it was his car."

"It's his car, Benny." I silently cursed the idiot who thought he was doing the man a favor. It's bad enough when a cop and a priest pound on the door at two in the morning. There was no call for this.

"The hospital," Benny said, pathetically hopeful. "They'll take him to the hospital, won't they?"

"Yes. Maybe you should go there and wait. I'll have Deputy Bishop take you down."

He made for the door handle, and before he could

15

pull it, I snapped down the electric locks. "Benny, let the deputy take you down. You're in no shape to drive. I'll make sure one of the other officers takes your car down for you." He slumped a little, then nodded, beginning to give up. I flipped on the PA switch of the radio. "Deputy Bishop," I said, and thirty feet away, Howard turned around. I waved him over. "Would you drive Mr. Fernandez down to All Saints'? I'll handle things up here."

Bishop nodded, and Fernandez was gone before they started to bring up the body bags. The thought struck me later that Benny hadn't even asked if his son was dead. And like a gutless wonder, I had avoided being the one to break the news. No more parents showed up at the site. But by then, Bishop would have found a telephone and called the names to Gayle, and she would have started lining up the appropriate clergy. At eighteen minutes after two, Les Atawene backed up his big diesel tow truck so that the rear duals were within a foot of the embankment. Bob Torrez and I cleared the crowds back.

"Damn it, aren't any of you folks sleepy yet?" I shouted at a group of stubborn ones. "Why the hell do you make us work around you!" One of them persisted in standing in the wrecker's way, and Les tapped the air horn. The guy said something obscene, and I heard it. "Just run over the son of a bitch," I barked at Les. The man flashed his middle finger at me, but he stepped out of the way, so I ignored him. Les hauled the heavy cable down to the wreck and saw right away that he had problems. If he hitched on to the only part of the car that was completely in the clear, about all he'd pull up the bank was a ruptured rear quarter. He stood and looked for a minute. The big wrecker's floodlights made it artificial noontime. He and his boy finally circled the cable completely around the wreck, from front to back, top to bottom. When the winch began to tighten, the cable pulled the wreck together into one not-so-neat ball. But it stayed together, and up the hill it came, groaning and twitching and smoking like some living thing.

As the mess crept up the hill, I saw Estelle Reyes crouching low, looking inside the car. She probed with the flashlight, then waved the beam quickly up the hill at Les. "Stop it a minute!"

Les did, patient as ever. "Careful around that, miss," he called. "Everything's kinda loose."

"You better believe that," I heard Estelle Reyes say. She stood up, face impassive, and waved a hand. "Okay, pull it another foot or so, and stop." She glanced around and caught my eye, then put her left hand in the crook of her right elbow and closed that arm tight, catching her hand between forearm and biceps. For a minute, I didn't understand, but then I nodded. It had been a while since I'd given blood, but I'd done the same thing when it was over, holding the small gauze pad in place over the needle hole. The tangle of metal lurched a little bit and stopped again. Estelle Reyes conferred with Torrez, and then she reached for the wrecking bar that Torrez still held. She worked intently, wrenching and prying, and Torrez stood back and watched. The whole ball of metal shook. When a piece of bodywork curled open just right, she took more pictures—she must have been on her fifth roll. She stopped taking pictures and scrambled up the bank. "No, not yet," she shouted when Les moved a hand toward the winch controls.

"Let me borrow your slicker, sir," she said to me. In the sixteen months she'd been with the department, she'd never called me anything but that. Not Bill, not Gastner. Just "sir."

"Is there very much?" I asked.

"A kilo, maybe." She took the folded rain slicker that I dug out of the trunk of 310.

"Grass?"

"No." She raised an eyebrow and shook her head. "It must have been under the front seat originally."

"With that kind of impact, it could have started out anywhere."

"True." Estelle Reyes took the slicker back down the hill, and I went with her this time, standing between her and the spectators. She made the transfer slick and fast, then backed away, holding the small bundle under her arm. "We'll have to take the car apart bolt by bolt. I'll have Les put it down in one of his bays. That way we can have a little security." She sounded as confident as a ten-year veteran.

Shortly after three, Estelle Reyes was satisfied that she had gleaned all she could until morning. She had an exhaustive inventory of personal effects. She had photos of skid marks, dirt tracks, grease blotches in grass, bent metal, and torn people. She was a methodical worker, and used a 35-mm with tripod, flash, filters, the works. A goddamned artist. And after each shot, she stopped to make notations in her field book. The rest of us, including me, did as she asked. And now, because the little package had changed the complexion of the crash, Estelle was extra careful.

Finally, the car was gone, the debris collected. When Detective Reyes was sure she needed no more pictures of the scene, she held up her hands. "All right," she said. "We can secure this area until morning. Daylight might find us something. Torrez or somebody needs to stay with the car. Locking it up isn't enough. I'll get down there when I can."

"He'll be there until Encinos relieves him. Eddie Mitchel is going to sit out here." Stealing from other shifts and double-timing was all we could do.

"And Bishop went to the hospital. I'll call him so he can put a lid on things down there. I should be back out about seven," Estelle Reyes said. Then she hesitated. "Before I go to the hospital, I'm going up to the lake for a quick look. Won't do much good in the dark, but you never know. Oh, and you might tell Mitchel to sit out of sight. Maybe just up the hill by the water tank. He might turn up something interesting. You never know. Somebody might be worried about their package."

"Fine," I said. "Be careful. And make sure your radio is on." We watched the rest of the traffic pull away.

"It's going to be a hell of a mess," Estelle said. "And all those poor kids."

"You'd better believe it. And we better be damn sure we don't make any mistakes. When we find out where that shit came from, I have a feeling some folks in this town will advocate a return to lynching."

"Maybe we should donate the rope." It was a line from a joke, but there was no humor on Estelle Reyes's pretty young face.

3

Sheriff Holman wasn't a cop. He spent his time playing politics and working innocuous civil cases, something he actually did pretty well. But that night he did something else that clicked my estimation of him up several notches. The dispatcher, Gayle "Wondergirl" Sedillos, had called him as soon as she knew that the crash was a multiple fatal. Holman left a small party he was hosting and drove to the office. He stayed out of our way, but when it came time for someone to notify next of kin, he took that job on himself, chauffeuring clergy here and there until the stunning message had been delivered to the four households that still remained innocent of grief.

He met with me, Estelle Reyes, and Bob Torrez around noon the next day, and he was serious. No veiled sex jokes to make Estelle blush, no cracks about my age, no ethnic jokes meant to rib Bob Torrez, who had a thin skin that way.

"Let's have it in order, short and simple," he said to me. I nodded at Estelle, who shifted in her chair, smoothed her khaki skirt, and flipped open one of the manila envelopes she carried.

"All right, this is what we've got. Four of the five kids in the car were eighteen. One, Hank Montaño, was a minor. Ricky Fernandez was driving. I think Tommy Hardy was riding shotgun. Pretty sure. Jenny Barrie was sitting left rear. Hank Montaño was sitting center rear. I'm pretty sure Isabel Gabaldon was sitting right rear."

"Why do you say 'pretty sure'?" Holman asked quietly. He held a pencil poised over a blank legal pad.

"I think what happened . . ." Estelle paused, searching for the right description. "I've heard that strange things happen sometimes in wrecks, Sheriff. In this case both Hardy and the Gabaldon girl were crushed up under the dash. Whichever one was riding in the back would have been forced past the front seat, between the seat and the collapsing door. I still need to get some details from the medical examiner. But I'm pretty sure. Both of his shoes were up front, for instance. Only one of hers was. Things like that."

Holman shook his head slowly, looking as if he wanted either to say something or vomit. He settled for, "Go on."

"There is evidence that Hardy may have turned off the ignition key."

"He what?"

"Turned the key. The driver never would, I don't think. Not at that kind of speed."

"What did the speedometer say?"

"Zero," Estelle said. "It didn't break at speed. Maybe it wasn't working. But trajectory and skid marks tell us that the car was doing well over a hundred. It had almost a quarter mile of straight road to wind out, and a big engine."

"So the kid riding shotgun got scared?"

"Maybe," Estelle said. "If Ricky Fernandez knew what was under the seat, he had good reason to panic when he saw the gum balls in his rearview mirror."

"Maybe he just thought he could get away," Holman said dubiously. "Hell, kids run from cops all the time. If they have a motorcycle, they usually succeed."

"That's true. But he must have known that the deputy got a good look at the car and knew who he was. And it should have become readily apparent that Bob wasn't pressing the chase."

"I stayed back," Torrez offered.

"So Hardy gets scared and turns the key. Wouldn't that lock the wheel?"

"No, not while the car is in drive. But it must have flustered Fernandez enough that he lost his concentration. It doesn't take much at that speed."

"And the cocaine was under the front passenger seat?"

"I think so. The way one corner of the package was wedged against the seat rail, it seems likely. The only other place is on the floor, between the Gabaldon girl's feet. That's unlikely."

Holman thought for a long minute. "So what you're saying is that it's possible that Fernandez was worried about the coke, and Hardy was just scared about driving so fast. If the drugs had been Hardy's, he would have been all for a clean, fast getaway."

"Maybe," Estelle said carefully. She reached a hand back and toyed with the bun of black hair at the back of her head, then frowned. "It's possible they all knew it was there. Or maybe just one of them knew. It's possible. We have no way of pinning the stuff on any of them, yet. When the medical examiner's report comes back, it may shed some light."

"What if they had it in their bloodstream?" Holman asked.

"Well, then obviously that ties them to it."

"And if not? If they're clean?"

"Then there's another set of possibilities."

"Including," I said, after clearing my throat, "that none of the five kids knew the coke was in the car. Maybe they were just trying to outrun the cops."

"If it isn't theirs, then whose?" When no one answered the sheriff, he added, "I mean, is Benny Fernandez a dealer now? And one more thing. Is there any possibility, any at all, that the ignition key could be turned off by the crash? Bounce back, somehow?"

"I suppose anything is possible," Estelle Reyes mused. "Especially in a crash that violent. I've never heard of it happening. Have you, sir?" She looked over at me. I shook my head.

Holman ran a hand through his salt-and-pepper hair. "So we wait until the medical examiner finishes. You found nothing else in the car?"

Estelle shook her head. "We had the warrant this morning, and tore things apart . . . what little wasn't apart already. An old roach clip in the front ashtray. That's all."

"And nothing more up on the hill."

"A couple of six packs they apparently ditched. Other than that, nothing."

Holman sat back and played with a pencil. "Wow," he said finally, like a preacher groping for a cuss word, "is there any reason why the discovery of the cocaine in the car should not be made public? The editor of the *Register* is waiting, believe me. He wants to know why we're being so vague about things."

Estelle Reyes looked over at me, and I said, "I see no reason not to make the report available. Simply say that nine hundred and fifty-three grams of a substance whose appearance is consistent with cocaine was found in the vehicle. Nothing else. Just 'investigation continuing.' That covers everything without hiding the facts."

"I see no value in that," Holman said.

"No value in what?" I shot back, not sure I understood him.

"No value in hiding anything." I relaxed. "And I like the way you phrase things, Bill. The 'appearance is consistent' bit is nice." He stood up. "What's that worth, anyway? Street value?"

Estelle shrugged. "If it's been stepped on, say ready

23

for the street, that's about a hundred and fifty thousand dollars."

"God Almighty. Five kids one month after graduation . . . and one hundred fifty grand worth of hard-core drugs. Terrific." He turned and stared out the window for a minute. "It's a long way from the big time, but it's enough for this little town. I'll talk to the press, then. I'll leave out the value until you're sure. But believe me, this is sensitive. Estelle, make sure whatever you do goes through Undersheriff Gastner." He pointed at me to underscore his serious formality. "Or myself," he added, almost as an afterthought. "You remember last year, when Dr. Sprague's daughter died from a drug OD? It about turned the good doctor into a basket case for a few months. Darlene was his only child and all . . . There was all kinds of talk, because it was the first instance in a long time that a kid in Posadas died from drug abuse, as far as we know. This is going to be worse, far worse. Bet on it. Shit like this is supposed to happen in the cities. Not out here."

It was obvious we were being dismissed, but Holman called me back when the others had left. "Bill, I want her full time on this thing, with you directly supervising."

I looked at him steadily. "All right," I said after a minute. That was the way we were organized anyway, but I said, "I've got more time than anybody else."

"It's not that," Holman said. He looked down at his desk. "You're also good at what you do." That surprised me. "And Reyes probably is too. But she's too goddamned young to . . . well, to have all the right perspectives. And I've got some ideas about this, too. Some directions that we can take if you don't turn something quickly. And I want this resolved fast. We're too close to the border for scum to get the idea they can just walk all over us. And if we don't move, the feds will, believe it. We don't need that kind of atmosphere in this town."

The more Martin Holman talked, the more he sounded like a man running after votes or a bigger county budget. Or both. But hell, I didn't care just then. I agreed with him. I wanted to hang somebody, too.

No amount of wishful thinking helped, though.
There was no evidence that leapt out of the wreckage
and shouted, "This is the way it WAS!" The medical examiner found no trace of any drug in the blood samples.
Ricky Fernandez, Jenny Barrie, and Tommy Hardy had
each consumed one beer. Whoopie. I was surprised at
that. A six-pack each would have been less surprising.
Deputy Torrez must have interrupted them at the beginning of the party. There was nothing to connect any of
the five with the bag of cocaine that had nestled down
near Isabel Gabaldon's once pretty feet.

Estelle Reyes found no fingerprints on the bag.
Nothing. Even the cocaine was generic. Nothing special.
A long way from pure, but still a pretty good deal for a
hundred fifty bucks a gram. It wasn't blended to kill
anyone instantly and it wasn't a cheap shot. Just garden-
variety, stepped-on shit that a kid could depend on.
Wonderful.

It was hard for any of us to accept that one or more
of the five kids had been into peddling junk on that
scale. The car was registered in Benny Fernandez's
name, and that was as good as any starting gate. I volunteered because I had known Benny for years, and
maybe because of some lingering guilt. Benny had taken

the time to corral me during the parade, fearful for his son's safety. We hadn't been much help. I desperately wanted to wait until after the mass funeral, but Holman gently but firmly nixed that idea.

"We need to move fast, Bill," he said, and so I found myself ringing the doorbell of 907 Mesa Crest Drive. It was a posh neighborhood, newly landscaped and as neat as something out of a gardening magazine. I parked well down the street. As I walked toward the address, I looked hard at the cars parked along the curb. About the time the folks would want some peace and quiet to deal with their grief, all the friends and neighbors would be swarming, trying to be helpful. Just before the front step, I straightened my Stetson and sucked in my gut. I took off my sunglasses and slipped them in my pocket. The doorbell was one of those multi-chimed affairs that sound like a symphony. First voices, and then the door was pulled open. I didn't know the lady who took one look at me and then squinted angry eyes.

"Hello, ma'am," I said quietly. "I'm Undersheriff William Gastner of the Posadas County Sheriff's Department. I know it's a bad time, but I need to speak with Mr. Fernandez."

"Oh, now what?" she said, first annoyed, but then with a combination of curiosity and weariness.

"I just need to speak with him, ma'am." Behind her, in the front hall of the house, I saw a couple of teenagers peeking around the corner. The woman was about to say something else when Della Fernandez strode to the door briskly, as if she were about to assault a door-to-door salesman.

"Now what do you want?" she snapped. Her eyes weren't so much reddened from weeping that I couldn't see the steel in them, even through the screen. She pushed past the woman and regarded me sharply. We knew each other enough that there was no need for more introductions.

"I need to speak with your husband, Mrs. Fernandez."

"Now? Is that really necessary?"

"Yes."

"He's with Father Vince Carey." Her thin lips compressed even thinner into two bloodless white lines. "You'll have to see him later."

I normally don't worry about tact, but this time, I actually took a second or two to weigh my options. I evaluated the stern face and said, "I need to speak with him now, Mrs. Fernandez."

She regarded me silently for a minute, then said, "I certainly wish you people would put as much effort into prevention as you do investigation well after the fact."

I took a deep, slow breath and let that zinger slide by, chalking it up to distraught emotions. "Mrs. Fernandez, before you slam that door in my face, I'll remind you of something that's common knowledge now around town. There was a kilo of cocaine found in that car. We have no idea who it belonged to. The car is registered in your husband's name. That is sufficient cause for him to be interviewed, at the very least. And when we're dealing with a felony of this magnitude, it is not something that waits, Mrs. Fernandez. In this case, it is Father Carey who will wait." I saw the lips compress some more, and knew I was making an enemy. What the hell. "Mrs. Fernandez, either I talk with your husband for a few moments now, or I return with a warrant for his arrest, and we talk down at the sheriff's office."

She muttered something in Spanish that I didn't catch, but turned away from the door. "Show him to the kitchen," she said to the woman, who remained silently fascinated.

Benny Fernandez tried hard, but he couldn't keep the reproach from his eyes or his voice. He walked into the kitchen followed closely by Father Vincent Carey.

Carey, tall and angular, touched Fernandez protectively on the elbow and nodded at me. "I'll stay, if that's acceptable with you, Bill."

"I really need to speak with Benny alone, Father. I'm sorry."

He didn't argue, just nodded and quietly left.

"I guess . . ." Benny began and stopped. He forced in a breath and looked away. "I guess it didn't do much good, eh?"

"Benny, I know it's hard, but give me five minutes, all right?" He nodded and locked his eyes on the highly polished bricks of the floor. "I'm going to be perfectly honest with you. You know about the cocaine found in the car. We have no idea who it belonged to. No link. Nothing." I paused to let that register. Benny Fernandez remained immobile, head down. "Do you have any reason to believe, any at all, that your son was involved with drugs in any way?"

Benny shook his head slowly, but looked up at me. He couldn't keep back the tears, and didn't bother to try. "Bill, you can't . . . can't imagine what it is like. It is bad enough to lose a child." He stopped and looked off through the window. "I had hopes. Some hopes. For him, I mean. Any father does, eh? But now . . ." he shrugged and turned back to me. "But to think now that maybe he was somehow involved . . ." He waved a hand helplessly in the air and sat down heavily on one of the kitchen stools. "That thought, it tears at me, Bill. And how can I know? Eh? How can I know? Sure, I can say, 'Not my boy. Ricky would never do something like that.' But in this day and age?" He reached over and yanked a tissue out of the counter dispenser and dabbed his eyes. "The only thing I can tell you, Bill, is that I pray to God . . . I really do . . . I pray to God that Ricky died knowing nothing about that stuff in his car. To think that he might . . ." but Benny Fernandez couldn't go on. He sat with his head down, hands feebly tearing at the tissue in his lap.

I patted him on the shoulder. "I appreciate you taking the time to see me, Benny. We'll do everything we can."

He nodded and pushed himself to his feet. He dabbed his eyes again and said, "I will tell you this. If my son was involved in some fashion, I will spend any time, any money, to find the people who pushed him to it. And there will be justice done for them."

"I think what happened is that Ricky just panicked, Benny. I checked the computer. He was not too many points shy of losing his license through speeding tickets. I figure he saw the lights come on and did what many kids would have done in the same situation. If he'd known the cocaine was under the seat, he would have played it cool. All the deputies knew him. They had no reason to suspect anything, except that he drove too fast too often. Benny, your son had to know that no deputy would bother to search his car."

"You cannot imagine how much I pray that you are correct, Sheriff. And tell me this. Is it true that the deputy slowed down? That he wasn't even speeding after my son's car?"

"That's what Deputy Torrez says. You know the road. He wanted to avoid exactly the kind of accident that happened."

Benny Fernandez grimaced. "Waste. Such a waste. I sit and think, how can I face those other good people? Knowing their children are . . ." He waved a hand helplessly in the air.

"I wish I had an easy answer, Benny. But I've taken enough of your time. I'll keep you posted, but I shouldn't have to bother you or your wife."

"My wife," he said, and almost managed a smile. He glanced at me almost apologetically. "She is my second wife, you know."

"I didn't know."

"Yes. Ricky is the son from my first marriage. His mother died when he was only two. With Della, I have the five daughters. The oldest is now thirteen."

"I see."

"She and Ricky never really . . ." He paused. "It was as if there was some kind of wall between them. I don't know." He straightened up, obviously realizing that what he was telling me was more in Father Carey's province than mine. His face hardened a little. "I intend to find out the answers, Sheriff. Ricky was my only son. He carried my good name. And when I find who was to blame . . ."

"The best thing you can do is stay in touch with us." I turned toward the door. "If you think of anything I should know, don't hesitate to call me, Benny. Anytime of the day or night. You have my number."

He nodded and I left the house. I always trusted gut feelings, and now my gut told me Benny Fernandez was clean as the driven snow. For my money, his wife was wacko, but that made little difference. Not the cocaine type—whatever that is. As I drove off, I tried to picture what had been going on in that charging Firebird during the last few seconds before it became tangled junk. There were too many versions, a tangled video I could replay in almost infinite variety. I thumped the steering wheel in frustration.

5

With so little physical evidence, about all we could do was talk to people. Estelle Reyes and I interviewed teenagers until they all blended together into a composite. We followed up on rumors, we upset a community of already upset folks. And we found ourselves wishing there were ten of us, instead of two.

We talked to those who hadn't been close friends of any of the deceased. They all expressed shock, of course, some for real and some because they figured it was expected of them. None of them knew anything about drugs, of course. Wide-eyed amazement that we would think such a thing. I suppose I was a little cynical. I didn't expect them to indict the whole county, but I had figured that someone would be touched hard enough to want to spill some names. Maybe that was naive on my part, but their collective innocence was irritating as well as frustrating. We figured somebody had to know something.

To interview the friends and intimates was another matter. Estelle and I compared notes frequently, and we came to the same conclusion. The incident had been a sledge between the eyes for many of them. Of course, they were depressed. Hell, they had lived through the initial shock, the talk, the rumors. They had all attended an emotionally brutal memorial service in the school gymnasium and heard the popular Father Vince Carey tell them that he had no answers for their grief and confusion. I went to the service too, but spent most of my time there just watching faces. I was in plain clothes, of course, but not so inconspicuous that I didn't collect an icy stare from Della Fernandez.

Carey had a tough time. Like most of us, he didn't know what to say. His soft voice drifted in and out of my attention, but I happened to be tuned in when he said, "And that the police investigation is continuing is ample evidence that somewhere, our generation has failed yours." That was the only mention of our work then, but of course as the days went by, the *Register* kept the coverage consistent, only shifting it to page 2 after a week when we hadn't found anything.

It wasn't all empty circles, though. I got my first hint during an interview with one of Tommy Hardy's friends. I talked to the youngster at Dial's Home Improvement Center on the west end of town, and after we were finished, my instincts told me I had hit pay dirt. I drove back to the office and prepared to play the tape for Estelle Reyes. The frustration of pounding the pavement and talking to folks who'd rather not talk had worn her nerves a little thin.

"So who is this?" she asked, as she plopped down in one of the cushioned chairs in my office.

"His name is Scott Salinger."

"I know him."

"Sure you do. So do I. If you attend a Posadas High School football game, you know Scott Salinger. He was reasonably close friends with Tommy Hardy." I punched the machine on, then sat back and smoked, feet up on the corner of my desk. Estelle sat back with her hands locked behind her head and stoically endured my cigarette smoke as she listened. Scott Salinger's voice was quiet, close to a monotone. Even though the microphone

had been held less that twelve inches from his face, it
sounded as though he were sitting across the room.

GASTNER: Would you state your full name for the
record, please.

SALINGER: Scott Alfred Salinger.

GASTNER: How old are you, Scott?

SALINGER: Seventeen, sir.

GASTNER: Did you know any of the five teenagers
killed in the accident last week?

SALINGER: I knew them all. [*Pause*] Everyone
would, in a town this small.

GASTNER: Were you friends with any of them?

SALINGER: [*After a long pause*] Tommy Hardy and
I used to hang around a lot.

GASTNER: And the others?

SALINGER: I knew them. They were a year ahead
of me in school.

GASTNER: But you and Hardy were friends?

SALINGER: Yes.

GASTNER: Close friends?

SALINGER: [*Long pause*] Yes. I guess so. We both
played football. He played basketball
and I wrestled. We were both on the
baseball team.

GASTNER: Was he your best friend?

SALINGER: [*Long pause, unintelligible word*]

GASTNER: I'm sorry, I didn't hear you.

SALINGER: I didn't say anything.

GASTNER: Was he your best friend?

SALINGER: [*Long pause*] What is it you're trying to
find out, sir?

GASTNER: We're just trying to learn all we can,
Scott. A major crime has been committed, and we have to learn all we can.

SALINGER: All right.

GASTNER: Was Tommy Hardy your closest friend?

34

SALINGER: Yes.
GASTNER: What was his relationship with the other kids in the car, as far as you know?
SALINGER: What do you mean, relationship?
GASTNER: Were they close friends?
SALINGER: He and Jenny Barrie had been going together for about six months. Pretty heavy.
GASTNER: Heavy?

At that point, Estelle Reyes shot a glance over at me as if to say, "You naive old fart, you." I shrugged. You have to ask.

SALINGER: He told me once he was thinking of getting married.
GASTNER: And what did you say to that?
SALINGER: I told him he was crazy.
GASTNER: Why is that?
SALINGER: He was in the top ten of his class. Three-point-something average, close to four. He was going to Purdue University to study electrical engineering.
GASTNER: And you thought his relationship with Jenny Barrie was going to jeopardize that?
SALINGER: I know it was. I know it did.
GASTNER: How do you know?
SALINGER: Do you know what his average was for the third nine weeks of this year?
GASTNER: Tell me.
SALINGER: He barely scraped a two-point.
GASTNER: So his love life put a dent in his scholarship. That's not unusual.
SALINGER: No. I guess not.
GASTNER: [*Long pause*] What did you think of

35

Jenny Barrie? [*Pause, no reply*] She
was a senior also, wasn't she?

SALINGER: Yes.

GASTNER: Good student? [*No reply*] I have to have
a verbal answer for the recorder, Scott.

SALINGER: She got by.

GASTNER: What does that mean?

SALINGER: She wasn't too interested in school.

GASTNER: What was she interested in?

SALINGER: You know. Playin' around.

GASTNER: She wasn't one of your favorite people,
was she.

SALINGER: [*Pause*] No, sir. She wasn't.

GASTNER: Will you tell me why? [*No reply*] Scott?

SALINGER: I've been thinkin' a lot about it lately.
The last week or so. I haven't made up
my mind yet.

GASTNER: About what?

SALINGER: [*Pause*] I don't know.

Estelle leaned forward and rested her elbows on her
knees. She watched the tape machine closely, as if she
could see the words coming off the reel.

GASTNER: We need to know, Scott. If it has anything to do with the accident, or the
contents of the car, we need to know.

SALINGER: It's just the pits, that's all.

GASTNER: What is?

SALINGER: Life. [*Pause*] Maybe it doesn't matter.
Probably be easier just to go away.

GASTNER: Go away?

SALINGER: [*Sigh*] This is my last year in school.
Get through that, then go away. College
probably. Or I was thinking maybe the
Air Force.

GASTNER: Scott, listen to me. If you have informa-

36

tion about this investigation, you'd be
doing everyone a favor by telling us.
SALINGER: Is there anything else you wanted? I
need to get back to work.
GASTNER: Don't hesitate to call me, Scott. When
you decide. Anytime of the day or
night. It doesn't matter.

I reached over and snapped off the machine. I lighted
another cigarette and Estelle stood up. "Something
there," she said. "I wonder what he knows?"

"Or," I said, "it could be that he was just bent out
of shape about Hardy. They were close friends. They're
both scholars."

"That doesn't surprise me. I knew his older
sister . . . she was also a brain."

"The school guidance office shows he's held a three-
point-eight GPA since his freshman year. Right now, he
stands about sixth in his class. He and Hardy were a
year apart, but best friends nevertheless."

"And so your theory is that he resented his friend's
infatuation?"

"Could be."

"You think there's more?"

I stood up and tucked in my uniform shirt. "Each of
those kids checks out. They seemed to be pretty much
normal, party-hardy teenagers, Estelle. Some maybe
more than others. Salinger's open dislike of Jenny Barrie
is the first hint of a crack. It may be nothing, who
knows. Probably is nothing. But I think we need to pry
a little deeper into her background. A couple other kids
said she was known as something of a wild hare. And
maybe we'll get lucky. Maybe the Salinger kid will decide that it's time to talk."

"And if he doesn't, then we're going to have to turn
up the heat. Holman's getting impatient. He keeps say-

ing he's got some ideas. He was breathing down my neck all morning."

I glanced sideways at Estelle, wondering if she was making one of her rare jokes, but her face was impassive. "Spare us from a politician who thinks," I said.

I was prepared to protest whatever harebrained idea our political sheriff was concocting—it wasn't that I actually disliked Martin Holman. But old dogs become stuck in ruts. I was used to the oldtime expertise of Holman's predecessor, Eduardo Salcido. Salcido chased criminals—he didn't chase block grants. I knew that modern departments without money didn't function worth a shit. I knew that the civil load of most sheriff's departments was ten times the criminal load. But it seemed to me that Holman spent too much time talking, and not enough time doing. And as far as I knew, the sum total of Holman's law-enforcement background was a two-week FBI school for sheriffs-elect.

Still, since he held the life of my contract in his hand, it seemed prudent to hear him out.

"Let me tell you what I plan to do," he said one afternoon when he'd managed to corner me in my office. Estelle Reyes had tried to slip away down the hall, but he waved her inside. It was very hot, maybe 105 degrees out in the sun. "Yeah, but it's dry heat," some airheads might say. One hundred five is hot . . . dry or not dry. Despite the air-conditioning in the county building, my uniform shirt was a mess of dark circles. Holman, dressed in a lightweight summer suit, looked 60 degrees.

"You no doubt are aware of the interagency drug task forces that have been pretty successful in various parts of the state." Both Estelle and I were aware, of course . . . more so than Holman. We were both polite enough not to say so. Estelle had worked records for them for two weeks shortly after she joined our department. I had been half-tempted once to work for the narcs, but the two weeks away from my hovel seemed an awfully long time. Old dogs . . . Holman continued, "I thought a minor version of that is something to try. You know Artie White up in Gallup? Chief of Police?" We both did. "I had some time at one of these law-enforcement conventions recently, and we got to talking. I was telling him about all of your experience, Bill, and he laughed and said he had the other side of the coin."

"How's that?" I asked politely.

"Chief White said he had a freshly minted patrol-man on his force who just turned twenty-one, for one thing . . . the kid couldn't even buy a legal beer until a couple months ago. And the chief said what makes it worse is that the kid is one of those long, tall bean poles who looks sixteen. Believe it or not, he's proving to be a good, careful cop."

I chuckled gently. "I wonder how he's going to do when he goes to his first bar fight and his backup never shows."

"I asked Chief White the same thing. The kid's been to a couple. The first one, he walked into this real tough joint. The two guys who were dukin' it out stopped, took one look at him and broke up laughing. He put the cuffs on both of 'em. Pretty effective. He got called to a second one, and damn near got a charge of police brutal-ity on his head. I guess he's pretty good with a night-stick. Fast as a rattlesnake."

"And so . . ." I prompted.

"And so," Holman said, "I got to thinking. Some un-dercover work is what we need, and not by some DEA hotshot, or big-time narc from the big city or from the state police. We obviously can't use our own people. They're too well known. So, I thought let's get the kid down here. Hell, we maybe can even plant him in the high school. Who's to know?"

"Some folks at the school should know, for one thing," I said.

"Why? What if the dealer is one of them? Hell, what if the damn principal is running drugs? Stranger things have happened."

"You got a point," Estelle said. "Would this guy really fit in? I mean, does he really look like a high school kid?"

"That's what White says." Holman was obviously pleased with himself.

"Let's get him down here," I said. "Maybe he'll get it all wrapped up before he has to enroll in school. And that reminds me of something we may be forgetting. Whose kid is he? I mean, he's got to be living with somebody. Nobody's going to believe a high school kid living by himself in an apartment somewhere."

Holman grinned and held up an index finger, apparently ready to make his grand point. "You have four grown children, correct?"

"So?"

Estelle had already covered her mouth with a hand to conceal the grin. She saw through Holman before I did. "So, your oldest son is what, thirty-nine?"

"So?"

"It's no secret that for the last ten years, he's had nothing but trouble with his oldest boy. A summer vacation for the rotten kid, away from home, is just the ticket. Who better for him to visit, in lieu of going to some paramilitary camp, than his old granddad, Undersheriff William C. Gastner, famous for his many exploits along the border?"

I looked at Estelle. "Have you been letting this man snort the evidence, or what?" I turned and frowned at the sheriff. "My oldest son doesn't have a son of any description. Five wonderful girls, yes. A son, rotten or otherwise, no."

"So who's to know? I mean that. How many people in this county, in this town, keep track of your grandchildren, Bill? Hell, you never talk about them."

"That's because I think that people who corral innocent bystanders with pictures and tales of their grandkids deserve to be shot."

"Bill," Holman said patiently, "even you are not that much of a curmudgeon. And once, not more than a month ago when we were all happier and more relaxed than we are now, you showed me a picture of one of yours."

I shook my head. "I would never do that."

"Then how do I know that down in Corpus Christi, Lieutenant William Gastner, Junior, and his wife Edie managed to keep little Kendal and Tadd clean long enough for a family picture? Lieutenant Gastner resplendent in flight suit? T2C Buckeye jet trainer in the background?"

"Checkmate, sir," Estelle said quietly.

"I showed you that picture?"

"Yes."

"It was a good one, wasn't it?"

Holman laughed heartily and nodded. "Thank you. That was the first time I've felt good in the past two weeks. Anyway, I want White's peach-fuzz to stay with you. What better yarn for local kids to swallow? A heavy metal shithead of a kid from out of town, occasionally bad-mouthing you as an old, worn-out symbol of law and order. Hell, that line alone ought to be worth five sales."

Estelle nodded. "Good idea. Better that than trying to hide him in the back room here. Or putting him with strangers."

"Big help you are," I muttered.

"You'll do it?"

"Do I have a choice?"

"Of course you have a choice."

"I bet. And I suppose you're going to coach him on how to treat me as an old and worn-out . . . symbolically, anyway."

"Bill, your skin is entirely too thin."

I ignored that. "When's he coming, Sheriff?"

"I called Chief White yesterday. The officer will meet you at Albuquerque International Airport Saturday at eleven A.M.

"Albuquerque! That's almost three hundred miles from here!"

"Huh," Holman said, pretending to be astounded. Then he turned reasonable. "It would look great for the kid to drive into Posadas in a Gallup patrol car, wouldn't it? Or to drive into town at all, for that matter. Your son wouldn't let him drive all the way from L.A. by himself, would he?"

"And so the idea is that he has supposedly flown into Albuquerque, and I go pick him up."

"Right."

"What's wrong with Las Cruces?"

"The major airlines from L.A. don't fly there, for one thing. Bill, picky, picky. Look, if you meet him up in Albuquerque, that gives you six hours or more for a private confab, right? Six hours to lay things out."

"He's right, sir," Estelle agreed. "And besides, between now and then, you could drop a word here and there about picking up this kid. No big deal, but any scat helps."

I looked at Estelle Reyes in astonishment. "'Any scat helps?' Where the hell did you hear that line? Christ." She grinned, looking about fourteen years old herself. I held up my hands in surrender.

"Great," Holman said. "And feel free to use a county credit card for gas."

"You are all heart, Sheriff," I said. A goddamned

kid chasing kids, I thought. Hell, maybe Scott Salinger would talk to him. Maybe Salinger would sell him a nice, fresh kilo and the kid-cop would bust the case wide open. That's all the little town of Posadas needed.

6

I reached the airport nearly an hour early, figuring to have time for breakfast and a leg-stretch before the long return drive. The place was busy. Everyone from real weirdos with turbans to an aging—relatively speaking—deputy U.S. marshal I recognized. He didn't see me, and seemed in a hurry, so I didn't bother hailing him. I probably missed some good war stories. In the corner of the restaurant, sitting back where it was dark, was a man who looked a lot like the city's mayor. He was in earnest conversation with another man who looked a lot like a popular U.S. senator. After a few minutes, a local news crew complete with minicam arrived and interrupted the quiet meeting. The senator gave them five minutes, then he and the mayor went out to the plane.

A big family pushed their way into the restaurant: fat father, pudgy mother, and an assortment of youngsters who ranged from three feet six to six feet three. I munched on the wonderfully huge, sloppy Danish and made bets about where the family was from, and where they were bound. From Terre Haute, going to Marine Land. Best bet. They headed for a table back in the area just vacated by the senator. The oldest boy—he was doing a good job of pretending the rest of his family didn't exist—changed directions without a word and headed straight at me. He was grinning from ear to ear and looking at me.

"Granddad!" he said altogether too loudly. "Here you are, hiding over behind the Danish!" I almost choked.

I wiped my mouth and stood up slowly. He extended his hand, still beaming. I had to take his hand, or it would look as if I were turning away my own kin. He gripped my hand in one of those hard two-handed squeezes, and to prevent him from shattering the arthritis I had been culturing in my right hand, I had to squeeze heartily in return.

"Gosh, you're lookin' well," he said, and motioned at the chairs. "Don't let me interrupt." He sat down first, still with that goddamned grin all over his face.

"You're observant," I said flatly, and went back to the Danish.

He dropped his voice several levels, all the while looking for the waitress. "Your sheriff told Chief White that all I had to do was just find a man who had an old-fashioned military brush cut and a mustache like Don Ameche's. I mean—" and he spread his hands expressively—"how many of you can there be?"

"That's all he said?"

Peach-Fuzz grinned. "No. But . . ."

"But what?"

He waved a hand in amusement. He was tall and skinny all right, but with the conditioning of a mid-season track star. Fighting with him would be like wrestling a steel spring. He looked sober. "Undersheriff Gastner, it's going to be a pleasure working for you. I hope we can run this thing to ground."

"Run to ground?" I said. "You've been reading too much Sherlock Holmes. It's a damn mess, is what it is. But we're grateful for any help. So, Officer Hewitt, what does a grandfather call you? Arthur? Art?"

Hewitt grinned. "My real granddad called me Punk."

"Smart man. Is he still alive?"

"No."

I nodded. "Grandparents have a way of getting old."

"He didn't die of old age. He got shot."

"Cop?"

Hewitt turned on that electric grin again. "No. He landed an oil company plane in the wrong place down in Peru. The natives were unappreciative."

"You don't seem overly grieved."

The young cop shrugged, and when the waitress finally brought his coffee, he took several minutes finding enough sugar. "He wasn't my favorite person. I'll tell you about him sometime."

"And there's got to be something better than Punk, too."

"Art would be fine." He drained the coffee. "You ready to go? I'm looking forward to hearing all about the case."

We left the restaurant and rode the escalators downstairs. A large crowd had gathered around the baggage conveyor, all hoping their suitcases hadn't gone on to Fairbanks or Miami Beach. Art Hewitt slid through the folks, watched for thirty seconds, then darted a hand out. He came back with a large brown suitcase.

"You went to all the trouble of putting that on the baggage-claim conveyor before coming upstairs?" I asked in wonder.

"Sure. Neat touch, right?"

I stopped and looked at him. "You're as much of a fruitcake as Sheriff Holman. Who in hell is going to tail me six hours north from Posadas County, Art? And for what reason?"

"You never know. Anyway, it saved me from carrying it upstairs. Where are you parked?"

I walked through the electric door and pointed. "Short-term lot."

He squinted. "The Blazer, right?"

I chuckled. "What other background information did you dig up on me?"

"Lots and lots. Your oldest son doesn't have a son, for instance."

"Aren't computers wonderful?" I put the key in the door of the Blazer. "And now you can forget all that and concentrate on what I'm going to tell you for the next six hours." He climbed in and we rolled. As he snapped the seatbelt, he said,

"So tell me."

7

Holman was waiting for me when I got to the sheriff's office the following day.

"Good trip?"

"Yup. Hewitt is a smart kid."

"What's he doing now?"

I shrugged. "Hanging out."

"Doing what?"

I chuckled and poured a cup of coffee. "I'm not sure what one does as a teenager hanging out, Sheriff. It's been a while since I was one. If you told me to hang out now, I'd probably go home and go to bed."

Holman looked a little concerned. "It's been a long week."

"And will get longer."

"Did you hear about the citizens' task force?"

"The what?"

"A certain Mrs. Wheeler has taken the bull by the horns, so to speak. She's organizing a bunch of parents. Their aim is to do something about drug abuse."

I sipped the coffee and slowly settled into my padded swivel chair. Holman sat down in the straight-backed chair under the window. "That sounds like something out of one of those dumb brochures. What is it that they plan to do?"

"I don't know. They want someone from this department to help coordinate their efforts."

"You mean someone to tell them what to do."

Holman sighed. "Yes. I suppose it would be a waste of breath to ask you if you're interested."

"All too true."

"They mean well, Bill."

"Of course. But has anyone told them that *we* don't know what to do?"

Holman smiled faintly. "No. No one told them that. I was sort of hoping that we wouldn't have to."

I tipped back in the chair as far as it would go and dug out a cigarette. "We have no leads, Sheriff. Maybe Hewitt will be able to dig up something by 'hanging out.' But I can't believe that's going to happen quickly. He told me this morning that he figured he'd break the case just about the time we were ready to kill each other."

"He's really ready to play this 'difficult grandson' bit to the hilt, then?"

"You'd better believe it. And I think he's more than half looking forward to enrolling in school here. And remember, it was your idea."

"I'll remember." He stood up. "You won't refuse to talk to a parent group if they make a specific request, will you?"

"Of course not. But they might not like what I have to say."

Holman looked wary. "And that is?"

"Well, for instance, five gets you ten that the meeting would be some evening, right?"

"Sure."

I spread my hands. "It might be more productive for them to stay home and talk with their kids, instead of leaving them alone one more time."

Holman grimaced. "Maybe I'll ask Reyes. By the

49

way, the DEA is in town. They're going to be running a chopper out of the Posadas Airport."

"Doing what? Running the border again?"

The sheriff shrugged and sidled toward the door. "Who knows. They didn't want to talk to me. Maybe they think I'm the ringleader."

I grinned. "Isn't interagency cooperation wonderful?"

"Terrific," Holman said. "Get some rest. Soon. You look awful." He left and as the door closed behind him, I muttered, "Thanks." I was tired, but I needed to think. If I stretched out for two seconds, I'd be asleep, and I didn't think well unconscious. I tossed away the coffee cup and grunted to my feet. It was a wonderfully clear day, hot and bright with puffy cumulus trooping out across the sky in even ranks. Within a block, I passed the village police unit. One of the part-time specials was sitting behind the wheel. He was reading something. Probably a Conan comic. Three months before, I had passed by and he was blowing z's, right there in public, in broad daylight. I had done the only thing possible in the circumstance. I idled the county car right up beside him, so that my right headlight was just about even with his car's door handle. Then I reached down and tapped my siren yelp. Had his head hit the roof any harder, it would have knocked him unconscious. He didn't think well of me after that.

The memory of that incident woke me up a little, and I swung east and north, planning to loop around Consolidated Ore and then head on over to Tres Mesitas, where I could find a shady, isolated spot under a piñon tree for uninterrupted thought. Or sleep.

"Three-ten, PCS."

"I don't want to," I moaned aloud, and reached for the mike. "Three-ten."

"Three-ten, ten-twelve, ten-nineteen."

"Ten-four. About four minutes."

I had no idea who was sitting in my office, waiting to talk to me, but it might bring a change of pace. Maybe my errant grandson was already in trouble. I turned around and flogged 310 back to town, driving too fast just for the exhilaration.

George Payton was waiting in my office. George was short, fat, bald, and seemed like a heart attack waiting to happen. Whenever we both lit up cigarettes in his store, we usually joked about which one of us was going to kick off first. At least we were smart enough not to make bets.

"You taking me to lunch, George?" I said as I hung my Stetson on the peg behind the door. He wiped his flushed forehead and slumped a little more.

"Gets any hotter I'm going to melt. No, no lunch. I could have called, but I was over in the Motor Vehicles office, and decided to kill all the birds at once. Your dispatcher took pity on me and agreed to hail you in."

I sat down. "So what gives?"

"Look, this is none of my business, Bill. But I guess you're discreet enough that I should tell you." He had my interest, and I leaned forward a little to encourage him. "You're a good customer at my gunshop. Hell, I got lots of good customers. But Benny Fernandez has never been a customer of mine, right?"

"How would I know that?" I said, but a nasty feeling was beginning to settle in my gut. "What happened?"

"He stopped by this morning. He spent an hour looking, very carefully. I asked him if I could help him, but he waved me off. At one point he looked at me and said, 'I've been doing some reading.' Whatever that meant. Anyway, when he was finished, he bought an entire setup."

"Meaning?"

George ticked it off on his fingers. "Nine-millimeter Beretta, that new one, like the one adopted by the army. Five boxes of ammunition. Not cheap plinkers, either, Bill. Two extra clips." He stopped and looked at me anxiously. "Hell, it isn't any of my business what people buy, as long as they can answer all the questions on the federal form. But, hey, I know what state of mind Fernandez has been in since that accident, or at least I can imagine pretty good. A man like Fernandez doesn't buy hardware like that for busting rabbits."

"No, he doesn't."

"I just thought that maybe, maybe one of you guys should know. I probably shouldn't have told you, but hell, I'm no priest or no lawyer. There's no law I can't mention it to you, is there?"

"I appreciate it. I have no idea where I heard it."

Payton got to his feet and pulled his golf shirt away from his sweaty schmo-like body. "Yeah, well. The last thing we need right now is one of those gun-toting vigilantes who goes around blowing everyone away, you know what I mean?"

"I know what you mean."

"I mean, if you came in and bought that stuff, I'd just think that maybe the county gave you a raise. And there's about fifty other good customers who might buy it and I wouldn't turn a hair. But Fernandez?" He scoffed. "I just thought you should know."

I reassured him that he'd done the right thing, and started to show him out. He suddenly stopped and turned, hand on the doorjamb.

"You remember Cuffy Oates?"

"Yes."

George nodded. "Man like him, never owned a gun in his life. Comes in the store, talkin' about how he's worried about snakes, and wants something for that. So I sell him a little inexpensive thirty-eight revolver. Remember that?"

"It wasn't your fault, George."

"No, but I never thought to question him any, either. So he goes home, turns on the television, sits down in

52

the rocker and blows his brains out." George shook his head, heaved a great sigh and turned away. "I'll see ya, Bill. Take care."

I watched him waddle off down the hall. It wouldn't have made George feel any better if I'd told him that Cuffy Oates had tried suicide about five different ways before taking the sure way out. George wanted me to do something about Fernandez. I could have gone over to the restaurant and confronted the man, asked him what the hell he was planning to do with a 9 mm cannon that could fire fifteen rounds from one clip. But he had a right to it, just like anyone else. At least we had gained a little edge if he was after something other than rabbits.

8

Hewitt and I had arranged to meet at home for dinner, and he showed up just about the time the lamb chops turned to charcoal. I had forgotten about teenage—or near-teenage—appetites. He finished three chops to my one.

"You coming off a week-long fast, or what?" I asked.

"I think I got a tape worm or something," he said. "You cook good, though."

"Most people who live alone do. It's either that or eat out all the time. I do too much of that as it is."

"Your wife died eleven years ago?" He looked at me over the top of an ear of corn.

"Yes."

"Airplane crash, wasn't it?" He had done his research thoroughly, but I had no intentions of discussing the past—especially those few minutes long ago when the airliner had fought a wind shear and lost.

"Did you make any progress today?" I asked, ignoring his question. He glanced down at his plate, embarrassed, then shook his head.

"Not really. Well, maybe some. I don't know. Tonight, maybe. I found out a couple places to check out. The burger place on Grande is one. I can probably even get me a job there. Kids hang out in that parking lot like flies on a dead dog. And there's a place out in the National Forest, too. I don't know just where."

"You mean out at the lake? Up past the old Consolidated mill?"

"No, no. Way the hell and gone out in the forest. There's some place where they can have campfires and a bunch of rocks keeps the fires out of view of the fire tower."

"Oh." I nodded and rescued another chop before they all disappeared down the human garbage disposal. "That's out County Road 21. Turn on Forest Road 420. About a mile, and turn off on Forest Road 562. Big limestone outcrop on the south side of the canyon. They call it 'the Rec Room.' They don't use it much anymore after the forest fire three years ago. That kinda spoiled the view. And the Forest Service sits on it pretty hard. If you get on the right road, you can't miss it. All kinds of graffiti on the rocks around there. You got a map?"

"Yeah. But I got to work on getting somebody to take me out there. No way you're going to let me take your Blazer, is there, Gramps?" He grinned widely.

"You got that right, punko."

"Maybe I can just hot-wire it sometime."

I ignored the thoughtful look on his face and asked, "Who'd you talk to, anyway?"

"I only found out this information after hours of resourceful digging."

"I bet. Who?"

"I stopped by the library. One of the clerks seemed to know all about it."

"If it was Mary Ellen Coburn, it's because she has three high-school-age kids. Hefty gal with freckles?" Hewitt nodded. "I'm surprised she talked to you."

"I was my most persuasive self," Hewitt said and grinned. "And speaking of persuasive, you never told me your department had the best-lookin' detective in the state. I saw her riding with Bob Torrez today."

"You mean Estelle Reyes."

Hewitt wagged his eyebrows. "How'd someone like her hook up with you guys?"

"She's lived in Posadas County all her life. Graduated first in her class at the Police Academy in Santa Fe. Hell of a good cop. She does more good in plain clothes than in uniform . . . spends most of her time as our juvenile officer."

"Plain clothes . . . no clothes," Hewitt said, and grinned some more.

"And her fiancé will slice you thinner than salami," I said.

Hewitt groaned and looked sickened. "Tough dude, huh?"

"He's a vascular surgeon in Las Cruces." I smiled pleasantly. "Keep your mind on your work."

Hewitt nodded and held up his hands philosophically, then pushed his plate away and stretched like a contented cat. "God, that was good. I wish we could get sweet corn like that up in Gallup." He glanced at his watch. "Got about two hours till dark. Guess I'll roam a little, then maybe twist some headlights or something."

"Twist headlights?"

Hewitt looked startled that I didn't know. "Yeah. Twist 'em. You get a Phillips-head screwdriver, and when the cop goes in for coffee, or in the office or something, you twist the hell out of the adjustment screws on one headlamp." He crossed his eyes wildly and cackled. "The cop car cruises around looking moronic. They can never figure out why the kids always know it's them coming up the street."

I looked skeptical. "And the cop doesn't notice? They're that stupid up in Gallup?"

"No, but, you'd be surprised. With the streetlights and all, it works pretty good with city cars. Not for the country, of course."

"Of course. I can see that the younger generation of

Posadas is going to profit mightily from your sojourn here, however short."

"You betcha." He stood up and shook his pant leg as if he had a dog attached. I glanced down and then did a double take.

"You're kidding," I said, pointing. He looked down, then up at me, puzzled. "An ankle holster?" I asked.

"Why not?" He pulled up the leg of his jeans. The little Smith & Wesson Model 19 rested in a suede holster with the Velcro strap just above his anklebone.

"You can run with that on?"

"Sure."

"And you can get it out without dancing around on one leg like an awkward ballerina?"

"Sure." He demonstrated, bending at the waist and pulling up his knee at the same time. One hand pulled pant leg, the other pulled S&W, all in one fluid, practiced motion. He snapped it back in.

"Huh," I said, noncommittal. "I've seen 'em in the movies." I started to gather dishes. "I don't think I'd be happy with one." Hewitt's expression of polite amusement told me that he could imagine the result as well as I. Grab down, suffer back-muscle spasm, throw out trick knee, stagger sideways and sprain other ankle. Fall and land on left wrist, refracturing an old break. At least I would be left with a good right hand and the S&W for permanent pain relief.

"I wasn't going to carry one at all," Hewitt said, "but then I got to thinking."

"That's a good idea, thinking. And by the way, just for passing interest, I found out today that the father of one of the teenagers in that wreck purchased his own arsenal. His name's Benny Fernandez. He owns the Burger Heaven you were talking about, down on Grande."

"No shit? I mean, I know who he is, but he bought a gun?"

"No shit."

"Who's he going to blow away?"

I shrugged. "No one, we can hope. Perhaps it will rot in his closet until he gets tired of it and sells it."

"What'd he buy?"

"A Beretta. The big kind. Like the military one."

"Terrific."

"He drives a white older model Cordoba, Yankee Charlie Xray one-thirty-six. He also owns a year-old charcoal-gray Continental, Charlie Delta fifty-nine-ninety. Keep an eye peeled when you're floating around. I don't know what he's up to, but it isn't quail hunting."

Hewitt nodded and repeated the license-tag numbers, firmly planting them in his youthful memory. I added, "And a reminder about the Salinger kid. He's mooning over something. Keep that in mind, too. I don't think you'll find him out and around much. He works at the home center days, but I don't think he's much of a night owl. But you never know."

"And what are you going to do?"

"I'm going to sleep for a couple hours or so, then cruise around some."

"Don't you have regular-shift deputies out?"

"Yes. Two on the road, four to midnight, and then one, midnight to eight."

"But you still work all day, and then most of the night?"

"Yes." I was about to say something more, but just shrugged. It never did any good explaining that work was also hobby, pastime, relaxation, and maybe even a little therapy. "If I see you twisting headlights, you'll have your first experience trying to undercover yourself out of jail."

He started with mock horror. "You'd do that, Gramps?"

"Certainly. Let them try to feed you. Probably bankrupt the county."

* * *

I slept so hard I awoke soaked with sweat, feeling as if I'd been slugged. The old adobe house was dark as pitch, and I turned to stare at the digital clock on the nightstand. By squinting hard and really concentrating, I could make out that it was after ten. I got up, showered and put on fresh clothes. The hall light near the front door was on so that Hewitt wouldn't stumble over the uneven floor bricks and break his neck. I left it on and went out. The air was velvety soft, black as pitch with no moon and no streetlights on my block. Not a breath of moving air stirred the cottonwoods that formed a thick umbrella over my house.

I slid into 310 and turned on the radio. It was silent. I almost pressed the mike to go 10-8, but decided against it. Miracle Murton was working, and if he knew I was out on the road, he'd do his level best to find something for me to do. Let him live in blissful ignorance . . . as usual.

Grande Boulevard dropped out of Posadas toward the east, and as I drove 310 out past the lumberyard, D'Anzo Chrysler-Plymouth, Laundromats, junk shops, tourist traps, and motels, and Benny Fernandez's burger joint right in the middle of them all, I chuckled. There were about ten youngsters lounging around that parking lot, including a group of four who sat on the hood of a big 4-by-4 suburban. Leaning against the fender of that same vehicle, looking at home like the rest of them, was my "grandson." Maybe he would do some good after all.

In another block, I had proof that the kid worked fast. The village police car idled out of a side street, another part-time patrolman at the wheel. The car was comically wall-eyed, its right headlamp skewed downward. I didn't want to be on the radio just then, but someone would tell him before the night was over, I was sure. The village was his problem, not mine. The village department was tiny, but the cops were sensitive. We always had to be careful not to step on their turf, unless asked. My plan was to swing east, gradually taking in the top half of the county.

"Three-oh-eight, PCS. Ten-twenty?"

"PCS, three-oh-eight. I'm about three miles up County Road 43, northbound."

I listened to the exchange with interest. Bob Torrez couldn't help sniffing around the accident site. He wanted to find something as bad as any of us.

"Ah, ten-four," Dispatcher Murton said, and there was a long pause while Miracle's brain churned. Predictably, he then went through the same routine with Howard Bishop in 307. Bishop responded that he was twenty-one miles southwest of Posadas, which meant he was probably cruising through the little hamlet of Regal. Even Miracle Murton could figure out that Torrez was closer to home. "Ah, three-oh-eight, swing around and ten-sixty-two at Chavez Chevrolet-Olds."

"Ten-four." As it happened, there was little that we, or any department, could do about the folks who sat in front of their scanners, listening to our dull number routines. With a half-measure of diligent listening, anyone could know with fair accuracy what we were doing at any given time. That in itself wasn't so bad, unless the person had the scanner in his car, which was illegal but convenient. Only the big metro sheriffs' departments had good patrol coverage, especially during the night hours. One deputy, or even none, to cover several hundred square miles was not unusual for us.

On impulse, I swung around and headed north, intercepting County Road 43 just as Torrez flashed by. My radio barked twice as Torrez keyed the mike to acknowledge that he'd seen me. And now any chance was better than none. If someone roaming up on the hill was listening to a scanner, he now knew that both deputies were busy and that he was as safe as church. In a few minutes, I passed Consolidated's mill. The road was deserted. I slowed down to fifteen, punched off the headlights, lowered the windows and turned off the air-conditioning. The radio crackled, and I reached down and turned it off, too. Smooth as silk, 310 purred up the road, and after a minute my eyes adjusted to the faint light cast by the single small bulb on the underside of the left front bumper—a light Holman liked to call my "perpetrator light." Hell, it was rinky-dink, but it worked. It threw just enough light in this case to catch the orange center line of the macadam road. The quarter-moon was peeking over the mesa, and before long I could make out outlines here and there.

Two miles below the lake, I damn near rear-ended a parked car. I swerved just in time, not so much because they were almost on the highway but because the sudden shape had taken me by surprise. I could see, faintly silhouetted as I went by, two heads merged as one low on the passenger side. After continuing on a few feet, I stopped, knowing that the flash of my brake lights would spring the two apart. I backed up the Ford until my windows were even with theirs and swiveled the spotlight until it bounced off the hood of their car. I could see clearly the two young guilt-washed faces. The girl was Beth Paige, a kid who worked as an office receptionist for the Forest Service. The boy was a stranger.

I looked Ms. Paige in the eye and asked, "Are you all right, miss?"

It was hard to tell in the harsh bouncing glare of the spotlight, but I'm sure she blushed. "Yes, officer," she said, and managed a sheepish grin.

I wasn't too bad at reading faces, and hers told me things were fine. "You might find a safer place to park," I said. The boy nodded, and had the good sense not to retort that it might be safer if I would turn on my headlights. The spotlight snapped off and I cruised 310 on up the road. I glanced in the rearview and didn't see any motion. No point in appearing too eager to comply, I suppose.

A few minutes later, gravel crunched under the tires as I swung in the lake road. Even if it's washed with a full moon, there's nothing much darker to me than an old quarry. That night, there was no full moon. The water was just a dull, black, shadowless hole. With 310 blocking the road, I turned on the spotlight. The beam lanced out and touched rock palisades, water, trees . . . and shiny metal. The car was parked well back in the shadows, and I wouldn't have seen it at all with normally aimed headlights. I didn't linger with the beam, but let it pass on by. Even in the brief flash, I had recognized the car. Without rolling forward, I turned on the radio and reached for the mike.

"PCS, three-ten."

Gayle Sedillos's voice cracked back, bless her. She must have come in early, and had taken over from Miracle. I told her where I was and that I would be 11-96 with Yankee Charlie Xray 136. She wouldn't bother to run the plate, since the number was on a small note on the bulletin board right above the radio.

"Ten-four, three-ten," she said crisply. "Three-oh-eight, did you copy?"

"Three-oh-eight, ten-four." Torrez sounded unexcited. "I'm ten-eight."

I had ten minutes, or less. I was willing to bet my pension, such as it was, that Torrez was more than just "in service." He would be on his way through town and up County Road 43, covering the ground a whole lot faster than I had. If the two neckers were still parked on the shoulder, his jet wash was just a few minutes away from rocking their locked lips apart.

People park in the midnight timber for several reasons, but only one or two fit Benny Fernandez that night. If he was out cheating on his wife, I was going to be embarrassed and so was he. But I didn't even consider that the occupants of the Cordoba might include the steely-faced Mrs. Fernandez.

A Forest Service access road allowed me to circle around so that I could park a few yards behind Fernandez's Cordoba. The duct tape plastered over the patrol car's dome light eliminated the blast of light when I opened the door. I walked slowly toward the Cordoba, letting my eyes adjust as much as they could. Benny knew I was coming—unless he was blind drunk or dead. And he would have heard me idle up behind him, as quiet as the night was.

When I reached the back fender, I stopped, flashlight still off. Cigarette smoke wafted out his open window.

"Benny? It's Bill Gastner."

"How you doin', Sheriff?" he said.

"Fine. Crack your door so I can see, will you?" He did, and the dome light flooded on. I moved up and relaxed a little when I could see both his hands. One held a sandwich of sorts, the other a plastic cup filled with coffee. "Long night?" I asked pleasantly.

"I figure this is as good a place as any," he said.

"For what? You got insomnia?" I tried to keep my tone light, but it was hard. I could see the black butt of the Beretta. The rest of the gun was covered by his right leg.

"You're out late too," he said. "You want some coffee?" He hefted the cup and looked up at me.

"Sure." I watched him reach for the thermos bottle and the cup-lid. He started to pour and then heard the noise at the same time as I did. "Boy," he said, "somebody is sure pushin' it hard on that highway."

I decided it was time to cut the gab and get on with it. "That's Deputy Torrez coming up the hill," I said. Fernandez looked sharply at me. "Standard procedure," I added. "A cop doesn't usually go talk with a man with a gun unless there's some backup . . . even if they're all good friends." Fernandez finished pouring and handed the coffee to me. I laid the flashlight on the roof and took the cup. "Benny, what are you doing up here?"

Fernandez took his time. I had always thought of Benny as something of a marshmallow. He had reminded me of all those Mexicans in the "B" Westerns, the folks who wore white cotton and were always being beaten and whipped by the bad guys. In the end, they rose up, armed with scythes, axes, and garden hoes. Maybe that was Benny's mood just then. There was a certain hardness about the man. I saw the muscles of his cheek twitch, and he looked down into the dark depths of his coffee cup.

"Is there something illegal about sitting out in the night, Sheriff?" he asked.

"No. And there's nothing illegal about carrying a gun in this state, either, Benny. Like the one under your leg there. But I kinda start wondering what you have in mind. It's hard to see rabbits in the dark. It's illegal to jacklight deer. This isn't good snake country." I paused and sipped my coffee, keeping my eyes on his hands. "But as long as the weapon isn't concealed and loaded at the same time, you can walk down Grande Boulevard with it. You might make a few folks nervous, just like you're making me nervous right now. You're hunting, Benny, and that makes me nervous. Who?"

Fernandez reached down and picked up the big Beretta. I wasn't familiar with the gun, but the hammer was down. Then I saw that the trigger was far forward, and that meant it was double action. I got nervous again. He turned it this way and that in his hands thoughtfully. "You know, Sheriff, for two, maybe three days after Ricky died, I could think of nothing but my own loss. I guess you could say I was feeling sorry for myself. Ricky . . . I'm sure he felt nothing." He snapped his fingers. "A fraction of a second, maybe. No more." He tapped the rim of the steering wheel with the

Beretta's barrel. "But then your people found that bag of cocaine under the seat." He stopped and shook his head. "For the past few days, I've been thinking, Sheriff. That much, it's worth a lot of money. It's more than just— what do the kids call it now, a little hit? I mean, somebody is dealing heavy. Maybe not like in L.A. or New York, where they bring it in a ton at a time. I still don't believe it was my Ricky, but it was in his car . . . my car. I believe he knew it was there, and ran because of it."

"Maybe."

"And I tell you this. I know from when I lived in Phoenix. Once the dealers move in, they move in for all they can take. That cocaine you found was not the last of it. Sometime, those bastards will try again."

"And you plan to be there with that thing when they do?"

Fernandez made a funny little noise that sounded like an effort to laugh. "People who deal in kilos aren't Boy Scouts, Sheriff." We both turned our heads as Bob Torrez's car turned into the lake road.

"Hang on a minute, Benny." I walked quickly back to my car and fumbled the radio. A minute later, we saw Torrez turn around and head slowly back down the hill. "I think you can appreciate that what you're doing makes us all a little nervous, Benny," I said when I returned. "I mean, this is our job, not yours. You're not trained for it, you're too involved to think straight. Now let's suppose a couple cars pulled in down there by the lake and parked door to door. What would you do?"

Fernandez just stared ahead at the imaginary cars. I continued, "I mean, it's dark, Benny. Are they just necking? Having a beer? Telling dirty jokes? What? And you're telling me that you're going to charge down there with a fifteen-shot semi-automatic pistol at the ready? How are you going to know who they are? Are you going to threaten them and force them all out of their cars and then search them? And if they bring suit against you, you'll probably lose. And I mean lose more than you can imagine. I don't know how many civil suits you've ever been involved in, but take my word for it, avoid them. And what will you do if they just laugh at you, Benny? Shoot them all? Then you've got manslaughter charges against you. And if they're drug dealers, Benny, what will happen is this. We'll find what's left of you lying on the gravel down there the next morning." I stopped. He was looking down at the gun. "Use your head, Benny. When I came up here, I did it knowing I had backup. I had a light. You don't even have that. If I hadn't recognized Yankee Charlie Xray one-three-six, I would have called in the plate and had a bunch of information before I stepped out of the car." Spouting out his license plate like that made a dent. He looked up at me, a little sorrowfully. "And, Benny, I've done this before. I don't think you have. We don't want to see you hurt, or anyone else."

He nodded and offered the Beretta to me, butt first. I shook my head. "That's not necessary, Benny. Take it back to wherever you bought it tomorrow. For now, just unload it and shove it under the seat. Go home and get some rest. Let us work. Hell, I may be fat and old, but I'm pretty damn good at what I do. The deputies are better still. We've got some leads. The sheriff told me today that he's planning to bring in a specially trained dog. The beast sniffs drugs, believe it or not. Even if you just smoked a single joint as much as forty-eight hours ago, this critter will nail you. We're going to publicize that, and some people are bound to get nervous. The Drug Enforcement Agency is working with us." That was a lie, but Fernandez didn't need to know. "Something's going to break, believe me. Soon."

He nodded and sighed heavily. "You just feel so helpless sometimes," he said.

"Sure." I groped for something to lighten his spirits

a little before sending him down the hill. "And my bet is that when this is all over, it'll be obvious that Ricky wasn't involved as anything other than maybe an innocent bystander. You'll be proud of him."

"You really believe that?"

"Yup. I know what kind of a home he came from." Even if I didn't buy that one, Benny Fernandez did. He looked grateful. I pressed the advantage. "I'll pull back so you can get out of here, Benny. There's other things I need to check up here. You go on ahead. Go down and get some rest. Being the midnight vigilante isn't your style." He laughed and sounded a little relieved.

"Thanks, Bill. I'll get rid of this thing tomorrow, first item of business. Sell it back to George Payton."

"I'm sure he'll give you back every nickel," I said.

"A man can be stupid sometimes," Fernandez said.

It was only in retrospect that Benny's last line really haunted me. If I had been able to replay that scene, I would have grabbed that Beretta at the first offer. But when I next saw the weapon, it was in a plastic evidence bag.

9

Meeting Fernandez had set me on edge. I was as wide-eyed as one of those lemurs you see in picture books about the jungle. Any notion that this night might be one with six or eight hours of sleep was just that . . . a notion. The road down the hill was empty. The night neckers had gone elsewhere. About five miles north of town, I jogged west on State 78. A housing development of new ranch styles sprawled up the side of the mesa. Most of them had "For Sale" signs in front, and a few looked pretty ragged. The mine and mill closing had caught many developers overbuilding. Maybe drug trafficking was the new industry, I thought as I followed the road up the mesa until it topped out by the airport. With headlights off, I drove along a hundred yards of fencing and passed the airport parking area and an apron access gate for pedestrians. The main gate that led to the hangars was wide open. That was normally the case during the daytime when the airport manager, Jim Bergin, was on the premises. But at midnight or after, it was a little unusual unless some charter flight had just come in.

I drove through the gate and saw that the big padlock was hooked loosely through the chain link above the gate latch. Farther on, one arc light blazed, casting hard shadows around the hangars. Light streamed out from one, and I drove over. Bathed in the harsh fluorescent wash from overhead was a pretty tan-and-white Cessna. Its cowl was off, and from an open door on the passenger side a leg and foot projected. As I stopped the car, Jim Bergin pulled himself up far enough so he could see my car, and then he untangled his long frame from the innards of the airplane. I got out and walked over. My left hand groped automatically at the cigarette pack in my shirt pocket.

"Don't smoke in here," Jim said immediately. In mock threat, he waved what looked like wire nippers.

I laughed. "You know me pretty well, Jim. How you doin'?" I patted the pocket flap back in place, fighting that strange reflex that smokers have when they're meeting someone and about to talk. I saw the pan of oil under the plane's nose and the neat cans of Aeroshell lined up on the floor.

"I'm tired and cranky and tryin' to keep the customers happy. How about yourself?" Bergin said.

I glanced at my watch. It was twelve forty-six. "Damn picky customers to make a man work this late."

Bergin offered one of his easy smiles. "Nah. There's a big bird coming in to pick up about five tons of milling parts from Consolidated. Maybe you saw the truck over on the north side of the parking lot?" I shook my head and Bergin added, "Their plane blew a tire in Pueblo, and that, plus thunderboomers, puts them about five hours late." He glanced at his watch. "So I figure about three o'clock."

"And you get stuck waiting for them, huh?" I ran a hand over the smooth alloy of the Cessna's prop.

Bergin shrugged and wiped his hands on a clean rag. "They want a fast turnaround and fuel. I'll help get them squared away and sell 'em a few hundred gallons of fuel besides. Hell, might as well make a dime. I don't have anything else to do." He grinned. "Corporate schedules assume people are not mortal, you know. What are you sniffin' around after?"

"Just out, Jim. Swung by here and saw a light. Whose plane is this, anyway?"

"Doc Sprague's."

"No shit?" I thumped the end of the spinner. "I didn't think he was still flying."

"Oh, yeah. He quit for a little while. About the time his daughter died. Just as well. A man's got to keep his mind on business up in the air. He just wasn't in any shape. But he picked it up again about eight months ago. In fact, he just bought this bird in June."

"Bunch of moola."

"You'd better believe it."

I walked around and looked inside at the fancy fabric and all the dials, knobs, and levers. "Wow." There was a messy hole in the middle of the dash, though, where Bergin had obviously been working. "Something break?"

"Putting in a new radio. He's got to have the best, you know. I figured I might as well change the oil while I was working and waiting for the charter. It's due."

I muttered some pleasantry in agreement and looked back along the fuselage.

"You seen anything of the government yet?" Bergin looked quizzical, and I added, "The DEA is going to be running a plane out of here."

"That's good news," Bergin said, and flapped his eyebrows. "There's nothing like government credit cards to boost gas sales. I hope they use a helicopter, and not some gas-sippin' bird. They're going to push the border again, huh?"

"Yup."

"I wish 'em all the luck. But unless they can cover the whole thing twenty-four hours a day, it isn't going to do much good. What are they flying, do you know?"

I shrugged. "I don't know anything about it. Just that they're coming."

Bergin nodded. "Probably bringing in one of their mix-masters. Complete waste." He shook his head sadly. "You know, if they'd go down into Mexico and bribe the right people, they'd probably be provided with a flight plan for each drug runner. But what the hell." He waved the wire cutter in disgust, then grinned again. "At two dollars and nine cents a gallon for av-gas, I hope they work the border for about six months. Then I can retire."

I was about to say something when I heard a car blasting down the state road past the airport. It caught my attention because the sound was that of a big engine being pushed until it howled. About the time I half-turned to look outside toward the road, we saw the flash of red lights. It was a county car, and flying low.

"Your boys are hotdogging it," Bergin observed dryly.

"Young blood, eager beavers," I replied. The door of 310 was closed, and I hadn't bothered to put the radio on PA. "I better go give a listen."

"Take care." Bergin went back inside the airplane and I walked out to the car. He called after me, voice muffled, "There's coffee if you want it." I waved a hand and then pulled open the door. The night air instantly was filled with radio traffic.

"Three-oh-eight, what's your ETA?" The voice was shaky, and I recognized it as one of the village part-timers.

"Posadas, three-oh-eight is six minutes out." It had been Torrez who flashed by.

I was already in gear when Gayle Sedillos came on the air, finding Deputy Bishop as well. "Three-oh-seven, ten-forty-nine Posadas Village Park code three. Three-ten, PCS."

I keyed the mike as I swerved around the hangar and out the gate. "Three-ten."

"Three-ten, ten-forty-nine Posadas Village Park code three. Ten-seventy-one."

"Ten-four. ETA seven minutes." Every muscle in my body was steel-tight. The innocent numbers Gayle enunciated so clearly on the air meant that somebody had just put bullets into somebody else . . . and maybe was ready to continue doing so.

I concentrated on driving, nervous because I knew Bob Torrez would arrive at the park first. The part-timer wouldn't provide much backup. His chief, Dan Martinez, wouldn't either, since he was off on a week's vacation. I reached the intersection of State 78 and County 43 and swept down the yield ramp at close to eighty miles an hour. There were three miles of straight paved road to the outskirts of Posadas, and after the first one, 310 felt light on its toes. I didn't bother to look at the speedometer.

The village park was a triangular affair of two acres, grass and swing sets and a statue or two. It even sported a welded-up, World War I vintage tank—supposedly left over from Pershing's fruitless dashes across the border after the outlaw Pancho Villa. If Pershing had used that tank in hot pursuit, it's amazing Villa hadn't laughed himself to death. The tank faced Pershing Street, and that's where I saw Torrez's car, parked diagonally in the street, lights flashing. Beyond was the village car, headlights askew. Pulling in from the other direction was a state police cruiser, no top-light bar but the grille lights pulsating. I skidded 310 to a stop altogether too close to 308. A crowd of people were gathered over on the grass about thirty yards behind the tank. I saw Torrez push someone hard, and the deputy gesticulated toward the village car.

Only after I had gotten out and was trotting across the grass did I recognize the man Torrez had pushed as the village cop. He ran past me, eyes wide. "Ambulance," he yelped, and sprinted on.

I reached the first knot of people, folks from nearby houses and the rapidly gathering cars. "Move it, move it," I snapped, and shoved through. The victim was lying on his face, but I recognized him immediately. My gut wound itself into a painful ball. The Beretta was in the grass, under the victim's left shin. Benny Fernandez didn't need an ambulance.

I stood up. "Now I want you people back. Way back," I shouted. The state trooper didn't hesitate to cooperate. He was five times bigger than me, and probably twice as mean. Crowd control was his thing, and he pitched in. I let him work, because Bob Torrez had me by the sleeve.

"Sheriff, over here," he said. I turned quickly and almost fell, suddenly and violently dizzy. I stopped in my tracks and took a deep breath, waiting for my eyes to clear. The night air hadn't felt so close and stuffy before.

"Who'd Fernandez tangle with?" I managed, but Torrez just pulled me along. I recognized one of the paramedics from the fire department, crouched and working furiously. He was off duty, and didn't have much to work with. Just as intent, and obviously in charge, was Dr. Harlan Sprague, Jr. I recognized first his unruly white hair. His face, unevenly illuminated by the bright sodium vapor lights of the park, was soft and puffy, like that of a man just jerked out of bed. I couldn't see much of the victim at first, but then I saw the ankle holster, and tasted the bile that welled up in my throat as I bent over.

"Ah, no," was all I managed to say. Art Hewitt lay on his back, arms outflung. By his right hand was the stubby Magnum.

"Where the hell is that ambulance?" the paramedic muttered. "There ain't a thing we can do until he gets here." In the distance, we could hear another siren building.

"How is he?" I said, dropping to my knees beside Sprague.

"His pulse is good. Breathing is ragged. There's no way of knowing where the bullet went. But I think he'll be all right." He was holding a pad made from Hewitt's own T-shirt against the young officer's right flank. "He's conscious."

Hewitt's features were rigid, and his eyes were staring wildly up into the night, shifting first one way and then another as if he were searching the heavens for an answer. "Art?" He looked over at me, obviously having trouble focusing his eyes. "Art, what the hell happened?"

He wet his lips and swallowed hard. "Damned if I know," he whispered. "I was talking with some kids and . . . and . . ."

"And what?" The ambulance screamed up to the curb. "And what, Art?"

"He was talkin' with some guy over by the corner."

"Who was talking? Fernandez?"

Art Hewitt nodded slightly and swallowed hard. "And then he just came over and jumped me."

"Jumped you? You mean he threatened you with the gun?"

"No. He just . . . he just charged me, pushed me real hard. I tripped and fell backward."

Footsteps pounded toward us, and I looked up. The ambulance crew was sprinting across the grass. I put a hand on Hewitt's shoulder. "They'll get you fixed up, Art. Just lie easy."

"I'll be okay, Gramps."

Sprague, an internist by training, and far from being a trauma specialist, stood aside and let the well-equipped EMTs take over.

I moved to give them room to work and gasped

74

aloud, so vicious was the combination of pain and pressure that suddenly and relentlessly clamped me in a vice. "Holy shit," I breathed, and stood bent over with my hands on my knees.

"Are you all right?" It was Sprague.

"I think so," I said, slowly straightening up. Air came a little easier and the pain subsided. "Too much running around."

Dr. Sprague's eyes narrowed as he looked closely at me. "Chest pain? Pressure?"

Everything was coming back to normal, and I knew that if I answered the doc truthfully, there'd be complications that I couldn't afford just then. "No. Just a little dizzy. I'm all right."

Sprague had me by the wrist, and it was only after a few seconds that I realized he had been expertly but unobtrusively taking my pulse. I pulled away. "I'm all right." They were loading Art Hewitt into the ambulance. "I need to get to the hospital."

"Probably for more reasons than you think," Sprague said dryly. "Who's your doctor?"

I looked at him impatiently. "None," I said truthfully. I had been ill so rarely that I had never seen the need for a regular physician.

"Find one," he said cryptically. "If you make it through this night, find one. I mean it."

I nodded and said, "Sure. And I'm going to need to talk to you. You saw this?" I nodded at the flattened spot in the grass. Even as we talked, a second unit arrived and Fernandez's corpse, covered with the usual white sheet, was loaded.

"No. I heard the shots. That's all. As you know, I live just over there." He indicated a row of town houses that had been built on the east side of the park. "I didn't even have time to put together something for my bag. I haven't been in active practice for some time."

"All right. We'll want a statement."

"Certainly."

I saw that Bob Torrez and the village part-timer were working the other five eyewitnesses. I left Sprague and joined them. In the next few minutes, Estelle Reyes arrived, as did Howard Bishop. "I want statements from every living soul within a block of this park," I snapped at Reyes. I could see, even in the vague light of the park's sodium vapors, that her face was pale.

"How is he?" she asked, and I shrugged helplessly.

"I'm going on down to the hospital. I'll call Holman and tell him to get his ass out of bed."

"He's already on his way down," Estelle Reyes said, almost in a whisper.

"Fine," I said. "Take this place apart. I mean it. I'll be back to help just as soon as I can."

I strode across the grass toward my car. But what I'd told Estelle Reyes wasn't true. It wasn't fine. I had the goddamned feeling that absolutely nothing was under control.

10

Martin Holman walked stolidly toward me. The hard heels of his finely polished boots clicked on the polished hall tiles of Posadas General Hospital. His hands were thrust in his pockets, and he stared at the floor as he walked, ignoring others, letting the few nurses dodge him. I didn't bother to get up. He stopped a pace in front of my chair and surveyed me with tired, bagged eyes.

"You look like shit," he said finally.

"Thanks."

"So what the hell happened?"

"I don't know yet. Art says Benny Fernandez ran at him. 'Jumped him' is how he put it."

"You got a chance to talk with him, then?" Holman said, relieved.

"Briefly. I didn't get the whole story. There were at least five witnesses, it looks like. Estelle and Bob Torrez are taking their statements now."

"Benny Fernandez was killed instantly?"

"Yes."

"And how does it look for Art Hewitt?"

"I think he'll be all right." I glanced at my watch. "He's in surgery now."

"Where was he hit?"

I jabbed my right index finger into my side under the ribs. "He was hurting bad, but it's just about impossible to tell anything, you know. I don't have any information whatever."

"We'll just have to wait," Holman said. "I called Gallup, by the way. Chief White says the boy's parents live in Tucson. He said he'd take care of contacts there."

"That's good."

We both fell silent, and after a long moment Holman said, "Hell of a thing."

"Yes." A nurse walked by pushing a jingling tray cart. She looked at us and smiled helpfully.

"Hell of a note," Holman said. I just looked at him. "So Benny Fernandez was killed outright?" he asked.

"Yes. It looked like he'd been shot once in the face." Holman winced. "You talked to the widow?" The blank look that settled over my face told Holman all he needed to know. "Christ, Bill, how long's it been?"

I glanced at the wall clock. "Twenty-five minutes."

Holman was already on his feet. "I'll take care of it. You stay here." I watched him hustle off, and shook my head. I must have figured the dead could wait attendance. I didn't worry about explaining my preoccupation to Holman. What was going to be tough was explaining why I hadn't taken the Beretta when it was offered to me.

After a while, the hospital didn't even smell anymore. I didn't notice the polish on the floor. Holman had returned, and for an hour or more we talked. Now he sat with his hands clasped between his knees, head twisted, slightly to one side, eyes staring without registration at the old issue of *Sports Illustrated* on the table beside him.

Estelle Reyes and Bob Torrez had shifted their operations from the park to the sheriff's office, and every twenty minutes one or another of them called us and got the same negative answer. At a quarter to five, when there still wasn't the faintest hint of dawn behind the curtains, Estelle Reyes walked into the waiting room. She looked so goddamned prim, like a grade school teacher ready to lecture the troops . . . except there was a little fatigue tremor twitching her lower lip.

"Officer Hewitt was apparently talking with the five teenagers," she said without preamble. "Three of them say he was trying to buy grass. Two of them think he was really after something harder. A couple of the kids were just hangers-on. They don't know what the hell was going on. One of them said they all thought Hewitt was 'funny,' whatever that means. I think they were just hanging out, no particular, cohesive group. If any of them had actually been into drugs, been ready to sell, Hewitt would have suckered them in, that's for sure."

"And if all this was going on at midnight or after, where the hell were the village police?" Holman asked bitterly.

"And then Fernandez arrived," Estelle Reyes continued, ignoring the sheriff's question. "One of the kids was so shook when the shooting started that he crapped his pants. He ran home. Howard Bishop went to talk to him."

"Who wouldn't panic?" I muttered morosely. "I'm surprised it was only one."

"And then?" Holman said.

"They all say that Benny Fernandez came across the grass like a man possessed. From the east side of the park."

"Over by the apartments?"

"Right. Now, even in the dim light, Officer Hewitt would have been easy to recognize. The tallest of the five kids was five feet six inches. Hewitt is six-three." Estelle looked at the paperwork on her clipboard, and took a deep breath.

Holman looked at me. "Did Fernandez ever have a chance to meet Hewitt? Did he know him?"

I shook my head, and Estelle continued, "They agree that Fernandez said something, but none of them understood him. It's possible it was something in Spanish, who knows. He pushed Hewitt very hard. 'Violently,' one of the kids said. Like a football player. Hewitt apparently was caught off guard and stumbled backward and fell. He wasn't able to catch himself, and went down hard. Two of the kids said that they saw Hewitt's gun strapped to his ankle as he fell. Apparently, Fernandez did too. One of the five youngsters saw Fernandez pull out a 'very large automatic.' That's how he described it. At that point, three of them agree that Hewitt said something like, 'Oh, shit.' Fernandez fired once. None of the kids are sure what happened, but it seems likely that Hewitt tried to roll out of the way. At the same time he pulled his own revolver from his ankle holster. Fernandez fired twice more. One of the youngsters says he heard the bullet hit Hewitt." Estelle looked pained as she thumbed through her notebook. "'It sounded awful,' the kid said. They all agree, and this is important: that Hewitt fired once, while lying on his back, after he was wounded. We'll get the autopsy report later, but I was just down at the morgue. The bullet hit Benny Fernandez just above his left eyebrow."

Holman nodded slowly. "You just never know, do you." He looked at me. "And up on the hill, Fernandez was cogent? Even calm, you said? Rational?"

"All those things," I replied. "He even seemed relieved to be going home, relieved that it was over."

"But apparently it wasn't," Holman said.

I looked at Estelle Reyes. "None of the five kids saw Fernandez before he started running across the grass toward Hewitt?"

"No, sir. They said that there were several people out all around the park. Apparently the late hour didn't

80

bother anyone. Certainly not the kids. They said they were getting nervous, though, that the village police might drive by. But they said Hewitt laughed and told them he'd fixed that up good. Something about cross-eyed headlights."

"He did that, as a matter of fact."

Holman asked, "Did Hewitt make a buy from any of the kids?"

Estelle Reyes shook her head. "Apparently not. We'll have to ask him, to be sure. But those kids were scared enough about the whole thing that I think they would have told me. I get the impression they thought he was some kind of big-city freak. He made them nervous."

"He enjoyed playing the undercover role to the hilt," I said. "Maybe too much so. He had nowhere near enough experience. We should have realized that. I should have monitored what he was doing much more closely."

Holman slapped the arm of his chair lightly. "This is no time for self-flagellation, Bill. Sure, maybe he was inexperienced. Maybe you should have confiscated Fernandez's gun. But that's all wonderful twenty-twenty hindsight. What we need to know is what triggered Fernandez. When he left you, he was mellowed out and homebound. What, about an hour later? About that? You had time to go out to the airport for a while. An hour later, he dashes into a park, charges into a gang of kids, and blows one of them away. We have to know exactly why."

"There's only one person who saw Fernandez before he ran into the park, and that's Art Hewitt," I said. "He was able to tell me that he saw a person he thought was Fernandez talking to someone on the sidewalk on the east side of the park. Now, Doc Sprague lives over there, in those new apartments, and he says that he heard the shots. But there was no reason for the doc to

be looking out beforehand. He says he didn't see anyone."

Holman looked up at Estelle Reyes, and he put his
fingers against his lips, deep in thought. We waited, and
finally the sheriff said, "But there's no reason for Hewitt
to make something like that up. So what do you plan to
do?"

Even though the question wasn't addressed to me, I
was ready to answer, but Estelle put her small notebook
back in her pocket and said, "Until we know exactly
what happened, we keep digging. There are a lot of people who live around that park. We'll talk to all of them.
And somebody might come to us." She turned at the
sound of footsteps coming up the polished hallway behind her. Dr. Alan Perrone's gown was blood-spattered,
but he was obviously too tired to care. With him was
Eva Young, a middle-aged surgical nurse who would
manage to look stylish and groomed in the middle of a
volcanic eruption.

She nodded at us and headed off toward the nurses'
station.

"We're transferring Mr. Hewitt to Albuquerque,"
Dr. Perrone said. He held a manila envelope in one
hand, and motioned down the hall with it. "Come on into
the office for a minute."

The three of us obediently followed, and he closed
the door behind us.

"How's he going to do?" Holman asked, and Perrone
pulled out the X ray and snapped it into the wall light.

"We've got some real problems," Perrone said, facing the X ray. "But to give it to you in a nutshell." He
pulled a pen from his pocket and used it as a pointer.
"You can easily see the largest fragment in situ way
over here, right behind the heart."

"Christ," Holman muttered.

"The point of entry was over here, exactly under
the last rib on the right side. There was minimal dam-

age to the ascending colon, but considerable to the right kidney. About this point, the bullet began to shatter." He shot a quick glance at Holman, frowned and turned back to the X ray. "Considerable damage to this lobe of the liver. Then tearing of the central tendon here. The diaphragm." His index finger traced a diagonal, upward path. "Most worrisome, of course, is the cardiac damage. This is the bullet's center core and part of the brass jacket. It shows up very plainly. We've managed to achieve some stability with the patient, but arrangements have already been made to fly him to Albuquerque. They have far more advanced facilities there, and in addition"—Perrone raised an eyebrow—"they have Dennis Chatman. He's the best cardiac surgeon I've met. Luck was with us because he was in Las Cruces, and he agreed to meet the air ambulance and ride over. That way, he can be with the patient en route."

"Odds?" Holman asked.

Perrone shrugged. "It's hard to imagine how a single pistol bullet could have been fired to inflict more damage. But the prompt emergency assistance certainly helped. We were able to stabilize the patient, and he seems to be responding well. He lost an incredible amount of blood, as you can imagine, but by good fortune, our blood bank has an adequate supply of his type." He made a wry face. "Or at least it did." He put the pen away and slid the X rays back into the envelope. "One of the Medivacs is in Las Cruces, by good fortune. I imagine it will be here before we have Officer Hewitt transported to the airport. Sheriff Holman, I can't give you odds. I am optimistic. We have a few things in our favor."

"A few."

"That's right."

"Is there any chance that we'll be able to talk to him?"

"That's very unlikely. He's just been through almost

six hours of surgery. He won't even be out from under the anesthetic for some time. On the flight north, he'll . . . well, you don't need to know all that, but I can appreciate your concern. I'm also aware of the investigation and the delicacy, no doubt, that is warranted by that. If one of you needs to ride in the airplane, by all means do so. I would suggest to you that they probably have room for only one of you."

"Bill?" Holman asked, and I nodded.

"You'll need to be out at the airport now," Perrone said, glancing at his watch. "Although the patient hasn't yet left the hospital, it will only be a couple of minutes. They won't wait for you, believe me." He nodded at us and left abruptly.

"Let's move," I said.

Estelle Reyes paced me out of the building and in the parking lot handed me a small tape recorder. "You might need it if he comes around for a minute or so. We want to know who was standing with Fernandez before the shots were fired."

"I know what the hell we need, Estelle," I snapped and climbed into 310.

"Sorry, sir," Estelle said quietly.

I slammed the door and buzzed down the window, already sorry I'd barked at her. "Have someone come out to the airport and pick up three-ten so it doesn't get a stone through the windshield," I said. I tried a smile, but it didn't work.

"You want me to make arrangements for your trip back?"

"No, I don't know when or how that'll be." I looked in the rearview mirror and saw the ambulance lining up at the hospital's emergency doorway. At the same time, we could hear the synchronized moan of the air ambulance's engines as it circled over the mesa and turned toward Posadas County Airport. Such goddamned good timing, I thought. The plane would arrive exactly on time, and would still have its engines idling for a quick transfer. Why was it, I thought, that timing, or fate, or whatever you chose to call it, couldn't work in our favor beforehand? Why couldn't Art Hewitt's frantic roll on the ground to dodge the bullet have been better timed, or Benny Fernandez's gun hand been less lucky?

"Just don't miss anything, Estelle. Don't overlook a goddamned thing," I said, and then the ambulance began to move. The detective stepped away from the car, and I pulled out onto the street, lights and siren in concert.

11

The transfer was flawlessly executed. The ambulance pulled up alongside the airplane as I was trotting across from the patrol car. It took a moment of careful jogging and shifting of the gurney, and then patient, medical staff, and paraphernalia were aboard. The ambulance pulled away promptly. I recognized everyone except a rail-thin nurse and a man who was almost tiny in stature. There was no time for introductions, but I guessed, correctly, it turned out, that the diminutive man was Dr. Chatman. Even as the door locks were thudding into place, the boarding-side engine came back to life.

One of the aircraft officers recited instructions to us about buckle-up, and I noticed that the crew up front was performing whatever checks were needed while the aircraft rolled down the long taxiway. From where I sat, I could turn and see only the right side of Hewitt's face and neck, down to the white sheet. Tubes and plastic packets of drip joggled and vibrated. Three people were obviously planning to spend their every moment tending and monitoring, and I shifted a little, trying to relax for the takeoff. I must have looked even less assured than I felt, because a hand patted my shoulder and one of the flight officers smiled reassuringly.

"He'll be fine, Sheriff. We'll really be hoofin' it, so it's only an hour and a half flying time to Albuquerque. And the weatherman promises smooth skies. So relax, huh? He'll be fine."

For a good hour, I believed him. And then things fell apart. The first sign was a slight stirring from Hewitt. He hadn't regained consciousness, but one leg flexed slightly and his head turned to the left. The emergency crew went to work, and I had sense enough to stay out of the way. I had to watch, though. I tried to will their efforts to success. At one point, the EMT officer who accompanied the aircraft slid forward past me.

To the pilot, he said clearly and loudly, "Straight in, Tom. We got a cardiac arrest."

We were in a gradual descent, and by the high pitch of the engines, it was apparent that the flight crew was taking every advantage of power and gravity, booting that airplane through the sky for all it was worth. In back, I saw those awful electric paddles that come out as a last resort in all the movies and jolt the patient back to life. Chatman vetoed their use this time, though, with a quick shake of the head. At the same time that I saw the doctor plunge an enormous hypodermic into Art Hewitt's chest, I heard the pilot, just a couple of feet behind my head, say, "Albuquerque approach, Air Ambulance Niner-one-niner is forty south, request change to priority straight on three."

"Double Alpha niner-one-niner, plan straight in on three. Are you declaring a medical emergency?" The voice of the controller was as calm as ice.

"Niner-one-niner, affirmative."

"And niner-one-niner, where do you want the ambulance? He's parked by the Aero Club now."

"Albuquerque, have him right at the intersection with eight. Can you do that? It'll save us taxi time."

"Roger, niner-one-niner. We will hold traffic commencing in five minutes until you're down."

"Roger, Albuquerque. Thanks for the expedite."

"Niner-one-niner, you're cleared straight in. Report twenty south and then proceed at your discretion. Tower has you."

I have no idea how fast that Piper Navajo was traveling on the final approach, but any lineup with the runway was done at a dead run. Working at his own dead run was the doctor in back. He had given up the needles and my stomach tightened and churned as I saw him shifting position, face intent and scalpel in hand. With a single, decisive slash, the doctor cut into Art Hewitt's rib cage. Blood welled up along the eight-inch incision that started just below the left nipple and curved down his side in line with the ribs. The EMT was at Hewitt's head, working the masks and tubes there, and faintly, over the steady bellow of the plane's engines, I could hear the click and hiss of the medical machinery. The nurse was hovering beside the physician, and the doctor, sweat now running down his cheeks, had his hand inside Art Hewitt's chest, rhythmically massaging the young man's crippled heart. I think, at that point, that the only person breathing in the airplane was Art Hewitt, and that was only by dint of mechanical assistance.

Suddenly the doctor's face cracked in a grin. "All right!" he cried jubilantly, sounding like a high school football coach after a touchdown. As if in answer, the engines dropped in RPM. I closed my eyes and rested the back of my head against the bulkhead. Alan Perrone had said something about the Albuquerque surgeon's being the best he'd seen. I wondered how often Dennis Chatman had done cardiac surgery in a plunging aircraft.

The flight officer squirmed forward and then back. "Touchdown in about a minute," he told the doctor, and the crew made only brief preparations. Everything was already as tied down as it could be. The EMT at Hewitt's head stayed close and put both hands on the patient's shoulders. The doctor ignored them all. His patient's heart was beating. It wouldn't have mattered to Chatman if they had been in a balloon floating over the Eiffel Tower. He was working to field-dress the incision and was lost in his own world. I heard the engine beat decrease, and seconds later, the transition from air to pavement came as only the slightest jar.

I found out later that runway 3, from the initial touchdown point to the intersection with runway 8, where the ambulance sat waiting, was almost eight thousand feet long. Our pilot used it all. Slow taxi was not in his book. He let the Navajo roll under considerable power. I opened my eyes and saw the big intersection of two other runways flash past. We must have been humping along at close to seventy miles an hour. Finally the nose dipped and we braked, not violently but insistently. Before the aircraft was stopped, the flight officer had the door unlatched. I looked out as we rolled up toward the ambulance and saw that the aircraft engine on that side was already windmilling to a stop.

"Let's move it," the doctor snapped, and in seconds the transfer was made. If I had taken time to blink I would have been left behind. I did see the Gallup police car, and the two men in it. I assumed one of them was Chief White. I could have ridden down with them, but I stuck with the ambulance. The explanations could come later.

It wasn't many minutes to the downtown hospital, but the nurse found thirty seconds to offer me a handful of facial tissues. I mopped the sweat that ran freely on my face.

"Are you all right?" she asked.

"The hell with me. How's he going to be?"

The nurse nodded and smiled slightly.

"I thought we'd lost him back there for a minute," I said.

She pursed her lips and looked as if she was going to scold me. "Dr. Chatman does not allow that to happen on his airplane," she said.

"Damn right," Chatman said without hesitation.

I suppose the logistics of what they had done was simple for them, but all I could do was sit there and wad Kleenex. Punk, I thought, you're on a roll. Keep those numbers clicking.

Once inside the hospital, all I could do, along with Chief White and Detective Stan Buchanan of Gallup, was sit, talk, and wait.

12

The nurse sneezed discreetly, but it was enough to jar me awake.

"You look like you could use about forty-eight hours straight," Dr. Harlan Sprague, Jr., said quietly. He was sitting nearby, a slender briefcase leaning against the chair leg. He let the journal he was reading fall closed, but kept the place with his thumb.

I rubbed my eyes and pushed myself upright in the chair. "Must have dozed off." I looked at my watch. Two hours of dozing. "When did you come up?"

"About an hour ago. I flew in." He fully closed the journal and put it in the briefcase. "Your two compadres left?"

"They had some kind of problem they got called on. Someone else from Gallup was supposed to be here by now."

Sprague nodded. "I've got a two-day conference that promises two days of boredom. Had I known you were going to make the trip, I would have offered you a ride in my plane. More comfortable, I suspect, than the air ambulance."

"It wasn't too bad. I appreciate the thought, though. About all we've been doing is waiting. Hurry up and wait."

"I can imagine," Sprague said gently. "Anyhow, I saw you here and thought you probably wouldn't be asleep too long." He glanced up at the wall clock. "I have about an hour, if there's anything else you need. I'm impressed, by the way, with how thorough your Detective Reyes was, however."

"We appreciate your cooperation," I said, trying to marshal my thoughts. What I wanted was a chance to clean up. I was still in uniform and acutely aware of how scruffy I must have looked.

"I wish I could be of more help," Sprague continued quietly. "Apparently the young officer saw Mr. Fernandez with someone just before the incident. On the sidewalk near the town houses." He shook his head ruefully. "Had I only looked outside. But, at that hour . . ." He shrugged.

"I never had much of a chance to talk with Hewitt," I said. "We're anxious to do that."

"How long has he been in surgery now?"

I looked long and hard at my watch, numbed by the passage of time. "God. Would you believe almost six hours?"

Sprague grimaced. "And almost that long down in Posadas?" I nodded. "Well," the doctor said, "if they finish up right now, it'll still be a number of hours before there's any chance of coherent consciousness. I would guess that it's wishful thinking to expect anything before late this evening. Better tomorrow, even."

"I'll wait," I said. Hell, it was getting to be a habit, waiting. Easier that than anything else. No news was good news, goes the cliché. Sprague nodded in sympathy and glanced at the tape recorder that I had with me.

"Why don't I go find out what's happening for you?" he asked. "I suspect I'll have an easier time of it than you."

"I'd appreciate that."

Harlan Sprague was gone for perhaps twenty minutes, and when he returned he smiled some reassurance. "You can relax a little. The officer has been out of surgery for nearly twenty minutes. I'm sure they would have told you, but there's been no opportunity. Apparently a messy traffic accident. Anyway, the officer is in ICU recovery. The nurse there says it will be at least six hours before they'll even think of letting you in the room."

"Six hours?"

Sprague nodded. "And the chance of him being awake and coherent is just about nil, I can tell you that."

"But he's doing all right?"

"The nurse said the surgery went 'fair'. That was her term. There are always so many complications in this sort of thing that that's about the best you can hope for." He stepped up closer to me and frowned. "Now listen. I know a man who's dead on his feet when I see one. And I also know a mild coronary when I see it . . . or at least an acute warning of one. And that's what you had in the park down in Posadas. Sheriff Gastner, you're a basket case. Go get some rest before you end up in ICU yourself. You're not doing yourself, or anyone else, any favors." He looked down at the table. "And for God's sakes, stop smoking those damn cigarettes."

I laughed. "Thanks."

He wasn't amused. "I need to go. If you're still alive tomorrow at four P.M., I'll be flying back to Posadas. Unless you've already made arrangements, I'd appreciate the company."

"I'll have to see what happens. But thanks again."

He tipped his head and looked at me for a long moment, then slowly shook his head and sighed. "Leave a message for me at the desk at the Hilton. I'll check there just before I leave for the airport."

I watched him walk off down the hall, slightly

stooped, briefcase swinging rhythmically. I went to the restroom and tried to freshen up. The grizzled face that stared at me from the mirror wouldn't freshen much. Neither would the rumpled clothes. I tossed the paper towel in the bin. "Who the hell cares what you look like," I muttered to myself. I turned to leave. The swinging door almost caught me in the head as Chief White walked in.

"Christ, you look awful," he said.

"I think the next person who tells me that is going to get punched," I said. I pushed past his bulk and patted him on the arm at the same time. "Hewitt's out of surgery. The nurse says it will be at least six hours before we can see him."

"The best we could hope for," Chief White said slowly. "His parents are on their way from Tucson."

I nodded. "I'm going to go across the street to the motel and spend some of the county's money for a bed," I said. "Give me a call if anything changes. Otherwise I'll be back around suppertime."

The walk revived me a little . . . just long enough to attend to chores. Half a block down the main drag I bought a pack of underwear and a pair of socks at an Army-Navy store. At the motel, I talked the taciturn desk clerk into having the maid run my uniform across to the one-hour dry cleaner's. I called Posadas and filled Holman in.

"Bill, hang on a minute," Holman said at one point. "Estelle wants to talk to you."

Her voice was soft on the phone, and I had to concentrate to hear. "If you fly down with Sprague tomorrow, talk with him about his daughter," Estelle suggested. "She overdosed in January of last year. His wife apparently left him a couple months after that. The interesting thing is that according to a couple of people I

94

talked to, one of Darlene Sprague's best friends was Jenny Barrie."

"That doesn't surprise me," I said. "It's a small community. Everybody knows everybody."

"I just think it's interesting that Doc Sprague's daughter OD'd, and then one of her good friends dies, involved with drugs as well."

"You're saying Barrie is our connection?"

"No, I'm not. It's just something, that's all. It might be interesting to lead the doctor that way, and see what he says."

"I'll see," I said.

"The sheriff wants to talk to you again. Hang on."

The connections clicked and then Sheriff Holman said, "Bill, I'm making a request of some of the other people that we set up an interagency task force here. We thought we could take the simple, limited approach, but it didn't work. I think a mass undercover operation might flush something out."

"It might."

"You don't sound overwhelmed with enthusiasm."

"Not right now, I'm not. I'm too damn tired to think straight."

"Well, when you get back here, we'll talk about it."

"Fine. Tomorrow, probably." We rang off and I headed for bed. With all its heavy curtains, the motel room was dark as night, and I burrowed in. It couldn't have been more than five minutes later that the phone rang.

I had been sleeping so hard that I jerked almost upright. Four rings later I managed to find the damn thing.

"Uh?"

"Sheriff Gastner? Chief White."

I rolled on my back and stared up into the darkness. "Yes."

"Art Hewitt died a couple minutes ago."

For several seconds I didn't say anything. Finally I shifted the phone and mumbled, "Did his parents ever make it up from Tucson?"

"They were with him."

"Okay. I'll be over in a minute." I hung up and rolled my legs off the bed until I was sitting. I dialed the front desk and asked that someone check on my uniform. The puzzled desk attendant replied that it had been placed at my door some time ago. I retrieved the bundle and tossed it on the bed. Then I went to the heavily curtained window, pushed the draperies aside a little and looked outside. I was stunned to find the street lights on and the sky inky.

I let the draperies fall and found the light switch. My watch said nine thirty-seven. I stared at it and then muttered something profane. A few minutes later I was dressed. I buckled on my Sam Browne belt and glanced in the mirror. I saw an aging cop with bags under his eyes. That didn't concern me. I was thinking about the son of a bitch who had brought that kilo of cocaine into Posadas. The death of five kids I blamed on him. And Benny Fernandez. Now Art Hewitt. "You got seven, you bastard. No more."

The hospital seemed a lot quieter when I walked in for the second time that day.

13

It was shortly before midnight when I returned to my motel room. The desk clerk looked up, saw me and reached into the cubbyhole for room 207.

"The gentleman who telephoned said to be sure you got this," the clerk said helpfully, and I took the small message. It was from Sprague.

> Sheriff: I'll be flying back to Posadas first thing in the morning. Leave a message for me if you want a ride. Flight time anytime after 9 A.M. Plane is at Sultan Flying Service at the International. Sorry about Hewitt.

"He made me read it back to him word for word, so I know it's right," the desk clerk said. For the first time I noticed how young he was . . . probably a high school kid earning a few extra bucks.

"Thanks," I said. I handed him five dollars. "And thanks for getting it right. It was important. And will you set up a wake-up call for seven-thirty?"

"Sure thing." He tucked the money away and wrote out a time note to stick in the slotted board behind him.

I called the Hilton and left a message for Sprague that nine o'clock would be fine. After more than an hour of tossing and turning, I fell asleep. I awoke only once, apprehensive as hell about nothing. I lay still, listening. Normal street traffic rumbled up and down Central Avenue. In the distance, a jet thundered off to the west. By turning my head slightly, I could see the faint glow of my watch. Four-sixteen. The air-conditioner kicked on. About time, I thought. The room was stuffy, the air filled with the cloying aroma of that gunk that room maids spray in an effort to make things smell better than Calcutta streets. My mind drifted from one thing to another, and the outside world began to fade a little. The wake-up call interrupted a dream in which Harlan Sprague was vehemently telling Posadas Airport manager Jim Bergin that cracked aircraft engine pistons could be detected with a stethoscope, if only Bergin would take time to listen carefully enough.

I watched the mountain just west of Socorro slide by smoothly. "There are towers on top of every mountain in the southwest," I said, and Sprague laughed shortly.

"Seems like it, sometimes, doesn't it."

"As long as we clear them all." There was little cause for concern. The Cessna obviously had power to spare, and Sprague was evidently not the sort to buzz treetops. I turned from the window and winced a little. I pulled at the knot of my tie and took a deep breath. The discomfort, nothing more than an annoying fullness that seemed to settle behind my sternum, subsided after a few seconds.

"You all right?" Sprague asked.

I nodded. "So the conference was a bust, huh?"

"Total," Sprague said. "A new low in boredom." He heard something through his headset and said, "Mike Bravo one seventy-eight." Immediately he reached forward and changed radio frequencies, then took off the headset and put it on the floor just in front of his seat. "Some peace and quiet," he said. "If I can't find Posadas in this kind of weather, something's wrong. I get tired of all the yammering."

The sky was magnificently clear, cloudless and the sort of deep blue that always made me think that some of the black of outer space was leaking through. We made a slight turn and then the Cessna settled into a straight course for Posadas. We sat without conversation for another ten minutes, each caught up in our own thoughts, content to watch the rumpled geologic oddities of New Mexico slide by.

"He never regained consciousness, did he," Sprague said. I just shook my head. Sprague puffed out his cheeks and let out the air in a loud sigh like a leaky tire. "At least he didn't suffer." I didn't respond to that. I could have said that lying in the wet grass of a village park with his insides torn to pieces was pretty close to my definition of suffering. And who the hell knows what the unconscious, or semi-conscious, mind thinks as first one set of synapses and then another shuts down. It sure as hell ain't party-time, Doc. But I didn't say any of that, because Sprague didn't deserve it.

Instead, I shifted a little so that I could talk without twisting my neck. I leaned a shoulder against the gentle vibration of the door and window. "Do you mind if I ask you a couple questions?" Sprague glanced quickly at me and shrugged. I smiled faintly. "No interruptions up here."

"Feel free," Sprague said.

"When your daughter died last year . . ." I saw the flicker of pain on the doctor's face, just a brief tightening of the muscles and an extra blink or two. "Do you mind?"

"Go ahead." He didn't look at me, but continued his regular scanning of the sky ahead of us.

"It was after a party with some of her friends, wasn't it?"

"Yes."

"Did you know her friends very well?"

Sprague turned and looked at me steadily. "Obviously not. Had that been the case, she wouldn't have been . . ." He hesitated, then said, "The incident wouldn't have happened."

"Was Jenny Barrie one of her close friends?"

Sprague was once more scanning the sky, this time looking out to the east, and for a moment it appeared that he hadn't heard the question. I was sure he had, though, and let the silence hang.

"She and the Barrie girl became friends during their freshman year." He said it to the window, then reached forward and wiped a speck of dust from the rim of one of the gauges. He seemed to settle a little. "That was a hard year."

"In what way?"

"I didn't like the direction I saw Darlene going."

"And how was that?"

He waved a hand at the familiarity of it. "The usual. Minimal effort at things I thought important. The sort of daily dress that . . . I'm sure you're familiar with the whole process. You watched four of your own grow up. First thing you know, there seems to be a gulf growing, and be damned if there's anything to do about it. Pretty soon the gulf's too big to cross." He glanced at his watch. "Too damn big."

"And the Barrie girl?"

"I tried to ignore her. That was a mistake, in retrospect."

"There was never any decision about where the cocaine came from that killed Darlene."

"No, there wasn't. But you would know that better than I."

"What do you think?"

Sprague eyed me skeptically. "You're serious?"

"Of course."

"For months, I agonized over that question, Sheriff.

Agonized. Over that question, over my daughter's death. You're a parent. I'm sure you can empathize. In fact, if I read you right, you're finding it hard to write off Art Hewitt as just another cop killed in line of duty. He's not so far removed in age from your youngest, right? And he was even living under your roof."

"Go on."

Sprague shrugged. "My first thought was to blame Barrie and her circle of creepy friends. Hell, not my first thought. My only thought." His lips compressed grimly. "It would seem that your department has found evidence supporting that notion."

"The accident that killed Barrie and her friends, you mean."

"Certainly."

"So you think the cocaine found in that vehicle was hers?"

"Maybe, maybe not. But it wouldn't surprise me if that's how it turns out. The common denominator is Barrie. Or her friends."

"Do you have any notions about which one? Or ones?"

"Detective Reyes asked me the same thing a day or two ago. Whenever it was. No, I don't. In fact, of the five youngsters who died in that car crash, I knew only two fairly well. Jenny Barrie, obviously. Tommy Hardy was a patient of mine when he was very young." Sprague blinked rapidly a couple times. "He was in leg braces for almost a year. A two-year-old in leg braces. He walked like a goddamned duck. It worked out all right, though. And now this. What a goddamned waste." He looked over at me and shrugged. "I knew the Fernandez boy only tangentially. I knew Hank Montaño only as a name and a kid in a long line of fall sport physicals. I did that for a few years, as you no doubt remember."

"I remember. My youngest son came home one day

after his and told me that you dipped your hands in buckets of ice water between each kid."

Sprague laughed loudly. "They always think that, don't they. God, that was years ago when he went through it."

"Something like nine."

"You know"—and he squirmed down a little in his seat, a touch more at ease—"I know I'm from a generation light-years removed, but for the life of me I can't figure out how a run-of-the-mill high school kid gets ahold of a kilo of hard drugs. That puzzles me. No kid has that much money. Do they?"

"Evidently one of them did. Either that or they were set up."

Sprague grimaced. "Set up? A teenager?"

"Or being used. It's possible none of the five knew the coke was there. It's conceivable that someone else was just using the car as a stash. That's possible."

"There aren't many other choices. Either they were dealing, or someone was using their car innocent of their knowledge, or someone was framing them. I don't see any other choice."

"I don't either."

"And so what do you plan to do?"

I shrugged. "Detective Reyes has been digging during my absence. I'll see what she's come up with. We've got a couple leads, and we'll thrash those out." Sprague didn't ask what those leads were, and that was a good thing. I didn't know, myself.

"Will you be returning for the funeral? Officer Hewitt's?"

"Yes."

"His parents are from Tucson, you say?"

"Yes."

"Is that where the funeral is? Tucson?"

"The family affair is. I won't make that one. Just the one in Gallup."

"And when is that?"

"Thursday at two."

"Another flight upstate, eh?"

"No. Holman and I will drive. The car will be in the procession. For some reason, cops seem to believe that it's a comfort for the grieving family to see the brotherhood assembled."

"Is it?"

I held up my hands. "Who knows. I can't imagine that anything is a comfort, except passage of time. Maybe the fanfare makes for a less painful memory, I suppose. Beats standing in the rain by yourself. We all need things like that sometimes."

Dr. Sprague toyed with a couple of things on the dash. "It makes you wonder, doesn't it."

"About?"

"At what point folks will stop accepting that it's a part of life to see their young buried."

"I'm not sure any of us accept that as a necessity, Doctor. We'd all pay a fancy price to avoid it."

Sprague looked at me for a long minute. Even without this attention, the Cessna drove a straight rail through the sky. "I don't think so, Sheriff. I don't see much evidence of willingness to do that."

"Wouldn't you do about anything if it were possible to have your daughter back?"

"That's what I mean," Sprague said so softly I almost couldn't hear him over the engine beat. "In retrospect, it's so simple. But before it happens? Did I do enough? Did any of us? We all know fast cars can kill, and we know they especially kill the young. And yet we allowed five youngsters to pack themselves in that vehicle . . . with alcohol included. We don't require much training for a driver's license. We allow parties. And all the time, what do we do? We gamble, Sheriff. We gamble that the ones who are killed—and we know they will be, every year—we gamble that they aren't

103

our own." When I didn't respond immediately, Sprague added, "You see? It costs, doesn't it? Let me give you one simple example. You're a law officer, and should appreciate the simplicity of this. Suppose that if you were caught driving while intoxicated, no matter what your age, you lost your driving privileges for life." I raised a skeptical eyebrow. Sprague smiled. "You see? We are not willing to pay the price yet, are we? The convenience of driving is more important to us . . . more important . . . than a stiff penalty to clear the roads of drunks."

"People would drive anyway."

"Even if they knew that if they were caught without a license they would have to perform five years of full-time public-service work?"

"And let their families starve?"

"So whose fault is that? Did they have to drink and drive? I don't mean to be argumentative, Sheriff. I'm just making the point that we aren't willing to pay the price. Yet. It just isn't important enough to enough people. We all think we can dodge fate. I stand down from my soapbox now." He grinned. "You asked for it." He gestured at the airplane. "There's nothing like having a captive audience."

"If you ever figure out the answers," I said, "be sure to let me in on the secret."

"Be assured," Sprague replied, nodding vigorously. Then he added, "But don't hold your breath. Humans are strange creatures. It takes a catastrophe of royal proportions to drill through the average person's complacency. I lost a daughter and a wife, and saw little stirring in the community. A car crash kills five teenagers." He shrugged offhandedly. "Still, not much. A few feeble efforts to form a parents' awareness group. A prominent merchant is killed after he mortally wounds an undercover police officer." He looked at me and raised an eyebrow in question. "What's it take, Sheriff?"

"I don't know."

Sprague looked off ahead, then pointed. "That hump on the horizon there is the mesa north of Posadas. We'll be home in about fifteen minutes."

Home. I thought about Posadas, and felt uneasy. For a hundred years or more, a sleepy, tiny border hamlet. For thirty years after that, a booming mining town, jerked so fast into the twentieth century that it lost almost all of its former color, culture, and dignity. A two-bit, booming mining town. Now the mine was gone, the mill closed. And what was left was struggling under something ugly and threatening. I looked up at the bright blue of the sky. Harlan Sprague was absorbed in his own thoughts, and we flew the final miles in silence.

14

"What do we know about David and Theresa Barrie?" I asked Estelle Reyes when I walked into the office early that afternoon.

Even if the detective noticed my lack of greeting, she didn't miss a beat. "I talked to them."

"I know you did. What did you find out that's new?"

Reyes shrugged and rummaged for her notebook. She flipped pages and said, "Personally, I think David Barrie is a first-class creep. His wife is a mouse. She lets him walk all over her." Her venom surprised me, but I wasn't in the mood to discuss other people's marital problems.

"Dr. Sprague blames Jenny Barrie for his daughter's death last year."

"That's the impression I got, too."

"I spent three hours with him in his airplane. It wasn't just an impression. He blames himself for letting it happen. What did David Barrie have to say?"

"Indignation is his game, sir. No matter what question I asked, he bristled. I think he figured he could scare me off. He also likes to threaten law suits. If we try to pin anything on the memory of his daughter, he promises to sue. I had a hard time keeping my mouth shut. I get the impression he would have liked the

chance to sue Benny Fernandez, too. He said he still
might sue the estate."

"Because the son was driving the car?"

"Right. He's a great guy."

"That's all he said?"

"Just about. Except that he told me we should
check the trucks that bring in food-service supplies for
Fernandez's restaurant."

I sat down heavily. "Hell, why not? It's a waste of
time, but why not."

"You don't think Fernandez was involved?"

"No, you're right. I don't. I don't know why he
came unglued in the park, but I sure as hell intend to
find out. But no, I don't think he was running drugs."

Estelle watched me light a cigarette and then
pushed an ashtray toward the extended match. "It was
pretty rough up in Albuquerque?"

"Yes," I said. "It was pretty rough."

Estelle nodded, then changed the subject. "It was
convenient that Dr. Sprague was around to provide air
taxi."

"Yes. He had a conference to attend. He got bored
early."

"Is that what he told you?"

I looked sharply at the girl. "You should have been
a goddamned oriental. What's on your mind?"

"He didn't have a conference."

"You checked?"

"Yes. I called a friend on the Albuquerque Police
Department who called a friend whose best friend is an
internist, too."

"Tight line of evidence, there."

A trace of a grin crossed Estelle Reyes's pretty
face. I realized I hadn't really seen her smile in a hell of
a long time. "And I also called Francis," she said, refer-
ring to her fiancé. "Anyway, there was no medical conference in Albuquerque this week. Not even a meeting

of the tooth fairies. There was no conference for medical writers. Or medical salesmen. There was only one conference in the entire city scheduled for yesterday and today."

She paused and I prompted, "And?"

"The city school bus drivers are having a two-day workshop."

I frowned and stubbed out my cigarette. "So why would Sprague make up a story?"

Estelle shrugged and tapped the edge of her small notebook on the desktop. "Maybe he didn't want to have to explain to you why he was there?"

"Well, obviously. But why *was* he there?" I asked, and then answered my own question. "He made a point of seeing me at the hospital. And then a point of offering me a ride home."

Estelle nodded. "Now, I may be a little cynical, but it's a bit much to expect him to be that concerned about Hewitt's welfare. He didn't know the kid from Adam. When I talked to him that night in the park, Sprague did mention that you needed to see a doctor." She smiled slightly at the surprise on my face.

"Horse shit."

"But I don't think he would fly all the way to Albuquerque and back because of that. Unless he was your personal physician."

"Which he isn't."

"So that leaves us with three choices. One, he is a concerned citizen with plenty of money who flies great distances on the outside chance that he can be helpful."

"That's entirely possible."

"Two, he wanted to find out what you knew. Or what Art Hewitt knew. If that's the case, then he stands to gain or lose something by that information."

"And three?"

"We don't know why he did it."

"I had a feeling you were going to say that. Number

two is the most interesting. If he is trying to track down, after more than a year, the source of the drugs that killed his daughter, he would be interested. Vitally interested." Estelle nodded. "That's what you were thinking?"

"*Sí*," she said, making her slight accent a heavy imitation of José Jimenez.

I lighted another cigarette. "Why didn't he just say that, then? He had ample chance during the flight back down here. And what put the bee in your bonnet to check on Sprague?"

"Just a hunch. When I spoke with him first, he said, 'Don't hesitate to call me later if there's anything else you need.' Less than twelve hours later, I find out from your call that he's in Albuquerque. I just found it odd that he didn't mention his conference commitment when I talked with him. I mean, the odds were good that I would want to talk with him again."

"So? Everyone says, 'Don't hesitate to call.' That doesn't mean they really mean it. Especially doctors." I remembered her fiancé. "No offense."

"What can I say? It was a hunch."

"Follow up on it. Very quietly. If Sprague is off on a personal vendetta, I want to know about it. I don't want another Benny Fernandez. And if he's just a good samaritan, I don't want him harassed."

"What are you going to do?"

I stood up. "I'm going home to clean up and get out of this monkey suit. And then I'm going out to the football camp for the afternoon."

"Ah," Estelle said. "It's that time of year, almost. When you pursue the pigskin. May your team always win."

"I'm touched."

"I'm just practical. Last year, every time your team lost, we couldn't get a civil word out of you."

"You exaggerate. I'm not that bad. Anyway, this is

partly work. Scott Salinger has had a couple weeks to stew. He'll be there. Maybe he'll have come to terms with what he knows."

"If he knows."

"My instinct says he does and is just frightened to deal with it. He might have to step on a few friends. Some folks have a hard time doing that." I picked up my Stetson and headed for the door. "Oh, and tell Sheriff Holman, if you see him before I do, that the funeral is at two o'clock Thursday afternoon. I already committed him. We'll drive up in three-ten."

"I'll tell him. He'll be overjoyed about the drive. Bob Torrez says the sheriff still talks about the last time he rode with you."

I grinned and left the cubbyhole that Estelle called her office. On the bulletin board above the dispatcher's desk, I pinned a Magic-Markered sign. J. J. Murton looked at me and said, "Oh, you're back!" Then he looked at the sign and read aloud, "Wash and wax three-ten by six P.M. Wednesday. Yessir, I'll have the trustees get right to that. Wash 'er right up." I reached out and pointed to part of the message. "Oh, and wax," Miracle said. "Right. Wax."

I nodded and smiled at him encouragingly. "I'll be ten-seven until tomorrow noon, J.J. Don't call me unless the town is burning down."

"Right."

"And I'm taking three-ten," I reminded him. His eyebrows shot together, and he looked back up at the sign I'd stuck to the bulletin board. "That's for tomorrow, J.J., not today."

I left the office and headed home. I walked through the front door of my house for the first time in nearly forty-eight hours, and stopped short. Dr. Sprague had taken me straight from the airport to the sheriff's office, because it seemed urgent to talk with Estelle. Now I was home, and it struck me like a well-placed blow. I'd

110

forgotten that Art Hewitt's personal effects were still scattered around my home—a jacket here, pair of tennis shoes there, toilet articles on the bathroom counter. It's the kind of heartshot that makes for a rotten afternoon.

I packed his things and put the bundle by the front door so I wouldn't forget it come Thursday. Then I showered, changed clothes, and left for the mountain football camp.

It was a yearly ritual that marked the beginning of the sacred season, an advance peek at the high school team on whose behalf I would bellow myself hoarse during fourteen games. I figured it to be potent medicine for what ailed me.

The car only scraped bottom once as I drove carefully up the twisting Forest Service road. Where the elevation tipped 8200 feet, I thumped across a cattle guard that marked private property. The sixty acres were owned by a Posadas businessman. The attraction was a large open field, reasonably smooth, and a casually laid-out camping area. Every year, the Posadas head football coach hosted a week-long "football camp." On paper, the idea was to provide a camping and recreational opportunity for area youngsters who couldn't tell a football from a yucca. There was lots of camping, and hiking, and running, and ball throwing. In short, lots of pre-season football practice. By chance, the camp was well attended by any student who wanted a place on the team. Not mandatory, but next-best thing. Coach Fred Gutierrez figured that young lungs that survived a workout at 8200 feet would probably handle any strain down below.

I drove in the cow path that led to the only structure on the property, a small, neat log cabin known as "Coaches' Cabin." As I pulled up, I could hear shouts out on the field. I locked 310 and walked through the thick grove of Gambel oak and ponderosa pine that separated the field from the cabin site. Up at the other end

111

of the field I could see a straight row of tents, but it was the action out on the turf that interested me most. I picked a thick-boled ponderosa and sat down at its base with a comfortable grunt. I pushed the cap back on my head and rested my forearms on my drawn-up knees.

Gutierrez and his four assistants—just camp counselors, mind you—were running the forty campers through simple passing routines. There actually were some younger kids there, too. And the Posadas Jaguars' starting lineup, or I was watching fly fishermen. I sat and relaxed for nearly a half hour, picking out the lineup that was going to make other schools beg for mercy that fall. Enough brain cells remained stubbornly fixed on business that after a few minutes I realized Scott Salinger was not on the field.

One of the assistant coaches saw me, finally, and trotted over. Mark Tatman recognized a faithful booster and grinned widely.

"Sheriff, how are ya?" he said. We shook hands, and then he turned serious. "Say, that was an awful thing about that young cop who got killed downtown. Some of the kids were saying he was living with you. They thought he was some kind of relative until they read the story in the paper yesterday."

I just nodded, still watching the players. The coach asked, "What was he undercover for, drugs, or what?"

"I'd rather not discuss it right now, Mark." I nodded at the action on the field. "They look good."

The assistant coach turned so he could survey the players. "I think so. A good year comin' up."

"When do the official two-a-day practices start?"

"August fifteenth."

"Super."

"Did you need anything, or were you just cruisin'?"

"Just getting a pre-season peek, Mark. But say, where's Scott Salinger? I don't see him."

Mark Tatman shrugged. "He and Coach Gutierrez

exchanged a few words yesterday. He left and hasn't been back."

"No shit? What was the problem?"

Tatman held up his hands. "All I know is he was real moody. Depressed. Couldn't keep his mind on what he was supposed to be doing. Yesterday Gutierrez shouted some instructions at him and Salinger cussed at him. Nothin' real bad, but with the little kids around, you know, you can't let it slide." Tatman shrugged again. "Not very like Salinger, either. He left after that. Just got in his car and left."

"Well, I'll be damned."

"Couple of the guys say he's still pretty shook about that July Fourth accident. Him and Tommy Hardy were pretty good friends, you know."

"Yes, I know."

"He'll come out of it. Coach said just to let him go. Let him unwind."

"Probably best."

"If he comes back, should I tell him you wanted to see him?"

"No. If I need him, I'll find him." The coach was anxious to return to his players, and I let him go with a grin and a pat on the back. I watched for another ten minutes, then went back to the car. It was time to find out if Scott Salinger was as tough off the football field as he was on it.

15

Posadas cooked under the hot July sun. Downtown that late afternoon was quiet. Many of the shops were closed already. I came in from the east and noticed that the Fernandez Burger Heaven was open. I wondered who was running it. Farther on, with the traffic only one or two cars deep at each light, the town looked like what it was—a slow-paced southwestern town where the single wide main drag was a little unkempt and weed-strewn.

I had lived in Posadas long enough that I could accurately visualize the interior of every store and shop along that main drag. I figured I knew every clerk and owner, too.

As I drove past the intersection of Grande and Fourth, I saw David Barrie walking from his now locked and dark hobby-craft shop to the parking lot. He looked like a caricature of one of those World War II British officers. Very blond, he wore his hair long on the sides, combed so that it looked as if he were facing a strong wind. A long, slightly ski nose jutted below very blue eyes, and his not-quite lantern jaw was set resolutely. He marched with arms swinging vigorously and rhythmically, and when he reached his car, he unlocked the door and slid in gracefully.

By then I had driven past, and I watched in the rearview mirror as Barrie's silver Corvette eased out onto the street, heading east. The hobby business was obviously a good one.

Scott Salinger's home was well away from the main drag, in one of the older sections of town that had been established during the heyday of the silver mines forty years before. The place was small, overshadowed by the collection of vehicles in the graveled driveway. A big boat, its cockpit covered with canvas and the engine booted, rested with its stern close to one garage door. The trailer hitch was supported at a convenient height by a cinder block. Between that and the street was a motor home perhaps twenty feet in length. A small motorbike was obviously a permanent attachment to the vehicle's nose, secured with two padlocks and a hefty chain. A middle-aged Chevy Nova with Texas plates was parked beside the boat. Between the garage and the brown plaster wall of the house was an old Grumman canoe, two bicycles long past their prime, and something that might once have been a wire dog-run.

I pulled into the driveway behind the Nova. It didn't look like anyone was home, so I left the engine running when I got out.

"May I help you?"

I spun around, startled. The young lady was in grubby gardener's clothes that served only to enhance her lithe figure. She pushed the wide-brimmed floppy hat back and surveyed me with eyes almost the color of jade.

"I'm Undersheriff Bill Gastner," I said, and extended my hand.

She shook with a slightly grimy hand and no apologies for it. "I'm Amy Salinger."

"Yes, I know," I said. "I remember you as the lead in that musical that the high school put on a number of years ago."

She smiled slightly. "You have a good memory, Sheriff."

I indicated the Nova with a nod. "You're a Texican now?"

"I'm a nurse at Texas A and M. I'm home for a week or two vacation. I assume you wanted to see Scott?" Her tone was sober and businesslike. I nodded. "He should be back in an hour or two. He went hunting."

"Hunting?"

Amy Salinger took off her hat and scratched her head, further tangling her already wild mane of strawberry hair. "That's what he calls it. Mostly it's just hiking around the hills. He seems to need the solitude. Especially now."

"It's been pretty rugged for him?"

"Yes, it has," Amy said. "The car crash really threw him for a loop. Mom and Dad just get frustrated talking with him. Scott and I have always gotten along well, and they asked if I would come home for a while."

"It helps?"

Amy wiped her hands on her jeans. "I don't know. Maybe a little. He says he doesn't know what to do. I don't know what he could do, unless he knows something about the drugs you found. But he won't tell me everything, so I can't do much except be supportive in very general terms. He's always been the kind to keep things bottled up. Some kids are fortunate enough to be articulate. He isn't." She shrugged.

"I spoke with one of his football coaches a few minutes ago. He said Scott left the camp. The coach said Scott was pretty depressed a good deal of the time."

"Small wonder," Amy said, and her voice carried some of the professional steel that good nurses always seem to have at their disposal.

I chewed on the corner of my lip a little, wondering how to phrase the next question. There was no easy way. I moved a few steps and leaned against 310's fender. "He's not apt to do anything rash, is he? I mean, you know him as well as anyone."

"Rash?"

"Well, if he's really depressed, and doesn't know which way to turn . . ."

"You mean rash like suicide?"

"Yeah. I guess that's what I mean."

"I hope not." She hesitated. "I know it's crossed his mind, though."

"Really?"

"I mean before. When he's had problems before. A couple of years ago, in fact." She shrugged and added, "What adolescent doesn't entertain the notion at one time or another? We just hope it's a notion that passes harmlessly, or that we can make the kid see that it's unnecessary. All things pass. Of course, convincing even supposedly mature college students of that isn't easy. And if they're the kind who finally decides to go lights out, the odds of doing anything to stop them are nil."

"You said he's out hunting now?"

"That's what he said. Once he told me he likes to go out on top of the mesa behind Consolidated. It's quite a view from up there."

"He took a gun with him?"

"His old twenty-two rifle."

"And you're not worried?"

"Of course I'm worried, Sheriff. He's the only brother I've got. And I love him a lot. But you can't put a teenager in a cage. Scott's not self-destructive—just confused." She blinked rapidly and cleared her throat. "And you can't believe how much it hurts to talk like this. But I have faith in Scott. I really do. Other than that, about all you can do is love 'em and make 'em really believe there's something worthwhile to come home to. And when they do come home, there better be someone to talk to who'll just listen and not make them believe they're being judged."

I looked at Amy Salinger for a long minute, and she returned the gaze evenly. "Then he's a lucky kid," I said.

"Thanks. But I think it's just common sense."

I nodded agreement with that. "What's he driving? I really need to talk to him."

"A 1974 Bronco. Blue over rusty white. It's got four of those big chrome lights on the roof and a power winch in front that doesn't have a cable. You can't miss it."

"Would you do me a favor?"

"Sure."

"If he comes home and we haven't talked, would you ask him to call me?" I pulled a card from my wallet and handed it to her. "It doesn't matter what time. If I'm not home, have him call the office number. They'll find me."

"I'll tell him, Sheriff. But in some ways, he's a stubborn kid. He'll mull things around in his head and then finally decide what he's going to do. Try and force something on him and he'll just clam up."

"I know. But I got to give it a try. It's been two weeks or better since the accident. He's had time to think. I really believe he's got some answers we badly need."

Amy Salinger said she'd do what she could, and I believed her. I backed out of the driveway as she headed back toward her garden. I knew the odds of finding Scott Salinger up on the mesa were slim, but I was stubborn, too.

To reach the mesa top, I drove up County 43 past the mine and the turn off to the lake. The pavement almost immediately gave way to gravel, then to rough and rutted government surplus caliche—hard as concrete when it was dry and slick as silicon syrup when wet. I half-expected to meet Scott's Bronco on the way down. One of us would have to take the ditch, and it wasn't going to be me. The county car straddled ruts most of the time, but once in a while crunched down hard enough to make me wince.

The road wound up the mesa face and finally came out on top. I couldn't see anything through the piñon and juniper, but when the road reached a triple fork, I stayed left, knowing I was heading toward the rim. Another hundred yards on I passed a derelict refrigerator, ten miles from the nearest 110-volt outlet. I always wondered what strange soul would go to all the trouble to cart such a thing out there when the county landfill was only a mile from town. A quarter mile farther on, an old mattress and the backseat of a van rotted slowly into the dirt. At least I could figure out what they had been used for.

After another ten minutes, I could see only emptiness through the trees and knew I was making progress toward the edge. And some of the tire tracks in the dust looked fresh. The road skirted a thick grove of mixed piñon and juniper and ended in a wide spot liberally littered with beer cans, a disposable diaper or two, and two bright-yellow oil cans. Parked under a fat juniper was Scott Salinger's Bronco.

I switched off the car and got out. The keys weren't in the Bronco, and it was locked. I felt a little better. I walked slowly and carefully through the timber . . . not because I was stalking anyone, but because I didn't want to fall on my face. I broke out of the trees and involuntarily slowed, struck by the view. The mesa rim was a wonderful place. The rocks were jumbled into scores of the best benches nature could provide. You could look out and see hundreds of square miles—old and new mines, two villages besides Posadas, a score of human enterprises, and endless works of nature. I stood still and scanned the rim. After a minute I saw Scott Salinger.

He was lying stretched out on a large flat rock, using another as a pillow. If he had the rifle, it was hidden behind him. I walked across toward him, and when I was a hundred feet away he decided to notice. He turned his head just enough to see who was intruding. I was well aware of the effect uniforms had on people, especially youngsters, and was glad then that I had changed into casual clothes. As I walked toward him, I thrust my hands deep in my pockets, hoping the effect was that of a harmless old man out for a simple daily constitutional, and that the meeting was entirely by chance.

"Scott, how are you doin'?" I said casually.

"Amy must have told you I was here." He sat up and watched my progress across the rocks.

"Yup, she did." I started to lower myself to a rock, and hesitated. "Do you mind?"

"Pull up a chair," he said, and managed a smile. I felt better.

"She seems like a wonderful gal," I said.

"She is."

"She's a little worried about you. So are a lot of people. I talked with Coach Tatman today."

"Yeah. Well." Salinger looked out into the distance. A slight breeze ruffled his hair and he ran a hand through it self-consciously. The family resemblance was striking.

"What happened? With football, I mean." I asked that and the boy shot me a glance as if to ask what business it was of mine, but then thought better of it. He returned his gaze to the distance and locked it there.

"It just got so it wasn't fun anymore. That's all. I was having a good time playing with some of the little kids. Watching 'em try to throw cracks me up." He grinned and curled his hands as if he were spastic. "The coaches aren't supposed to spend more than about an hour with us each day. With the varsity team, I mean . . . some state rule like that. But push, push, push. You'd think we were going for the Rose Bowl or something."

"You don't think it's pretty important?"

"No. Not compared to other things."

"Like?"

He was a long time in answering, and obviously knew why I had bothered tackling the mesa. "Like that undercover cop getting killed. Like Mr. Fernandez getting killed." There was a tremor then in his voice, and he turned his head further so I couldn't see his face. "Like Tom Hardy. Ricky. Isabel. All the rest." He twisted and looked at me then, under control. "No. It's not important."

"Life goes on, Scott."

"So I've been told."

I lighted a cigarette and the breeze took the smoke back away from the rim. "I guess it's not such an original thought. But it's true."

"Yeah."

"Where did the cocaine come from?"

Scott let out a breath that was the beginning of a weak chuckle. "I saw you coming across the rocks there, and knew that's what you wanted to ask me."

"Well? Here I am."

"Where do you get the idea that I know?"

"That first interview. When I used the tape recorder. I listened to that quite a few times. So did Detective Reyes."

Scott Salinger grinned at the mention of Estelle Reyes. "You know what she said to me a day or so ago?"

"I have no idea. She didn't tell me she'd talked to you."

"I was downtown. She was walking out of the bank. She stopped and stuck out her hand, like she wanted to shake, you know? I was kinda embarrassed, but what the hell. So I shook hands and she wouldn't let go right away. She hung on for a minute, and put her other hand up here, on the side of my face. Then she said, 'I wish I knew what was going on inside that skull of yours.'"

I laughed. "That sounds like Estelle. What did you say?"

"I said, 'So do I.'"

"Fair enough."

"She's something else. She didn't say anything more than that. Just kinda smiled and let me go. I was embarrassed as hell." He glanced at me. "She knows my sister. Went to school with her." I nodded and remained silent. He reached out and stripped a grass stalk bare and chewed on the end of it. After a minute he said, "I think the cocaine belonged to Jenny Barrie."

"What makes you think so?"

Salinger shrugged. "You hear talk. And once, I think it was a couple weeks before the end of school, Tommy was talking to me and asked me if I thought coke was as bad as everybody was telling us it was."

"What'd you say?"

"I said I didn't care, one way or another. I told him he was stupid if he was messing with it."

"What'd he say to that?"

Salinger frowned. "I don't remember. I think he just kind of shrugged it off. But he was going with Jenny Barrie, and she was a space case. She always was, even in grade school. Tommy said once that her old man smoked pot. I thought that was kinda funny."

"Funny how?"

He glanced at me and his eyes drifted to my cigarette. "Somehow I just never think of older folks smoking joints. There he is, fretting over his income tax, or oiling his lawn mower, or building one of those model airplanes his shop sells, and he's sucking in for all he's worth." Salinger pressed thumb and index finger against tightly pursed lips and sucked the imaginary joint until his eyes bugged. He let out a hard breath and chuckled bitterly. "Funny."

"Do you have any direct evidence that the kilo of cocaine was Jenny's?"

He shook his head. "No. But I know Tommy wouldn't be able to afford even a down payment, even if he was into that shit. He couldn't even afford a dime bag. And Isi Gabaldon was so straight she squeaked. The only reason she was in the car is because Hank Montaño was. And Ricky only did what his friends told him to do. No, it was her. Count on it."

I took another long shot, now that Scott was talking. "Did you know Darlene Sprague?"

"Sure."

"What about her?"

Scott picked at the grass stem. "We all had ideas about who slipped her that shit. And you know the semester after she died? Last year? I had a creative-writing class. Space case was in it, too."

"Space case?"

"Barrie. She spent the whole time writing those damn sappy poems. Always the same thing. Death, guilt, suicide." He made a horrible, twisted face that would have looked about right on a corpse. "We always had to read our stuff in class, you know. And hers. Wow." He pitched a small pebble down the rocks. "It got so bad that whenever she read something in class, me and a bunch of others would pretend like we were playing violins." He looked over at me and grinned. "Pretty bad dudes, huh?"

"Well . . ." I said dubiously.

"We got on her case pretty hard. But it always seemed that she enjoyed it in sort of a screwball way. I got the notion that she just enjoyed being miserable and tragic."

"Miserable and tragic."

"Yeah. It got really bad one day, though. The vice-principal came to the door to talk to Mrs. Rosenthal about something, and this one kid, maybe you know him—Terry Semple?"

"I know the family. His dad's a rancher."

"Right. Well, Jenny'd just finished reading some damn thing, all full of oh-ah, pain and agony. Just real first-class shit, you know. I didn't think anybody was really listening, 'cause she was wearing one of those sweatshirts that's got all the cutouts in it?" Salinger grinned. "And absolutely nothing on under it. That was kinda neat. Anyway, old Semple, he leans across that dumb little circle we had to sit in and says when Jenny finished reading, 'If you knew you were going to feel so damn guilty and broke up, what'd you deal in that shit for?'"

"Ouch."

"Jenny just looked him right in the eye and said, 'Fuck you.' He turned about eight shades of red, because he didn't know what to say to that. Then Mrs. Rosenthal came back and we were all acting real normal, like nothing happened. The rest of us about split a gut."

"And you didn't have much use for the Barrie girl, did you?"

Salinger hesitated, then said, "Unless you were in her pants, I don't think there was all that much about her to like." He looked soberly at me. "I mean, she didn't deserve to get killed like she did, and I don't mean to be bad-mouthing her. But . . ." he looked away for a minute, thinking hard. "I just thought she was a fake, that's all. I didn't know her that good, and I never had anything to do with her, until Tommy took up with her." He still gazed off into space. "She really had him hooked. And now they're all dead, so maybe it doesn't matter. But hell. One more year, and then I'm gone."

Abruptly changing the subject, he pointed off toward Posadas. "I sure like country like this. You sit here long enough, and it seems like you can feel the earth turning. I think I can see the curve in the horizon, and then I can feel the movement. You ever felt like that?"

I didn't say anything, pretty sure he wasn't expecting an answer. "I do," he said. "Every time I come up here. It's just back down in town that things are all screwed up."

"That's where the people are."

"That's for sure," Salinger said with a short laugh.

"Scott, I've bothered you long enough, but will you do me a favor? If you think of anything else that we should know, will you call? Now that you kinda have things sorted out? Will you do that? I'd appreciate that. We don't have any concrete leads, and the last thing I want to see is any more people hurt. We could use the help."

He gave me the same patient, searching look that his sister had. "All right. I'm sure that stuff was Jenny Barrie's. But I have no idea where she might have gotten it. Not that much. I can't believe her family had anything to do with it. Hell, Mr. Barrie is a jerk, but nothing like that."

I stood up somewhat shakily, careful to stay well away from the jumbled edge. Scott picked up the short Ruger .22 that had been lying beside him. "I'll walk back with you. I got to get home for supper anyway."

We reached the vehicles and he stopped short. "I don't believe you drove that up here."

I patted 310's front fender. "Wanna drag?"

He laughed. "From here to the pavement, sure."

"No dice. In fact, let me go first," I said. "That way, if I break an axle, I won't have to walk back to town."

I carefully turned the heavy Ford around and idled and bumped out the path through the trees. Scott Salinger's Bronco stayed a respectful hundred yards behind me all the way. I hit the pavement feeling pretty sure that the kid would be all right. But I had been wrong before. I wasn't quite ready for a ground swell of confidence. I knew I'd feel better when I had somebody behind bars. But at least now I had some ideas.

16

The telephone rang five times before my sleep-fogged brain bothered to interpret the noise. Even then, it was slow to issue orders to move. We had gotten back from Hewitt's funeral at midnight, and even Sheriff Holman had been bone-tired. I had been almost comatose, and driven the last fifty miles by instinct.

I had no idea what time it was, only that the telephone sounded like a fire alarm exploding directly in my ear. Had it been noon already, I wouldn't have known. My bedroom would have made a good photographer's darkroom. Some years before, I had installed a really heavy pair of shutters on the window, with the logic that a cop who has to sleep at odd hours should be able to do so in comfortable darkness.

I groped for the nightstand, realized I was on the wrong side of the bed and groaned as the ringing persisted.

"Ga——" I coughed and then managed a squawky, "Gastner."

"Sheriff, sorry to bother you."

"Um," I murmured, more interested in drifting back to sleep than listening.

The voice said something about being Roger Downs,

and a lonely, alert synapse somewhere deep in my brain fired promptly. "Are you awake, sir?" Downs persisted.

"What's up, Roger?" I replied, finally close enough to the surface to remember that Downs was one of our own part-timers, a student at the community college thirty miles away, who found time to study between midnight and eight.

"Sir, Sheriff Holman said to call you. We've got a ten-sixty-five, and he says you'd want to know."

"Umph." I tried to sound as noncommittal as possible, because I couldn't remember what a 10-65 was, and found myself wondering what kind of eager beaver would use the cryptic 10-code on the telephone. "Give me a few minutes. I'll be down shortly." I hung up the phone without waiting for a response and promptly fell asleep.

"Sir, are you awake?" It was Downs again, and for the life of me I didn't know how the telephone receiver got up against my ear.

That was, finally, all the disturbance my aching brain needed. I snapped fully and completely awake. Through a narrow crack in the shutter I could see a sliver of white light as wide as a pencil lead that meant the sun was trying to burn off the paint. "What the hell time is it, Roger?"

"Eight-fifteen, sir."

"Jesus H. Christ. What's the problem?" I could only vaguely remember the first call.

"We've got a missing-person report in, sir. Sheriff Holman said you would want to know."

"You bet. Who is it?"

"A kid by the name of Scott Salinger, sir."

For a minute, I couldn't think of anything to say. Roger Downs finally said into the silence, "Sir?"

"Give me fifteen," I replied, already moving to hang up the phone. "And I'm awake this time. Thanks for the re-call, Roger."

Thirteen minutes later, cotton-mouthed and un-shaven, I pulled 310 into the small sheriff's department parking lot. Amy Salinger's Nova sat two spaces down from my reserved space. I hustled inside.

Amy Salinger was standing with our regular dispatcher, Gayle Sedillos, near the big wall map of Posadas County. They were in earnest conversation, with Gayle pointing out something on the map north of town. I saw no one else in the office. Apparently Roger Downs had already gone home.

"Fill me in," I said, and both girls snapped around. Apparently neither of them had heard me come in. "Miss Salinger, what's going on?"

Amy's face was pale, but she was under control. "Scott went out sometime yesterday afternoon, Mr. Gastner. He never returned." As simple as that.

"Where was he headed? Did he say?"

"No. None of us were home. This is his favorite time of the year to go hunting." She tried a semibrave smile. "For whatever screwball reason, he likes the summer heat. That's what we thought. I checked to see if he had taken his rifle. He never goes without that. It's still behind the door of his bedroom."

I turned to Sedillos. "Who's out and where?"

"Sheriff Holman left early this morning for a meeting in Las Cruces with the DEA. They're arranging the interagency task force."

"I know that," I said quickly.

"I sent Baker up the hill. Miss Salinger showed me on the map where some of her brother's favorite haunts are. Baker said he was familiar with the rim area."

"Where's the schedule?" I turned and grabbed the sheet that told me who was supposed to be working. "Terrific." Todd Baker was the only deputy on duty until 4 P.M. "All right. If we don't turn anything quickly, we'll call the others in. Miss Salinger, what was Scott's mood the last time you saw him?"

"At lunch. He seemed more relaxed than he has in a long time. He told me about meeting with you the other day up on the mesa. He didn't say what you two talked about, but whatever it was, it helped."

"That's encouraging. Does he have any favorite night spots?" She shook her head. "Any friends with whom he's apt to spend the night?" Again a shake of the head. "As far as you know," I prompted.

"As far as I know, no. And neither Mom or Dad could think of any place he might have gone. It's not like him to go out without telling someone. Dad went out to check a couple places where they used to hunt together. Mom stayed at home, in case he showed up or called."

I walked over and looked at the map. "The most likely thing is that he took a header somewhere, Amy. That happens. If a person's out a couple miles, it doesn't take much to incapacitate him to a point where he just has to sit, wait, and sweat it out."

"He's got a trick knee from football," Amy offered hopefully.

"There you go, then. He's probably sitting somewhere under a tree, waiting for us to find him. What was he wearing?"

"Jeans. Some freaky heavy metal rock T-shirt."

I smiled some encouragement. "Let's find him right now." I'm not sure she bought my feigned optimism, but I didn't give her a chance to brood. "Gayle, call Jim Bergin at the airport and tell him we're on the way. He gets to fly a county contract. If he's not there, call him at home and get him up. Amy, let's go."

Technically, I was giving the county commissioners about thirty-seven reasons to put me on the rack. Twenty-four hours hadn't passed, and Scott Salinger wasn't a missing person yet. Taking a civilian on an air search was another, especially on a county voucher. The list went on, but I wasn't about to sit around, waiting for answers. Amy Salinger and I were worried for the same reason—people like her brother didn't simply walk away without a word unless something was very wrong. We drove quickly to the airport.

"He's on the ball," I said, pointing as we drove in toward the parking area. "If your brother drove his car off a rough road somewhere, this is the quickest way to find him. You can see a lot from the air in country like this." On the apron in front of his small office building was Bergin's Piper Arrow. He had a small cowl flap up and was peering inside. When he heard us grind to a stop on the gravel, he snapped the flap closed and walked quickly around the wing. He stood at the trailing edge, and the cabin door was open.

"Morning, Sheriff. Your dispatcher said not to linger over coffee. That's a tough request."

"We appreciate it."

"Where are we going?"

"Local search."

"I guessed right, then. Marijuana field tip-off again?"

"Go ahead and get in back, Amy," I said, and she stepped lithely up on the wing, then squirmed inside the narrow confines of the airplane. "No marijuana field, Jim. Missing person. We're looking for a blue-and-white Ford Bronco. Probably one occupant. Probably went hunting. My guess is up on the mesa somewhere. Let's head that way, and then we'll play it by ear from there."

Jim Bergin nodded and climbed in. I followed, settling more stiffly than I would have liked. "You got to slam it," Bergin said after my first abortive attempt with the door. He reached over and whumped it shut, then stretched to push the top lock closed. He twisted around to make sure Amy was secure, glanced my way, and then busied himself with the plane.

"Amy," I said, turning so she could hear me, "does Scott usually park and then hike some distance, or is he a dyed-in-the-wool four-wheeler?"

"He loves to hike, Sheriff."

I nodded and watched Bergin. He was reading a plastic laminated check sheet methodically. After some twisting, pumping, and switch-snapping, he unlatched a small plastic window, craned his head to see as far around the airplane as he could, and then yelled, "Clear" so loud I startled.

"Who the hell are you talking to?" I asked.

"You never know," he said, and grinned. The engine came to life promptly and settled into a cowl-shaking idle. Bergin seemed to be running most of his checks as he taxied out, and then, with a healthy bellow, we were airborne.

Posadas lost a good deal of its significance from the air. Almost immediately, I could look ahead and see the main Consolidated Mining building to the north, up on the rise of the mesa. We passed directly over the lake and cleared the edge of the mesa behind it by no more than five hundred feet. Bergin came back on the power and began a methodical sweep pattern, flying east-west tracks a mile apart.

"You holler if you see a vehicle," he shouted. Almost immediately, I saw Todd Baker's county car, stark white against the brown and green of the mesa. I keyed the hand-held radio.

"Three-oh-six, Airborne."

"Three-oh-six, go ahead."

"We're over you now. See anything?"

"Negative, Airborne."

"Three-oh-six, is it possible to tell fresh tracks?"

"Negative. Too dry."

"Ten-four. I don't think there's much more you can do up here. Head back down and stay central. We may need you later somewhere else."

Baker acknowledged, and on our next pass up the mesa, we saw the dust from his patrol car spiraling up through the trees. "Do you know where your father went?" I shouted back at Amy. She shook her head and leaned forward.

"He didn't say."

"Where did they hunt?"

She twisted her face up in thought. "There's a bunch of old cattle drinkers north and east, over by Bailey. They used to go out there for dove, things like that. I think they hunted deer over by Las Notchas." I nodded. Bergin continued his tracking, smooth as silk. The wind was blowing slightly, and I noticed he held the plane in a slight crab. I saw a flash of moving metal and tapped Bergin on the arm, pointing. The Arrow immediately stood on one wing and turned so fast my stomach kept going west. We flashed over the treetops, skewed sideways against the wind, and I had a good view of a startled face looking up from the cab of a green Forest Service truck. If he had a radio, he didn't have our frequency. I bounced a message back to Gayle by way of 306, and shortly we had confirmation from the Forest Service that their man downstairs hadn't found an unattended Bronco.

All our efforts were concentrated in just *seeing* as the mesa fell away toward the open wide valley to the north. The mat of piñon and juniper below us was broken only by an occasional dirt road. Amy Salinger tapped me on the shoulder. "I know he used to come out here once in a while," she shouted, pointing at the flat hot prairie. "Rabbits." It was a rabbit heaven, all right. Stock tanks dotted the landscape, with barbed-wire fences stretching out across the thoroughly grazed bunch grass.

The country was a checkerboard of ownership . . . some private, some Bureau of Land Management, some Indian reservation. If a person wanted to get out away from everyone and everything, this was the place. But there was no Bronco. Jim Bergin looked over at me and raised an eyebrow.

I turned to Amy. "I hope somebody checked to make sure he didn't go back out to the football camp."

She shook her head. "He didn't. That was our first thought."

"How about flying back around the edge of the mesa," I suggested to Bergin. "Right around the edge." He nodded and the Arrow turned south. I scanned the trees and brush. I tried to climb inside the adolescent mind for answers, but that was a lost cause. I found myself thinking that as long as we didn't find anything, or hear from anyone, all was to the good. Deputy Todd Baker scotched that wishful thinking just as we rounded the west end of the mesa, with Posadas still hidden by its center bulge. The reception wasn't great, but he was understandable.

"Airborne, Three-oh-six."

"Airborne."

"Airborne, I have a blue-over-white Bronco, Sam Victor one, five, niner, niner. One-half mile east of County Road 43, on the Consolidated access." Before the deputy had finished, Jim Bergin pushed the throttle forward and we banked sharply toward the east. Todd Baker was one of those officers whose voice on the radio always sounded like a recording. He would have said, "I don't like cabbage," in the same tone as "The world is ending." Only his pregnant wife could get him excited.

Amy Salinger must have been watching my face, because all she did was lay a small hand on my shoulder. If she hadn't been leaning forward in her seat, she wouldn't have heard my exchange with Baker over the loud drone of the airplane's engine. But she had heard enough, and knew where the Consolidated access road was as well as I . . . close to town and close to a well-traveled highway. There was no good reason to be stranded there.

In another three minutes, we flashed over the lake at something like 130 miles an hour, and Jim Bergin reached out and pulled back the throttle. My stomach flopped a little as the Arrow nosed up. Our airspeed fell away and we started a big circle around the Consolidated Mines complex. The place had been abandoned for almost four years. A company security man drove through on rare occasions to check the locks. The access road swung off County Road 43 and wound around the complex, gradually dropping down to the huge "boneyard," where the detritus from thirty years of active mining filled a good five acres: junked machinery; probably thousands of feet of drilling pipe and cable; even a long, neat rick of aspen mine-shaft supports. The access road didn't belong to Consolidated. In fact, it continued down the hill, rough and rut-gouged, to peter out finally several miles later behind the county landfill. It wasn't picturesque country.

We looked down and saw Baker's car parked behind the Bronco. The small vehicle was pulled off the road, nestled in the shade of several small scrub oaks.

"Three-oh-six, any sign of the driver?"

"Negative, Airborne."

We peeled away toward Posadas, and I looked back over the wing. The sun was just right, brilliant on the back walls of the tin equipment sheds that were built practically on the edge of Consolidated's artificial mesa. Even though we were flying away at eighty miles an hour or so, I could plainly see the figure sitting in the sun, back against one of the shed walls like a Mexican sitting on the patio at noon. "Tight turn and head right for the lake," I shouted. Bergin did so, banking hard enough that I could feel the g's make my cheeks sag. As soon as we were wings-level again, he could see my target as well, and he pushed the nose down. We flew over the tops of the buildings low and hot, turning toward the south to avoid the rising hillside. When we flew over the figure, we were no more than three-hundred feet away. Whoever it was paid us no heed. His knees were drawn up with his arms resting on them, and his head was down. And then we were past. Bergin didn't have much room to play with, but he brought the Arrow around smoothly, concentrating on his flying and not the scenery out the window. I radioed Baker, and by the time we were lined up to make another slow pass, this time headed downhill, his car was rolling.

None of us in the plane said anything. Because of the fence, Baker had to park a hundred yards away from the shed. He clambered over the chain link, and we saw him trot across the open, sun-baked space. For a long moment, Consolidated was out of view as we turned again. Maybe it was just as well.

I keyed the hand-held. "Three-oh-six, is the subject the owner of the vehicle?"

"Ten-four, Airborne. Ten-fifty-five." My insides sagged again, and it wasn't from a tight turn.

"Get back to the field, Jim," I snapped, and he didn't hesitate. For the next thirty seconds or so, I kept busy on the radio, too gutless to turn around and say anything to Amy Salinger. When I did, I saw that words were unnecessary. She was looking out the window, staring at nothing. Her hands were balled into fists, held close to her mouth. She was crying. Amy Salinger had the training and the nerve, but there are limits for anybody. She had heard the confirmation from Baker that the figure seated against the building was her brother. And she had worked around emergency personnel enough to know that 55 was a call for the coroner.

17

The light plane touched down smoothly and Jim Bergin fast-taxied toward where I had parked 310. The propeller clicked to a stop and the Arrow rolled quietly the last few yards.

I unlatched the door while we were still rolling, and when the plane stopped I clambered clumsily out, then turned to help Amy Salinger while Bergin held the seat forward. "I'll get squared away with you later, Jim," I said, and he shook his head, face sober. He was watching Amy Salinger as she deplaned.

"On the house," he said quietly. "Let me know if there's anything else I can do."

I hustled Amy into the car, and we drove away from the airport. "I think I should go up there first," she said as the car pulled out onto the paved road. "I can't tell Mom and Dad without knowing for sure. I mean, there's a chance, isn't there?" She looked across the room at me. "There's a chance."

"Amy," I said patiently, "The deputy knows your brother. Baker's worked enough games at school, or seen his picture in the paper often enough."

Her hands were tightly clenched together on her lap. "I want to go up there first," she said simply.

We drove in silence for a couple of minutes as we

passed through Posadas. I didn't waste any time, but I avoided the red lights and siren. There wasn't much need. Only after we had started up the hill did Amy shake her head slowly and say, "I just didn't believe he'd really do this." She dug out a wad of tissue and through it whimpered, "I don't know if I can take this."

"I wish I could say something that would help," I said. She shrugged her shoulders simply and looked away, her body occasionally shivering like a little cold kid caught unhappy and out in the rain.

We turned into the access road, and I saw one of the county cars pulled diagonally across the narrow right-of-way. Eddie Mitchel, who had probably been just about ready to go to bed when he received the call, bent down as I lowered my window.

"Sir, you can drive through the gate just up ahead there on the right. We haven't located the security guard yet, but I took the liberty of cutting the lock off."

I nodded. "Don't let anyone down here except department personnel without my say-so, Eddie." I looked at him hard and added, "Nobody."

"Yes, sir."

"And you might move your car back up the road— right at the turnoff from the pavement. I want all of this closed off."

He nodded and made for his car. I picked up the mike as we drove down toward the gate.

"Posadas, three-ten."

"Go ahead, three-ten."

"What's Detective Reyes's twenty?"

"Uh, three-ten, I'm still trying to locate her." For the first time that I could remember, Gayle Sedillos sounded a little flustered. With good cause, I thought.

"Find her," I snapped, and hung up the mike.

Todd Baker had moved his unit to the gate, and he met us there. "Stay in the car," I said to Amy. My guess that maybe a brusque approach might be helpful paid off. She nodded quickly, responding to the desperate need for direction.

No one else had arrived, and I told Baker to stay with Amy Salinger until Estelle Reyes arrived. I didn't want Amy alone, and I certainly didn't want her alone at the gate, acting as a greeter for all the law-enforcement personnel who were bound to arrive during the next few minutes.

I started across the hot, packed surface of the bone-yard at a fast walk, and after the first fifty feet realized it wasn't just apprehension that was putting a garter around my insides. I tried for a deep, calming breath, and the pressure under my sternum subsided a bit. I swore pointlessly at the high altitude and slowed my pace, trying to calm my pulse. I reached the shed and turned the corner.

I leaned against the warm metal of the building and looked at Scott Salinger. I had investigated probably a dozen suicides during my years in the military and later as a cop. Some of those incidents seemed to be the result of spur-of-the-moment decisions. If the victim had given himself a few minutes, there might well have been some reconsideration. But others—they showed planning and determination. So twisted had their lives become that nothing anyone could say or do would have mattered an iota. That was the impression I had then.

When a wave of dizziness subsided, I stepped forward and knelt down. The body was in a sitting position, knees drawn up and feet flat on the hard-packed asphalt on which the portable sheds rested. Salinger's forearms rested just above his knees, as if he had been bracing the heavy revolver with which he had shot himself. The revolver was still in his lap, and his right thumb was in the trigger guard.

I heard footsteps crunching behind me and turned to see Deputy Paul Encinos and the county coroner, Emerson Clark. I pushed myself to my feet. "Hello, Doc," I said.

He nodded. "That's his sister out in your car, isn't it?"

"Yes. She wants to identify the body. I don't want her to see him like this. When they move him to the ambulance, maybe."

"Tough stuff," Clark said. He knelt down and peered at the corpse. While he was examining the body, I turned to Encinos and asked, "Is Reyes on the way up?"

"Last I heard, dispatch was still trying to locate her, sir."

"Shit."

"Does this weapon belong to the boy?" Clark asked. He looked at the gun without touching it.

"I don't know," I said.

"Well," Clark muttered, "as long as the bullet hole isn't from back to front, it doesn't make much difference. But that's your department, not mine, Sheriff." He pushed himself to his feet. "Is the young lady handling this?"

"Reyes? Yes, if we can find her."

"If she's not here soon, then it's yours, I guess. Unless you're going to have Miss Salinger sit out in the car all afternoon," Clark said. He grinned at me. "Us old buzzards sure get used to delegating, don't we?" He looked back down at Salinger's corpse.

"He didn't want there to be any doubt, did he? Couldn't have hit any more dead center if he'd laid it out with a T-square first." He shook his head slowly. "I wonder what was so special about this place that he chose it?" Clark turned and looked down the hill. "Maybe the view," he said with some bitterness. "Great view of the county dump way down there." He looked at me from underneath shaggy eyebrows. "Gastner, you're not saying much."

"What's there to say?"

140

His eyes narrowed. He was pushing seventy-five years old, and life didn't hold many surprises for him anymore. "And you also look damn near like a basket case yourself," he said.

By way of ignoring the comment, I said to Encinos, "Cover him up, Paul. Be careful not to move anything. Detective Reyes will want accurate pictures."

"Do you have any ideas why he did this?" Dr. Clark asked as he watched Encinos spread out the black plastic blanket.

I shook my head. "The last time I talked to the boy, he seemed to have things pretty well sorted out."

Clark grunted something. "You might want to ask the family if he ever mentioned suicide before."

"The answer to that is yes. His sister told me that."

"Well, then," Clark said. "Unless the medical examiner comes up with something pretty bizarre during the autopsy, it seems pretty cut and dried." He held up a hand as Encinos was about to finish covering the corpse. He bent down. "I'm no detective, but find me an answer for this before I have to make a ruling."

He pointed at the heavy caking of blood on Salinger's T-shirt. "Explosive exsanguination consistent with a close-range Magnum wound produces a lot of blood," Clark said. "And that's what we've got here." With his index finger, he carefully pulled the elastic collar of the T-shirt away from Salinger's neck. "Still, we ought to expect that gravity still rules, wouldn't you think?"

"What are you getting at, Doc?"

"If he sat here, as it appears, and pressed the muzzle of a heavy Magnum to his chest, as it appears, and pulled the trigger, then we would expect the blood flow to be outward and then downward from the wound, would we not?" Clark looked at me and raised an eyebrow. "Now, cotton shirts soak up a lot of blood. You could call it a capillary action of sorts. Like a wick. But this"—and he pointed at the area near Salinger's right clavicle—looks like a blood track to me." He shifted position. "There is no reason for blood to flow from the bullet hole in the center of his chest to nearly the top of his collarbone. Not only no reason. It would be impossible, if the body didn't move after the gunshot."

He looked at me blandly. "Do you see what I mean?"

"Yes."

"What you see here, unless I'm dreaming, is consistent with the body first lying on the ground, head perhaps slightly lower than the rest of the body." He stood up again. "Fluids flow downhill, Bill."

My forehead was wet with sweat, and one eye burned from the salt. "You're saying he was shot somewhere else and then propped up here?"

Dr. Clark held up his hands in protest. "No, I'm not saying that. I'm saying that these particular bloodstains puzzle me. There may be a perfectly simple answer. I want that simple answer." He thrust his hands in his pockets and stared hard at the corpse. "Unattended deaths are just that, Bill, as you well know. Unattended by anyone but the victim. We may never know. But if there is an interesting answer to be had, it would be a shame to ignore it."

He started to walk off, and then stopped. "I didn't want to move anything until you have all your photographs. I'm assuming from the lack of blood on the ground behind the body that there is no exit hole in the back. If there is, there also better be a hole in the back of this building. Keep me posted."

"I'll walk back with you, Doc," I said. "Paul, I'll be right back."

We almost reached the cars when Dr. Clark extended his hand. I shook and he said, "Sometimes these jobs are shit, aren't they, Bill."

"Yup."

"He was a good kid. I worked on his knee once,

142

about four years ago. Seemed to have the world by the tail then. But I guess things can go downhill pretty fast when you're that age."

"Any age, Doc," I said. He got in his car and left, and I walked over to the patrol car. Amy Salinger got out of the car, head bowed, and I offered her a hand. She was determined to see her brother, and we made our way back across the boneyard toward the shed.

"You don't have to do this, you know," I said.

"Yes, I do. Until I do, I'll never believe it's him."

When we turned the corner of the building and she saw the black cloth and Deputy Encinos, she stumbled and almost lost her balance. I guided her with one hand on an elbow. I curled a corner of the drop cloth back, just enough to reveal Scott Salinger's bowed head. Amy whimpered and stepped back. Paul Encinos protectively hugged her shoulders. After a minute, she nodded and turned away.

"Amy, I'm going to have Deputy Encinos take you down the hill. He'll stop and pick up Father Carey as well. Is that all right?" She nodded soundlessly. "I can't leave here, or I'd do it myself. I really need to be here when the detective arrives."

"That's . . . that's all right," she mumbled.

Paul and I escorted her back to the gate. I didn't say anything else to her. There was nothing I could say. I wasn't worried about Salinger's family. They would have to tackle their own grief in their own way. They'd have help. Right then I was more concerned with why blood would run uphill.

18

"Where the hell is Estelle Reyes?" I snapped at Todd Baker. Our department was one of those absurdly small organizations, and Estelle Reyes, still wet behind the ears, was our chief detective—she was also our only detective, if folks like myself and Sheriff Holman weren't counted. Violent deaths, whether homicide or suicide, call for the kind of expertise that sophisticated departments dish out routinely. For a small, rural department, it was a different story. I knew we'd all have our hands full with this one.

Baker was standing with one foot on the doorsill of his car, mike in hand. Had I been in a better mood, I would have said something about his Broderick Crawford imitation. He looked apologetically at me. "Gayle says Reyes went down to Tres Santos to help plaster her mother's house."

I stared at Baker, incredulous. "She what?"

"She's plastering her mother's house," Baker repeated hopefully. "The old lady lives in Tres Santos. Estelle took a day of personal leave, and she and her boyfriend went down there."

"Oh for Christ's sakes. Give me that." I took the mike from him and got Gayle Sedillos back on the air.

"Did you call Reyes?"

"Ten-four, three-ten."

I wiped my forehead impatiently. "Well? What did she say?"

"She's on her way up, sir."

"Wonderful." I tossed the mike at Baker. "What is that, an hour's drive or better?" Baker nodded. "Then let's get to work. I'm not going to sit around here on my ass for an hour. Watch the gate." The ambulance had arrived, and I took a moment to tell them that they might as well cool their jets. The corpse wasn't going anywhere for quite a while. Then I grunted into 310 and drove across the boneyard to the shed. I gathered my own equipment from the backseat—it wasn't much, and it all fitted into a slender briefcase. The little snapshot camera would have to do, because there were answers I wanted and I would have to move the body to find them. If Estelle Reyes found out I had moved a corpse without taking pictures from every angle, she'd bat her long black eyelashes at me, then she'd shoot me herself.

I burned up two rolls of film before I touched the body. The Magnum bothered me, and I worked under the assumption that the gun belonged to the boy's father, who himself was an avid outdoorsman and hunter. It really didn't matter to me to whom the gun belonged, as long as Scott's thumb had pushed the trigger. The boy had often taken his .22 rifle on hunting trips or even casual hikes. That rifle would have done the job, albeit not with the shattering finality of the .357 Magnum. That the youth had deliberately chosen the big handgun indicated to me that his mind had been thoroughly made up about its use. And of course, the coroner had his misgivings with his worry about bloodstains. Maybe someone had throw us all a curve.

I laid out a zip-top plastic bag, and with the eraser of my pencil pushed the boy's thumb out of the trigger guard until I held the Magnum with the pencil. I gripped the bloody front sight between two fingers and lifted the weapon up. After it was safely in the plastic bag, I filled out an evidence tag and attached it. I felt bad that I didn't have a big cardboard box. Estelle would give me gentle hell about not using one of her new-school stunts. The gun should have been suspended with stout twine in the box, with no part of the weapon touching the sides—at least until all the lab workup was done. But the evidence bag would have to do.

With both hands, I gently pulled the corpse away from the metal wall. It was like working with a stiff store manikin. There was no wound in the back, no mark on the wall. Something made me hesitate. Holding the body's weight with one hand, I knelt and looked closely. Scott Salinger's T-shirt was hiked up in back, with the cloth bunched up several inches above the belt line. The paint flecks on the skin of his lower back were obvious. Photographs, I though, and knew my small pocket camera was inadequate. I let the corpse rest back against the wall and stood up. I ran a hand down the wall of the building and looked at the white dust and flecks that my palm immediately collected.

I frowned. Were people intent on suicide as careful as anyone else when they sat down? To scrunch up the otherwise tucked-in T-shirt and dot the skin underneath with old paint meant that Scott Salinger would have had to plop himself down, first banging against and then actually sliding down the old wall, oblivious to the discomfort, even pain, of such a maneuver. I knelt down again, and had to wait a minute for dizziness to pass. By pushing the corpse forward and to one side, I could look closely at the wall. I could imagine that I could see vertical marks in the dusty paint, but eyes sharper than mine would have to offer a second opinion. It was only because I was waving my free hand at the flies that I looked down and saw the wood. It was sticking out of the youth's right back pocket. The portion that I could see was about half an inch long and curiously shaped. It attracted my attention first because, in the shade and difficult to see, it looked for all the world like the end of a fat skewed marijuana joint. The idea of Scott Salinger actually being involved with drugs twisted like a knife. Using just my fingernails, I caught the end of the object and pulled it out. It was not a joint. Rather, it was a three-inch length of wood, one long side flat and the other sides rounded. Both ends were rough, like a broken stick. Attached stubbornly to the wood by what had to be glue of some kind was a five-inch-long streamer of blue two-or-three-mil plastic, torn into an irregular banner shape.

Scott Salinger, or someone, had obviously thrust that piece of junk into his hip pocket. I turned it over without touching any part of it except where my fingernails pinched one end. Something, somewhere twanged in my mind, but I couldn't bring it to focus. I didn't have much of a grip on the wood, and I let the corpse rest back against the wall so I could grope for a small evidence bag with my left hand. I snapped the bag open against the slight breeze and dropped the wood and plastic inside. Instead of just dropping the light package into my briefcase, I made a point of sliding it into one of the pockets in the lid. With the article safely stowed, I rummaged for an evidence tag.

The contents of my briefcase seemed somehow confused and jumbled. I hesitated. What was I looking for? Dizziness returned, and I reached out a hand for support. Either my own vision was screwball, or the sun kept slipping behind clouds. My arms lacked the strength to hold me up. Even as I stumbled on my hands and knees like a poisoned dog, I heard vehicles. They would find me, of course, but somehow it seemed desperately important to meet them at the corner of the building. I staggered to my feet, unable to breathe. My left hand slapped the side of the building and I lurched toward the corner. My momentum carried me beyond support and out into space. I fell heavily, not unconscious but so weak that blinking took too much effort. I heard feet running on the asphalt of the boneyard, and then, with time confused and blending, sirens. In a moment of lucidity, I thought, Great timing, Gastner. Great timing.

19

Briefcase. The first word to worm its way back into my consciousness. A moment of panic followed. Had I lost the briefcase? And along with it my camera and film? Maybe the detective found it. Reyes. What was her first name? Reyes. Something Reyes. I opened my eyes.

Up on the wall was a softly cheeping machine, tiny lights blinking its intelligence. As if the pulsing lights were a catalyst, my connections came into sharp focus—a damn tube in each arm, bags hanging from poles and chemistry slowly dripping into my system. I lay absolutely still, assessing. Other than being weary and maybe a little buzzed from the drugs, I felt fine. I took a tentative deep breath. My breastbone ached as if somebody had slugged me, but other than that, nothing hurt. Everything seemed to work.

I turned my head and searched for the nurse call. This was no time to be lying around. I had work to do, and fast. But I couldn't find the damn cord. Wasn't it usually pinned to the pillow?

"May I get something for you?"

I started and grunted involuntarily as the nurse appeared in my peripheral vision. My voice wasn't working, that was for sure. I tried again and this time I managed a little far-away voice that sounded like a kid trying to wheedle another cookie.

"I need to talk with Estelle Reyes," I croaked. I cleared my throat and said it again, a little stronger.

The nurse moved so I could see her, and I recognized Helen Murchison—old and ugly and efficient. She had one gold front tooth that winked when she smiled. She didn't smile much. "How do you feel?" she asked.

"Weak," I replied. I tried to lift an arm and put it behind my head, but the tubes tangled. "What the hell is all this plumbing for?"

"Well, you're doing well, Sheriff. You just relax and rest."

"And you didn't answer my question. Where's Perrone?"

"Dr. Perrone will be in first thing in the morning."

"Then I need to see Estelle Reyes, Helen. Right now."

"Detective Reyes?"

"Yes."

She looked at her watch. "Would she be at the office now? It's three in the morning."

My chamber of tubes and machines didn't have any windows, so I had to take her word for the hour. "Three A.M.," I muttered.

"It's probably the first decent rest you've had in some time, isn't it? That's what Sheriff Holman said this afternoon."

"Yeah, well, do me a favor, will you, Helen?" I gagged a little and it took several minutes before I could talk. "Call the dispatcher and tell them that I need to see Estelle Reyes." I stopped again, marshaling my strength. "The minute she sets foot in the door. And tell her to bring my briefcase." She nodded. That was enough exercise for me. I let myself sink back into the pillow and bedding.

Later, the voices were an irritation, and I begrudged having to swim back to the surface again so soon. I had been enjoying my personal black void. Two men and Helen were standing near my bed. Even in the subdued light, I recognized Dr. Alan Perrone.

"Good morning, Sheriff." He smiled. "Nice vacation you got going here." The bell of his stethoscope was ice-cold. He straightened up and pushed the instrument back in his pocket. "Sheriff, this is Bob Gonzalez." I looked at the young man with Perrone. Maybe one year of med school at most. "He's one of our emergency-room rotation docs from Las Cruces. He was on duty when you came in yesterday."

Gonzalez hadn't taken his hands out of his pockets yet. But I felt as if I were being X-rayed by his unblinking black eyes.

"What we have planned," Perrone said, "is a session of complete rest first. We need to build your strength back up. You've been pushing pretty hard lately. Personally, I thought you looked like hell that night we worked on your undercover cop."

"Everyone goes out of their way to tell me that," I said, wishing I had the energy to put some gravel in my voice.

"You might start believing them. We consulted a little with Bud Sprague last night, too. He said the same thing."

"Dr. Sprague, you mean?" I asked, and Perrone nodded.

"Listen," I said, "I need to see Estelle Reyes. It can't wait." I looked at Helen Murchison. "Did you call like I asked?"

Dr. Perrone didn't give her a chance to answer, but said, "Reyes is waiting downstairs. She came in about an hour ago." Perrone smiled slightly. "And she understands that she has to wait. You need to understand that too."

"This can't wait."

"I'll let her come up for about fifteen minutes. That's it."

"How long am I going to have to stay here?"

"If all goes well, we'll probably move you out of this ICU room later this morning."

"ICU? What the hell am I doing here?"

Gonzalez wasn't amused. "You're here because you fell flat on your face yesterday."

"We need to run some tests," Perrone added. "We need to find out what's going on inside that old carcass of yours. And you need to start taking care of yourself."

"Are you saying I can't smoke in here?" I asked.

Perrone just laughed gently. "I'll send Detective Reyes up. Helen here will wait outside the door with a stopwatch. When the time is up she'll pitch the young lady out on her ear." He patted my knee. "And I was sorry to hear about the Salinger boy. That's rough when a teenager packs it in." He headed for the door. "Fifteen minutes with Reyes. That's it. Give yourself an uneventful day and night, and then we'll see."

I nodded weak agreement. Doctors always leave the full story hanging. What else could I do? The two doctors left, and I asked Helen, "What's Gonzales's racket?"

"Dr. Gonzalez is doing his residency in thoracic surgery."

"Oh." I thought I had detected something predatory in the young doctor's gaze. "Well, he's not practicing on my thorax, I'll tell you that."

Helen Murchison nodded, and smiled.

If Estelle Reyes had been busy plastering her mother's house when she got the call, there was no sign of it when she padded into ICU. She was dressed in one of her immaculately pressed outfits that might have been customed-tailored. I knew better. She didn't have any extra nickels to waste on clothes from what we paid her, but her trim, square-shouldered figure made even the cheapest rack clothes look good. She was carrying my briefcase, and there was a red paper seal across the lid seam.

"You'll sure go to some length to avoid work, sir," Estelle Reyes said. She laid the briefcase on the foot of the bed.

"How about that, eh?" I said, feeling better already with her in the room. I pulled the sheet up a little to cover my potbelly.

"You startled ten years out of my life when you came around the end of that building. I was walking across with Sheriff Holman and Bob Torrez, and there you came, flying on one wing. You crashed right in front of us."

"One of my better performances. Anyway, we don't have much time. I want to hear what you found."

Reyes sat on the side of the bed. She looked down at her fingernails and silently chewed on her lip. Finally she said, "It seems a damn strange place for a kid with as much to live for as Scott Salinger to commit suicide, sir."

"I agree. No place makes sense. You've talked some with Amy and his folks?"

She nodded. "I mean, he had a view of the city dump. And if he went up there in the dark, he could see the lights of Posadas, but there are more picturesque places."

"That's what the coroner said."

"Over the years, you've probably investigated— what, about a dozen suicides all told?" She looked sideways at me.

"Something like that."

"And I'm willing to bet that your experience supports what I've read. People who destroy themselves usually do it at home . . . right in the middle of their misery. Have you ever known one who went out into the

153

wilderness? I'm not saying it never happens, but it seems strange to me."

I nodded and tried to adjust the goddamned tubes. "And the Consolidated boneyard was not a haunt of Salinger's," I said. "Still, you never know what goes through a kid's mind."

"True. But there're a couple things about this case that bother me. I sort of wondered if you had seen the same things, because you evidently moved the body some."

"I lifted the gun," I said. "I checked the body for an exit wound."

"There wasn't any. Bob Torrez says that's not unusual for hollow-point ammunition, especially the lighter-weight bullets. Did you have a lot of trouble freeing his fingers?"

I shook my head. "No. His thumb was in the trigger guard, but I didn't have any trouble. His fingers were more or less in a relaxed position."

"Odd that a heavy Magnum like that wouldn't recoil back."

"They don't jump all that much," I said. "Not enough to fling the gun away, if that's what you mean."

"You'd just think that someone who was wound up tight enough to shoot themselves would be gripping that gun pretty tightly, is all. I mean, no matter what decision they make, no matter how resigned they are, there's got to be some apprehension. The grips of that gun were wood, with sharp checkering. There was little indenting on the skin of his palms or fingers." She shrugged and pulled a manila envelope off her clipboard.

"Doc Clark was talking with me, too. He said he'd mentioned the same thing to you." She pulled out a thin pack of five-by-seven photographs and held one up for my scrutiny. Salinger's T-shirt had been cut away, and it was obvious that most of the blood was below the ragged, dime-sized hole in the center of his chest. "That track isn't just from cotton soaking like a wick," Reyes said, pointing at the stain that marked a straight line from wound to collarbone.

"That's what Clark said."

"And then there's this," Estelle said, and found the photo she wanted. It was a close-up of the right shoulder of the T-shirt, taken from the rear. The fabric wasn't torn, but it was scuffed. Estelle handed me another picture, this one of the victim's shoulder. A small scrape, just a mild abrasion of the skin was visible. "Ordinarily I wouldn't have thought anything about that, but I also found this." She held out another photo. "That's a piece—small, I admit—of asphalt. A little pebble." I looked at the picture and frowned. "This is where it came from." The photo she handed me this time showed the right side of Salinger's head. A pencil was holding a spray of hair out away from the skull, and another pencil pointed at the fragment of paving in situ next to the skin. "My guess is that he fell backward. His head hit the ground pretty hard. The ME will have more for us, I'm sure. But he hit his head hard enough to imbed that gravel in his scalp. I could see the mark."

"Good work, Estelle." That's all I could think to say.

"On the victim's lower back is some paint residue."

"I saw that."

"The most interesting thing is what I found this morning." She looked at me, and I could see the excitement of the chase in her eyes. "There were powder marks on the outside of his left arm. The *outside*." She pointed to her own arm, and then handed me a picture. "They don't show up well. I asked the ME to take some that would. And to make sure to run the NAA tests there, too. I think that the gun was fired more than once."

"No shit?"

She nodded. "I talked to Mr. Salinger yesterday afternoon."

155

"How are they doing?"

"It's rough for them. But Scott's father said the gun is his, and that he hasn't loaded anything but jacketed hollowpoints for that revolver since he bought it more than four years ago. So it would be unusual to find lead residue in the bore, wouldn't it? If it only shot brass-jacketed bullets?"

"I would think so, unless the gun was so badly out of time that it shaved the lead tip before the slug got into the bore."

"The cylinder timing is almost perfect."

"Was there lead in the barrel?"

"Yes. I asked the crime lab in Santa Fe to do me a rush-rush. That's what they said."

"Rush is right. How'd you get the gun up there so fast?"

Estelle Reyes looked sheepish. "Sheriff Holman almost went into orbit when he heard. I had Bob Torrez take it."

"He drove it up?"

"No. Jim Bergin flew him up. I wanted an answer, and fast. A guy up there owes me a favor or two. We printed the gun, and he took powder samples. The only results I got back so far are the prints—they're all Scott Salinger's—and the positive test for bore lead."

My forehead was flushed, and the weariness was competing with my attention. Helen Murchison was going to tackle Estelle any minute. "So tell me what you think happened."

"There's a lot of unanswered questions, sir. But if I had to write a script, it would go like this. I think Scott Salinger walked into the middle of something. He parked just off the edge of the road. Whoever it was somehow either talked the gun out of Scott's possession, or took it from him without a struggle that left marks . . . unless that's where the lightly skinned shoulder and head bruise came from. Then the killer shot Salinger. There's a very small powder-burn corona around the hole in the T-shirt. It looks like the revolver barrel was almost actually touching him. The body was moved to behind the shed, and whoever it was had the brainstorm of making it look like a suicide. Maybe whoever it was knew the Salinger kid, knew that he was depressed. Maybe whoever it was even knew Salinger had talked about suicide."

At that point, Helen opened the door. Without breaking stride, Estelle turned and held up a hand. "Two minutes, Ma'am. Please close the door." Helen did so without question. I was surprised at the steel in Estelle's voice.

"Whoever it was plopped him down behind the shed, scuffing his lower back against the building. Then the killer got smart . . . too smart. He wanted the NAA to be positive. But he couldn't shoot the gun again with Salinger's ammunition. As dumb as we are, we'd notice two rounds missing. My guess is that whoever it was had a gun of his own. If it was any thirty-eight caliber, it would work. And that's the most common cartridge. So he took out a round, put it in Salinger's Magnum, folded the grips in the boy's hands and fired once off to the side. He pops open the cylinder, takes out his casing and puts the live round back in. Closes the cylinder and his tracks are covered. Real cute."

"One cold son of a bitch, if that's the case," I said quietly.

Estelle Reyes got up. "That's for sure. Gayle said you wanted your briefcase. I sealed it."

"No need, Estelle. In the top pocket is an evidence bag. The contents were in Scott Salinger's back pocket."

Estelle snapped the seal and opened my briefcase. "In the top pocket," I repeated, and she pulled out the small bag. She held it up and frowned.

"This was in his back pocket?"

"Right side. About an inch of it was protruding.

That's why I saw it. When I moved the body forward, I saw it there."

She turned the bag over and over, puzzled. "A piece of wood and a piece of what looks like plastic."

"Junk."

"Why would he pick it up and put it in his pocket?"

"If he was intent on suicide," I said, "I don't think he would."

Estelle relaxed back on the edge of the bed, leaning on one elbow. "It wasn't suicide," she said flatly. It was the first time either of us had come right out and said it. "And that leaves us only two choices for something like this. Somebody put it in Scott's pocket, maybe after the shooting, maybe before. Why, we don't know. Or Scott picked it up and put it there himself."

"Why?"

She tossed the bag back in the yawning briefcase. "Who knows? Good citizen picking up litter?"

"Just this, and not everything else that trashes up that mesa?"

"When we find out what it is, or what it was, maybe we'll have part of the answer," Estelle said. "Did the doctors say how long they were going to keep you cooped up here?"

"Tomorrow," I said. "What do you plan to do next?"

Estelle hesitated. "It's got to be somebody in town," she said. "That's what I think. I'm proceeding on the assumption that, one, it was murder,"—she ticked off a finger—"and, two, it was somebody from around here. Or at least somebody very familiar with the area."

"And you've given up any thought of its being suicide?"

"It wasn't," Estelle said immediately. "NAA and ballistics will confirm that. But for right now, I want that between you and me. I haven't told anybody else."

I frowned. "That's going to be a rough road for the family."

"Yes, it is. But I think it's to our advantage. Everyone I've heard talking assumes it was a suicide. I'm thinking we can just leave it that way for a while . . . just a few days. We might catch somebody off guard."

I shook my head. "I don't think I want to jerk the Salinger's chains like that, Estelle. They've got to know."

"If they know, so will everyone else."

"I think we can give them more credit than that."

The door opened and Helen Murchison marched in. She didn't give Estelle a chance this time . . . and next to Helen, Detective Reyes looked like a junior high school cheerleader. "Out," she said. "It's been far too long." She began checking me and my machines.

As my cheerleader moved toward the door, I said, "Talk to them, Estelle. Convince them of the importance of going along with you. And if they want to talk to me, encourage that. We'll just find a minute when Helen here steps out to lunch, if I'm cooped up in here that long."

"Lie back and shut up," Helen said cheerfully. "It's obvious you're going to trouble."

Estelle swung the door open. "I see you're in good hands, sir. I'll keep you posted." She held up my briefcase. "I'll let you know what the junk is."

I waved. Helen Murchison sniffed her disapproval. I guess I wasn't supposed to feel better.

20

They had promised to move me, and while I waited for that grand event, I drifted off. When I woke, the room was quiet and lonely, save for the patient, faraway hum of the machines above my head. No clock, no watch, no window—it could have been midnight or noon of July Fourth or Christmas. The chemicals still dripped into my veins. I felt like cloudy water.

"Ugg," I said, and shifted position. I wanted a cigarette. Was there enough oxygen in the room that if I lit up I'd risk blowing the side of the building out into the parking lot? Either that or Helen would knock me through the wall herself. I examined what I could see of the darkened ceiling. The room, a twilight tomb, was depressing. What were all the damn white curtains for? To remind the patient of heaven?

The fuzzy, disoriented, floating feeling had to be from the drugs. Or was that what dying felt like? Scary notion. Did things just fade to black without any awakening? Was death a special fade? Was its approach recognizable? Morbid. I couldn't help it. My brain kept casting back for other memories. What had Art Hewitt thought, as he lay on his back in the village park? When there's time like that, did the mind unwind slowly? Could the person feel things gradually coming apart, gradually shutting down? Did Scott Salinger have a couple of seconds of conscious thought after the Magnum shredded his heart? Or was it simply like a light switch . . . one instant full on, the next instant full off—permanently off, main line cut and wires removed? Who the hell knew? In frustration, I kicked the sheet that covered me. I wasn't going to lie there any longer and torture myself. I twisted my neck and this time found the buzzer cord. By moving carefully, I could flex my left arm, tubes and all, and press the button.

I waited about thirty seconds and repeated the call. And repeated. And repeated. Maybe the button wasn't connected. The door was open, even though I couldn't see it through the curtain. I heard activity of some kind down the hall, and I pressed the button again for good measure. A shadow materialized first, and then one of the nurses pushed the curtain back. She regarded me soberly for a second, saw that there was no panic on my part, and then smiled.

"What can I get for you, Sheriff?" she asked.

"Undersheriff," I corrected, and then wondered why I had bothered. I had never worried about the distinction before.

"Do people really call you that?" she asked pleasantly.

I let my arm relax back on the bed. "No. Too awkward. I was just wondering if there was anyone left on the planet."

She smiled a delightful smile. She was young, raven of hair and eye, and the name tag pinned to the right breast of her uniform was too small to read even in good light. "Just you and me, dear," she said.

"What a pleasant thought. How long have you worked here?"

"Longer than you've been a patient," she said, and I detected a little edge. If she couldn't melt a recalcitrant patient with those eyes, then there were other weapons in her management arsenal, I decided. "Are you feeling discomfort?" she asked.

"I just wanted some information," I said.

"It's six-fifteen."

"P.M.?"

"Yes."

"Good God. I'm supposed to be out of here. What's for dinner?"

She smiled and ran two fingers down one of the tubes. "You're on drip."

"How much do I have to pay for some real food?"

"You'll have to ask Dr. Perrone that. His orders."

"And I suppose a good cigar is out."

She just laughed mildly and adjusted the hanging hardware. I watched her for a minute, then said, "I need something to do before my brain turns to mush. I'm lying here thinking nothing but unproductive thoughts."

"You're not supposed to be thinking anything," she said. "You're supposed to be asleep. About a month straight would be about right. Nobody can work a dozen twenty-six hour days in a row." I wondered whom she'd been talking to. She put one of those warm, soft nurse hands on my forearm. She reminded me a little of my youngest daughter, and then of Amy Salinger.

"Am I allowed to use the telephone?"

"You got a quarter?" She flashed a bright smile, and patted my arm again. "Probably tomorrow, when they move you out of ICU. You know, we kind of like to keep you quiet."

"I thought today . . ."

The footfalls were so soft I almost didn't hear them. Harlan Sprague pushed the curtain back and surveyed me critically.

"Hello, Doc," I said. "Now you're going to tell me my internal plumbing is crapped out, too." Sprague laughed the polite little laugh that doctors use when you mildly insult their medical specialty.

"You're looking a little better, Sheriff. He nodded at the nurse. "Katie," he said, and then ignored her. "It's probably wishful thinking to ask if you're behaving yourself."

"Barely," I said. "See ya," I called to Katie as she slipped through the curtain. "She's a doll, isn't she? And you're the first doctor I've seen all day," I said, and Sprague shrugged.

"You're asleep most of the time, Sheriff. There's not much they can do right now, except monitor and adjust medication. Perrone's a good man, though. I always thought the hospital was lucky to have him on staff." He sat down on the edge of the bed and clasped his hands together over one knee. "No more discomfort?"

"No. Just buzzed. Why all the drugs? They're worse than anything else."

Sprague looked up at the IV tube. "Just relaxants. Maybe a blood thinner. The object is to create a situation where your heart has as little work to do as possible. No sudden surges, no spikes on the electrical chart. It's pretty standard. Given a chance, it's an organ with wonderful recuperative powers. Up to a point."

"What do you think they're going to suggest for me?"

Sprague smiled. "I hate to try and second-guess a specialist. Maybe in your case, just the required change in life-style might be enough."

"That's as bad as letting Gonzales in with his knives."

"Come on, Sheriff. There's got to be a way you can relax. I can see that I'm going to have to drag you off fishing sometime with me."

"I haven't baited a hook in fifteen years," I said.

"Once a fisherman, always a fisherman," Sprague said affably. "You ever fished in the surf?" I shook my head. "One trip to the ocean and you'll be a convert. Guaranteed."

"Maybe I'll have to try that."

Sprague stood up. "I don't make idle promises, Sheriff. When you're on your feet, off we'll go. I've got a little spot I like down on the coast in Mexico, a few miles from Bahia Kino. Therapeutic isolation. Sunshine, sand, maybe a few fish. Nothing like it."

"Sounds good," I said. And it did . . . a whole lot better than this white chamber they'd stuck me in for a little case of fatigue. There were too many unanswered questions for me to be sleeping the days away. I looked at the IVs in my arms, then managed a grin at Sprague. "As soon as they unplug me."

"It's a deal." Sprague patted my foot. "Behave yourself." He left the room, and left me wondering why a retired doctor was so damn eager to adopt new patients.

21

My IV needles were removed and my arms patched.
And in my new room, there was a window. A telephone.
Even a newspaper lying on the nightstand. But I wasn't
planning on staying.

"Dr. Perrone will be in to see you after a while," a
nurse whom I didn't know assured me.

"Terrific," I grumbled. It was nice to be able to roll
over without fear of ripping out connections. I lay on my
stomach and gazed out past mattress, bell cord, side
rail, glass of water, and pill cup. I had to admit that the
rest had been nice. It gave me time to think. Now, I
was bed-weary, eager to go. The newspaper on the
nightstand was turned in such a way that I could see
several headlines. A portion of one headline included the
name of our governor, and so I ignored that one. A
smaller head, low on the bottom half of the page, included the word "coroner" and I stared at it, trying to
read the whole thing.

The breakfast cart interrupted my concentration. I
rolled over and a candy striper beamed a good-morning
with impossibly straight white teeth and dimples. "How
about some breakfast?" she said brightly. I knew her
from somewhere. Her name tag said she was Beth Molina. She began to arrange the bedding so I would have

a fighting chance of finishing breakfast without spilling. "Can I buzz the bed up some?"

"Buzz away," I said. Fernandez. That was it. She was, or had been, one of the counter kids at the Fernandez burger joint.

"Are you planning a career in nursing?" I asked. She put the short-legged tray stand over my middle.

"Oh, maybe," she said cheerfully. "My dad said I should work here this summer to see how I liked it."

"Smart man. How do you like it?"

Her frown was the equivalent of a shrug. "I don't know yet. It's different than I thought."

"A lot of smelly, sick old folks," I said, and grinned. I felt an acute need for a shower and shave.

"Oh, that's not it," she said instantly, and with radiant sincerity. "I just never really liked science before."

She placed the tray of food on the stand. Something puddled in the middle that resembled limp, dead eggs. Two pieces of wet toast flanked an infant's portion of orange juice that was as far from fresh as east from west. I tried the juice, nearly gagged, and shook my head. "Not hungry," I said. "Maybe you'd move the tray and hand me that newspaper."

"Oh, but you have to eat."

"No, I don't. Maybe I'll go to the corner diner for something that's legal. Would you eat this stuff?"

She looked at the tray and cocked her head. Then her nose wrinkled, she glanced furtively at the door and shook her head. "Maybe lunch will be better," she said hopefully.

"Maybe. Don't count on it. If the food was good, there would be less incentive to leave this place—alive, that is." She dutifully removed the tray and stand and set them back on the cart. "The newspaper," I reminded her. "And if you ever get a minute, would you try and round up a copy of one of the Albuquerque papers for me?" I was beginning to feel downright alert, and on impulse I reached over, picked up the pill cup and tossed it at the food cart. It landed on my breakfast and bounced into a crevice between trays. If she noticed, Beth Molina didn't say anything. She handed me the *Register* and pushed the cart out of my room.

I needed my reading glasses, but by straight-arming the paper against my knees, I could see well enough to make out the story.

> Coroner Delays Ruling in Salinger Death Case
>
> Posadas County Coroner Dr. Emerson Clark today refused to issue a ruling in the recent shooting death of a Posadas teenager.

I looked up for the date of the newspaper. It was yesterday's. I continued reading.

> Salinger's body was found August 4 by Sheriff's officials after the youth had been reported missing overnight by family members. Clark said today that he would make an official ruling "only after a thorough investigation is completed."
>
> Posadas County Sheriff Martin Holman would say only that Salinger's body had been foundon property owned by Con-

167

solidated Mining, and that
the youth had apparently
died from a single gunshot
wound.

Holman refused to
answer questions about the
youth's death. The incident
is the latest in a string of
misfortunes to strike the
community in recent weeks.
Holman told the *Register*
today that comment on
the case would come from
Clark, or from the office of
Undersheriff William C.
Gastner. Gastner himself
was reported in fair but
stable condition this morning at Posadas General
after he suffered what hospital spokesmen say was
an apparent fatigue attack
during the initial investigation of Salinger's death
on August 4.

Members of the Sal-
inger family have refused
to talk with reporters
since the incident.

Salinger's death comes
on the heels of . . .

I let the paper fall onto the bed. I wasn't interested in
reading the rest—nearly a quarter page of recapitulation
reaching back to the July Fourth car crash. I knew it
would mention the discovery of the cocaine, the deaths
of Hewitt and Fernandez, and finally the death of Salin-

ger. Interspersed would be a review of the efforts to establish parent and counseling groups, talks with the school officials, maybe even the clergy . . . all of that.

What interested me was that the *Register* had obviously run a previous story on the youth's death—I reminded myself to ask for the papers from August 5 and 6—but that nowhere in this story was suicide even hinted. In fact, the context was such that a reader could readily make the assumption that Salinger's death was somehow related to something else . . . the cocaine? The efforts of undercover cops? It was no secret that my office—and that terminology was in itself a laughable attempt to make our county department seem something larger than it was—had been continuing its investigation into the cocaine, and into Hewitt's death. Hell, we'd interviewed people until we felt like door-to-door census takers, and I'd talked with the *Register* editor more than once.

But only two people from the department would have issued a statement about Salinger—Holman or Reyes. Clark, the old curmudgeon, wouldn't have said anything other than that one line attributed to him. With the press listening eagerly, our department spokesman would obviously have a choice. The information could be slanted so that the implication of suicide was obvious. That hadn't been done. I looked at the article again, and skimmed the parts I hadn't read. Nowhere did the words "self-inflicted" or "suicide" appear. In fact, comment from the Posadas County Sheriff's Department was noticibly lacking—surprising when one considered Martin Holman's love of public relations.

The telephone was on the nightstand, just out of reach. I grunted to the edge of the bed, grabbed the receiver, and dialed.

On the second ring, J. J. Murton answered.

"Get me Estelle Reyes," I said abruptly.

Murton sounded a little huffy. "Who's calling?"

"Gastner. Get Reyes on the phone."

"Hey, there," Murton said, and then began to babble what promised to be an endless series of questions— probably most of them warranted. I cut him off.

"J.J.—put Estelle on. Now."

"She ain't in," Murton said, sounding hurt. "You want me to call her on the radio?"

I almost said something unkind, then checked myself. A picture of Miracle Murton holding the telephone receiver up against the radio speaker came to mind. "Tell her to meet me over here at the hospital if she's ten-eight."

"I'll get right on it."

"I'll wait. Go ahead and call her." I closed my eyes and listened to the background noise. I could hear Murton on the radio, and it seemed like a year before 301 responded. As I lay there listening, a nurse came into the room. She looked at me and frowned. She obviously wanted to say something, but didn't, because reinforcements were right behind her. Dr. Perrone entered, accompanied by Gonzales. I heard the distant, electronic voice of Estelle Reyes say that her ETA at the hospital would be fifteen minutes.

"I heard," I said when Murton came on the line again. "Is Holman there?"

"He sure isn't. He's meeting with the county legislators this morning."

"About what?"

Murton had to think. "Uh, it's the regular county meeting, sir. Starts at nine. He left a few minutes early."

"Tell him to stop by when he's done."

Murton began a rundown on Holman's previous visits to my room when I had been unconscious, and I interrupted him again. "I appreciate it. I'll be awake this time." I hung up the phone. Perrone took it and set it on the nightstand.

"You're looking better," he said.

"That's because I'm not taking any more of those damn pills," I said. "The ones that make little white rabbits run up and down the walls. The ones that turn my brain to old Jell-o."

Perrone smiled faintly. "We're keeping the medication down to a minimum. You need to take what we prescribe."

"I do?"

"If you want to avoid complications, you do. Yes."

"Doc," I said wearily, "I got so damn many complications I don't know which one to ignore first. All I want from you is as much help at getting out of this bed as possible."

"I have no argument with that. But my advice is to let your department worry about the work load. There's nothing you can do about it here, anyway. I'm sure you have competent officers."

"It's not that simple, Doc."

"I think it is. If I became ill, I would expect another physician to look after my patients. I don't know the details of this particular case, and to tell the truth, I don't think I want to. I read the newspapers"—he indicated the one folded on the bed. "And as you know, the morgue and pathology lab are in this very building. So I have an idea of what's happening. I don't see that there's much you can do about it all from this bed. My job is to get you out of bed as quickly as possible. Your job right now is to help me do that."

"What's your proposed schedule?" I asked, still unwilling to give in completely.

"We want to run some tests. We need to know what your vital capacities are." He paused. "If there is an arterial insufficiency that warrants it, surgery might be indicated."

"What kind of surgery are you talking about? Bypass?" I asked, and Perrone nodded. I looked at Gonzales and said, "My impression is that you've already made up your minds about that."

Perrone laughed. "We're quite sure, yes. But we want confirmation."

"And what's the recovery time for surgery like that? Ten days? Two weeks?"

"In that neighborhood."

I frowned and looked out the window. "The timing of this shit is not spectacular," I said.

"It never is."

"And if I put it off?"

Perrone held up his hands. "I flunked Crystal Ball one-oh-one."

"I don't have the time to lie around here, Doc."

Perrone shoved his hands into his pockets. "Sheriff—let me put it to you this way. One of the most accurate ways to find out what went wrong in a body is to do a postmortem." He hesitated and let that sink in. "I really don't want to do an autopsy on you. I really don't. So you're going to have to trust me a little. And trust my schedule."

Estelle Reyes appeared silently in the doorway. "Come on in," I said. "The docs are trying to figure out where and when to stick the knife."

Estelle stepped into the room, nodded at the two physicians and leaned her large briefcase against a chair back. She could have been a real estate saleswoman.

Perrone put a hand on Estelle's shoulder. "Maybe you can convince your boss that there are other police officers in the world. Your case won't fall apart if he takes it easy for a while and lets us do our work."

She looked at me with those big, quiet eyes. "If things have to wait, they have to wait," she said softly. She turned to Perrone and the doctor dropped his hand. When she spoke next, her voice sounded as if it came from an emotionless dictaphone. "It's just that with Undersheriff Gastner being a material witness and all, there are some formalities that we'll be observing here. I'll do what I can to make the interruptions of your routine as minimal as possible."

"We appreciate that," Perrone said, obviously a little puzzled. He folded his stethoscope and added, "It would help if you kept your visits as short as possible."

The doctors left the room, and I took a deep breath. "Estelle, I think they're trying to make an example out of me, or some such crap. I want out of here." I swung my legs over the side of the bed and took a deep breath. I felt pretty good. "I've read where patients did fine until they went into the hospital . . . then they croaked. Hand me that robe." Estelle fetched the terry-cloth robe, and I put it on.

"What do you plan to do?" she asked.

"You're driving me home," I said. She frowned, and I lifted a hand. "Don't you start."

"If you're sure that's what you want," Estelle said.

"That's what I want. And what did you find out? You got anything?"

"I've got lots of goodies," she said, and smiled thinly.

"Then we'll spread things out on my kitchen table, and take our time over a decent cup of coffee." I rubbed my hands. "God, that's going to taste good. You wouldn't believe the crap they serve here." I walked to the closet—maybe a little more shakily than I would have liked—and found most of my clothes.

"Where's my gun belt?"

"Sheriff Holman took it. He didn't want it in the hospital."

"Good God. All that's going on, and he worries about things like that. You guard the door. I'm going to get dressed."

Estelle discreetly watched the traffic outside while I fumbled with my clothes. My brain was fuzzy, and I felt as if I'd had a bad case of the flu, rubber joints and all.

But I could move, and the cool, dark corners of my own home seemed more therapeutic than this white-walled cell. When I glanced at myself in the mirror, I damned near scared myself back into bed. Dark under the eyes, baggy wattles under my chin—hell, 122 years old at the least. "Did you hear anything from the lab in Santa Fe?"

"Sure did."

My pulse picked up at that. "Anything interesting?"

"Yes, sir."

"Then let's get out of here." I stood up and took a deep breath. "Where did you park?"

Estelle pointed out through the window. "Way over there."

"Then hightail it out there, and swing by the front door. Let's not give them time to call the cops."

As it turned out, I didn't get the satisfaction of confronting anybody. The gal at the information desk gave me a quizzical look, but that was it. I was out. And the air smelled good. And the suspense of waiting to find out what Estelle Reyes had dug up was the best medicine in the world.

I climbed into the Ford, and we shot out of the parking lot like two volunteer firemen.

22

We were still a mile from Escondido Lane when I saw the helicopter in the distance, its blades flashing in the sun. I could tell it was a Jet Ranger, and it was headed up the mesa toward Consolidated.

"State cops?" I asked, pointing.

Estelle shook her head. "Television. And we're going to have to be careful on that score. A couple of news units have moved in. Even one of the big papers from Albuquerque. A wire-service guy tried to pump Holman today at the office." She smiled wryly. "It's the first time I ever saw him squirm and try to dodge publicity. And Channel Three flew in late yesterday."

"Just what we need. The sheriff hasn't said anything about bringing in other agencies on this?"

"No, sir. In fact, late yesterday, he stopped me as I was leaving the office and told me that all he wanted from me was progress . . . not to worry about what other people thought. He told me to leave the public relations to him."

My eyebrows shot up. "Good for him. And he's going to have his hands full. I gathered from the newspaper that not too many people are accepting the suicide angle."

"The natural tendency is to link it all together," she

175

said. "There's a lot of talk on the street, and none of it is suicide, as far as the Salinger death is concerned."

"And so what are the city news hounds playing? The 'small town reels under big-city problems' angle? The 'once pastoral village goes to shit' story?"

Estelle nodded. "Exactly. And we're being pushed." She grimaced as she swung the car into my tree-shaded driveway. "Holman hasn't learned to bark yet . . . especially at the press. He's too concerned with image. But give him time. And we may be able to use all the publicity to our advantage. But let me outline what I've got. You'll be interested."

That was an understatement. I heaved myself out of the car. Even the cottonwoods smelled good. As I fumbled for the keys, Estelle turned this way and that, looking at the adobe house. "Beautiful place."

"Yes, it is."

"How old is it?"

"Built in 1914. I bought it in 1965, just before I retired from the service."

The front door was heavily carved wood in territorial style, and it swung open silently, like the door to a bank vault. Estelle Reyes had never been to my home, in recent years, few people had been. They'd probably carve "Gastner the Hermit" on my tombstone. What the hell.

"Come on in," I said. "I'll put on the coffee." We walked down the long hallway to where it opened into the kitchen, and off to the right, two steps down, into the living room with its enormous dark ceiling beams. Sunshine flooded through the big kitchen windows and bounced off the colorful Mexican tile countertops.

"Sir, this is fantastic."

"I like it."

"Did you do the work?"

"You've got to be kidding," I said, and rummaged for the coffee. "I'm allergic to handyman stuff. Every time I pick up a tool, I end up bleeding or bruised. No, I made a lot of money in the service, and we managed to save a chunk. We figured this place was payback for living in government tin for twenty years."

"It makes my trailer look . . . look like scrap paper."

"Hey, you're young. You and Francis will find something that suits you. Give it time." I put on the water. "And the last thing you want is for a dream to become an albatross around your necks. You've served enough civil papers to see that." I took a deep breath, glad to be home. "But the hell with all that." I indicated the kitchen table. "Let's see what you found out . . . before the alarm goes out, and we end up with company." I winked at Estelle. I knew that walking out of the hospital was stupid, even juvenile, but those are the breaks. None of their medicine had made me feel this good.

Like a gambler dealing cards, Estelle Reyes laid out a display of reports, photos, and evidence bags on the table. I pulled up a chair. "First of all, the Magnum was fired twice," Estelle began. "The ballistics lab report talks about two completely different powder residues. You can see here"—she held up a large close-up photo of the Magnum's cylinder area and pointed with a pencil. "That is a collection of unburned powder grains, all flat, disk-shaped. That right there, in the juncture of the top strap and the barrel's forcing cone, is an unburned powder particle that is almost rod-shaped. The chemical residue supports that conclusion."

"What kind of powder was responsible for the left-arm powder burns?"

"The disk-shaped powder. There were particles imbedded in the skin. It's a fast-burning powder commonly used in factory loads for handguns."

"But not home brew, you mean?"

Estelle turned the report over and read a paragraph to herself. "Right."

"And the other powder was consistent with Magnum performance, obviously."

"Yes. And it matches the kind of powder that Mr. Salinger said he has used for years. What puts the cap on it is the lead residue. There was a trace of lead along the lands in the barrel. I can't imagine how a brass- or copper-jacketed bullet could leave lead. The medical examiner also said the checkering on the grips would have left a deeper imprint had Scott actually held the gun when the Magnum was fired the first time. Especially since, with the expected apprehension and all, he probably would have been gripping it tightly."

"Prints on the gun?"

"Only Scott's. And some of his had been smudged. As careful as he was, though, the killer got through in a hurry." Estelle dug out another photograph. The image of a .357 Magnum cartridge casing had been enlarged to nearly poster size. The quality was incredible.

"Did you take this?"

"I wish I had," Estelle said ruefully. "No, the lab gave it to me. Look here." Her pencil tip touched the right side of the ten-inch-tall nickel cylinder in the photo. The dust that adhered to the partial fingerprint showed a clear pattern.

"I see it. Not the boy's?"

"No. And no match yet to anyone else. Plus, it's only a fragment. But I'm working on it. I think the killer got a case of nerves. He was sharp enough to know that two empties in the Magnum would draw attention. So he used one of his own cartridges. The Magnum is a common caliber, and you can shoot thirty-eights in it as well. Bob Torrez gave me a demonstration of all this. I think the killer removed a live Magnum round, put in one of his own, fired off to one side with Salinger's hands pressed to the grips. That would make the nitrate test positive in case we were smart enough to bother with the test. He took out the empty casing and put the unfired Magnum round back in. Closed the cylinder, wiped the gun a little, and he was all set. But he started to hurry. He forgot that he had handled the cartridge. He left that fat and clear partial for us."

"I hope the son of a bitch remembers that and doesn't get a minute's sleep right up to the time we knock on his front door. What about the bloodstain?"

"As obvious as can be," Estelle said, nodding. "The bump on the head with a bit of asphalt caught in the hair, the shoulder scrape . . . all consistent with going over backward."

"The killer must have moved quickly then. There wasn't much blood that went the wrong way."

"The medical examiner told me that he guessed the killer took enough time to look quickly around. He saw the row of buildings and took his chance. He didn't drag the body. If he had done that, evidence would have shown on the victim's shoes. I don't think you can drag soft running shoes across rough, broken asphalt and not leave something imbedded in the shoe material."

"No weakling, then."

"Well, no, but Scott only weighed about a hundred and fifty. With a little adrenaline pumping, most normal adult males could pick up that much weight and stagger a few steps."

"And then he dumped the kid behind the building."

Estelle nodded, and finally sat down. "What's to lose? It was a spot hidden from the road. Even if someone had happened along before the killer finished his business, the odds of the back of the buildings being checked were small."

I rubbed a hand over my eyes. "What was going on?"

"Something that the killer or killers were ready to murder to protect."

"I can't picture the boy turning down that road in the first place. Everyone knows where it goes. His favorite spot was the mesa top. And from the paved road, you can't see the boneyard, or the dirt road where it runs beside it. You have to drive down in there. He obviously did that, and then very deliberately parked his Bronco. Now, did someone intercept him up on the paved road and force him to drive down there?"

"It's possible."

"Did you turn up any prints on the Bronco other than Scott's?" She shook her head. "Then why? Why did he drive down there?"

"We don't know."

"And if they were concerned with not being seen, they would just have let him drive on by, like all the other county-road traffic."

"Right."

"So that leaves two logical choices." I got up to fetch the cups and coffee, and lit a cigarette. "One is that he was meeting someone down there. He wasn't into anything illegal. I'd stake my life on that. Maybe he was meeting someone with the intent of talking them out of something. Who the hell knows. Or, he somehow got wind that something was going on and just decided to show up."

"Carrying a three-fifty-seven Magnum?"

I grimaced. "That's the thing that's been bothering me all along. Why that gun?" We both fell silent for a minute, looking at the photographs and sipping the coffee. The cigarette didn't taste very good, and I snubbed it out.

"I don't think the gun had anything to do with his initial decision to stop there."

I looked at Estelle with interest. "Why not?"

"I talked with both his parents and sister today." She clenched her teeth. "Rough. You were right about jerking chains. You know, I've known Amy Salinger ever since we were in high school together. We were never in the same circle of friends, but I always thought she was a neat person. I couldn't play games, seeing the way they hurt. I just tried to stick to general questions that wouldn't give our investigative direction away. Sir, that family is swimming in guilt so deep, I felt like grabbing them by their necks and shaking heads. I guess it's natural. Finally, though, Ryan Salinger came right out and asked me if we were investigating this as a murder."

"And you said . . ."

"Yes." Estelle shuffled some of the documents and put them back in the briefcase. "You should have seen the look on his face . . . on all their faces. It was like they'd been waiting just to hear that from us. They're eager to help. Any way. Anything."

"What'd Salinger say about the Magnum?"

"Only that it was his, the ammunition was his, hand-loaded by either him or the boy . . . he doesn't remember which. Last deer season, he let Scott pack it. Had a shot and missed. Got a deer with the rifle. After that, he let the boy take the gun hunting or plinking whenever he wanted. The only stipulation was that it would be cleaned and then put away unloaded in the wooden case in the den."

"And they were convinced it was suicide before you talked to them?"

"I think so. That was my impression. All Ryan Salinger asked me was whether we were going to be talking to the newspapers."

"What did you say to that?"

"I told him that anyone with any interest in the case would have to talk to you. Or Sheriff Holman."

"Good. I'll get together with Holman sometime and we'll work out a statement. In the meantime, I appreciate all your legwork. And by the way, what about the wood and plastic? The junk that was in Salinger's back pocket?"

Estelle pulled the evidence bag out. She read the

brief report. "The wood is spruce. Its shape is consistent in cross section with the leading edge of an airplane wing."

"Model airplane, you mean."

She nodded. "Yes. The plastic is a commercially available heat-shrink material used in model building as a covering. There are several brands, and the folks at the lab weren't willing to guess which one this was."

We looked at each other, thoroughly puzzled. "Huh," I said finally.

"Huh is right," she said, but before she could say anything else, the telephone on the counter jangled. "You want me to get that?"

I shook my head and held up a hand. "You know who it is as well as I do. Someone wants to cuss me out for leaving the hospital. To hell with 'em . . . at least for a little while. I'm tired of all the goddamned inter-ruptions." I nudged the plastic and spruce with my index finger. The phone finally gave up. "We were talking about that."

"I don't see the connection between this and Scott Salinger's murder. No way. Was somebody flying a model airplane around up there? So what? You don't kill someone for stopping to watch you fly an airplane. I guess you could cause someone to crash a model, and he might punch your lights out, but murder?"

"Strange place to fly it, too."

"If you assume that's what happened. We don't know where Salinger picked up the scraps. They might have been in his back pocket for hours . . . who knows. Or why."

"We're not even sure that he knew. Was he into model airplanes? Did you ask anybody?"

"I asked Amy. Just sort of off-the-cuff. He was into sports . . . football, baseball, wrestling, you name it. And hunting. He wasn't much to build models. Never was. A plastic car once in a while when he was younger . . . that was it."

"Do you have photos of this stuff?" I fingered the wood through the thin plastic of the evidence bag. Estelle Reyes nodded. "I want to keep this, then," I said. "Let me do some checking."

The telephone rang again. I looked heavenward. "You didn't call in, either," I said. I got up from the table with a grunt and picked up the receiver on about the eighth ring. It was J. J. Murton. The simple son of a bitch actually started the conversation by asking, "Are you home now?"

I let that slide but cut him short. "I can imagine that Holman wants to see me, J.J. When he comes back into the office, tell him I'm home . . . and expect to stay here for a while. And I'll be sound asleep for about four days, so I don't want to be bothered. You got that?"

"I ain't sure what he wanted," J.J. offered, hoping that I'd fill him in.

"Couldn't guess. If it's about the Salinger case, tell him that Detective Reyes is working on it. Nobody needs to bother me." I hung up abruptly and turned to grin at Estelle Reyes. "J.J. is trying to think again." She was too polite to say anything about Murton.

Instead, she began gathering the evidence and putting it back in the briefcase. "Do you still want to see the Salingers?"

"Yes," I said. "That would be better than a phone call. Bring them over here, if you would. And I do need to see Holman." I glanced at my watch. "Maybe you could set it all up for tomorrow morning. That'd give me time to get this place in order, maybe even catch a little rest. I got a couple things I need to think about and sort out."

Estelle Reyes left the manila envelope that contained the plastic-and-spruce-model parts with me, and promised to check in first thing in the morning. I walked her out to the car, and when she was behind the wheel, I closed the door and leaned my forearms on the windowsill. "I think we're getting close, Estelle, I really do. I feel it."

She nodded and asked, "Are you going to need anything?"

I shook my head. "Just some time to let things gel in my mind." I straightened up and patted the car's roof. I watched the Ford back out and kick up dust on the main road. With my hands in my pockets, I ambled back inside, forehead wrinkled in thought. Something was lying at the back of my mind, nagging. I couldn't put my finger on it. I closed the heavy front door and turned the dead bolt. Back in the kitchen, I tossed the evidence envelope on the counter and poured another cup of coffee. I tried a cigarette, and it tasted as bad as the first.

"Damn, what'd they do to me?" I muttered. I looked at the envelope again. Nothing was clear to me. I didn't want to make a false move out of ignorance and spook somebody out of the country. What the hell, I thought. Sleep on it. And when it all came clear, the world was the wonderful pitch-black of three-thirty in the morning.

23

I fumbled the telephone, dialing a couple of times before getting it right. Eventually the phone rang, and I tried to picture my son's household in Corpus Christi being jarred awake. Buddy should be up, I thought. Four rings. How could he get to the 4 A.M. flight briefings at the Naval Air Station if he didn't get out of bed? After eight rings, I had just about decided that maybe my youngest son had found some leave time after his return from Spain and the family was off somewhere camping.

"Hello?" The voice was thick with sleep.

I immediately flushed with acute embarrassment. "You're going to be late for your briefing, Buddy," I said, trying to sound jocular.

There was a silence while a sleeping brain tried to digest that. "Who the hell is this?" Lieutenant William C. Gastner, Jr., asked. He was awake and ready to punch somebody, and then before I could speak again, he said with some disbelief, "Is this Dad?"

"This is Dad."

"Jesus Christ."

"Why, thank you."

"Well, shit!"

I laughed. "I jerked you out of bed, obviously. You aren't flying today?"

"No. I flew in about twenty-three hundred hours last night. But the hell with that. Dad, how the hell are you? I talked with Camille after I got in. She said you were doing much better. I was getting things arranged so I could zip over that way."

"Ah, wait until you can come with everybody," I said. "Hell, it's no big deal. Over and done with. I just got in a little over my head, is all. Overtired."

"Right," Buddy said a little skeptically. "I can believe that. Camille said it's been a hell of a summer in Posadas." His voice dropped a tone or two. "She was sorry as hell she couldn't get there right away."

"Don't start that," I chided him with a laugh. "If a man wakes up in the hospital and sees his family standing around him wringing their hands, he knows right away the doctors told everybody he's dying. It scares him so bad, he dies."

My son laughed. "You timed it really well, if you wanted it to remain a secret. One daughter's in South America, I was in Madrid, and Joel was over hobnobbing about transistors with the Japs. Camille is in Flint with a broken ankle." He cleared his throat. "If your sheriff . . . what's his name?"

"Holman."

"Holman, that's right. If he hadn't been persistent and finally reached Camille, none of us would have found out until you got around to calling. You did good, Dad."

"I try. But if Holman thinks I'm going to remember him in my will, he's got another think coming. Anyway, I needed to ask you a question."

"I had just about figured that out. Nobody calls at zero three-thirty hours just to chat, although I'm not kickin'. Which nurse is the one in question?"

"I wish. No, I'm home already. Not even in the slammer anymore."

"That's super news."

"You bet. But look. Is Kendal still building one airplane model after another?"

There was a slight pause as Buddy tried to puzzle his way through my abrupt change of subject. "Yeah, he's doin' that. He's a terminal airplane nut case. He even got me to join the base modelers' club so he could be a member."

"They fly those gas-powered jobs?"

"Right. Some of them are pretty sophisticated. Especially the radio-controlled ones."

"There's a Scout troop here in town that does that, too. They had a float in the July Fourth parade. I was just remembering how big they were. Nothing like those things you used to fly on the end of strings."

Buddy laughed. "Nope. Whole different world. Last time I flew with Kendal, I put one straight down into the pavement. Shot about three hundred bucks. What, are you thinking of a hobby, or what?"

"No." I reached over to the nightstand, turned on the light and pulled out the evidence bag. I held up the wood and plastic that had been found in Scott Salinger's back pocket.

"I've got a curious piece of evidence. I wanted to run a couple things past you."

"Shoot."

"First of all, what's the plastic stuff that people cover model airplanes with now? It feels like a very heavy, slick garbage bag."

"Hell, there's several brands. Just a sec." I heard muffled voices, and Buddy said, "It's Dad. He's fine." He came back on the line. "Edie just snuck up on me. She said to tell you to get back in bed where you belong."

"Tell her I am in bed. And tell her not to go away. I want to talk to her when I'm through with you. So tell me about airplane coverings."

"We use a brand called Unicoat. It comes in a roll

about two feet wide and in several lengths. Six, twelve, and twenty-five feet. There's three or four brands. Most of them are pretty much alike. I'm not into it as deep as some. Kendal would know more than me."

"But it's nothing like that paper stuff you used to use as a kid."

"Silkspan? Hell, no. Some people still use the silk and dope, though."

I turned the wood and plastic over in my hand. "What holds the plastic to the wood? The bond seems pretty tight."

"You put it on with a hot iron, or a hair-dryer kind of thing. There's some sort of high-tech stickum on the back side that adheres under heat."

"How would I tell one brand from another if I had a sample?"

There was a moment's silence. "Beats the shit out of me," Buddy said. "The only thing I know is that to put on Unicoat, we have to turn the iron up to its highest setting. That's not true with the others. I don't know if it's just because it's thick, or what, but it always seems to take a humongous amount of heat. What the hell are you working on, anyway? Did somebody back there Unicoat somebody's mouth shut, or what?"

"We don't know yet, Buddy. I found a scrap of model-airplane wood and covering in a murder victim's back pocket."

"So your victim built models?"

"That's something I'm going to check. I've been holding back for obvious reasons. The stuff in his pocket was just scrap. I can't imagine why he would walk around out in the boonies with that. My theory right now is that he picked it up . . . and because it wasn't crushed deep down in his pocket, my theory is that he picked it up just before he was murdered."

"Who was the victim? Anybody I know?"

"No, I don't think so. A high school kid."

"No shit," Buddy said in wonder, and he whistled softly. "The airplane stuff . . . what was it?"

"The crime lab said it looked like the leading edge of an airplane wing."

"Shaped into a taper, you mean? The front edge is rounded?"

"Right."

"How big is it?"

"The piece is about three inches long. I would guess about three-quarters of an inch thick at its widest point. Maybe a little more."

Buddy made a sound of surprise. "Balsa wood?"

"No. Spruce."

"A big sucker, then."

"What's big?"

"The model that the piece came from. Kendal's got an airplane now that has a wingspan of about sixty inches, and it uses a piece of quarter-inch dowel for the wing's leading edge."

"This is three or four times bigger than that."

"How long is the chunk you've got?"

I held it up close, as if Buddy could see it over the telephone lines. "About three inches. Maybe four."

"On the back side . . . the trailing-edge-side . . . is there a slot of any kind?"

"No. The wood is smooth. There's some glue residue. And a speck or two of white stuff. The crime lab said it was a kind of Styrofoam. No other marks of any kind. Why?"

"Well, it's from a foam-cored wing, then. Usually, if the thing is all balsa, the wing ribs glue to the leading edge. There would be a mark, or even more likely, a slot in the wood itself where the rib fits in. But if it was foam core, that wouldn't be the case."

"Nope. So what's the significance of foam?"

"It's used in models that are either of simpler construction, or are intended for pretty high performance.

Several of the new full-size airplanes—especially the aerobatic ones—have core wings. Composites, they call 'em."

"So your guess is that this is from a pretty big model, then."

"Yes. If it was balsa, not necessarily. But spruce or pine, yes. That spruce is put on there just as a leading edge, for a little stiffness and protection. Where's the rest of it?"

"Beats me."

"The piece is obviously broken out?"

"Yes. Both ends are fractured. There's a split that runs almost the length of the piece."

"The only thing that makes sense is that it got wrecked in a crash, or stepped on, or crushed by a car, or something. It took a hell of a thump. If it crashed, there should be other pieces. If it went straight in, they'd all be together. If it skipped around—and that's just as common—you might have a bunch of pieces in one spot, then some more many yards away. Who knows. Weird case you got, Pop."

"Yes, it is."

He laughed. "I've seen some fruitcakes in this club down here who would probably kill if you did something wrong and caused them to screw their plane into the ground. Some of them get pretty serious."

"I don't think that's the case here."

"How was the kid murdered?"

"One shot through the heart. Kind of a clumsy attempt at making it look like suicide."

"Well, you'll nail 'em. Anyway, if you want to tell if the plastic is Unicoat, just get a modeler's iron and turn it to the highest heat setting. If it takes all the iron's got to make it stick, it's Unicoat." He hesitated. "But now that I think about it, five gets you ten it's not. If you are ironing a covering onto foam, you don't want to melt the foam. You'd need low heat. So it wouldn't be

Unicoat, then. Probably not. You'd want a low-heat cover of some kind. I don't know what they are, 'cause we never use 'em. Something like Colorfab. I think that's one. I don't know the others. Kendal would. And the other thing I've noticed is that they all have favorite shades. What color is it?"

"Sky-blue."

"That should be an easy match. And a dumb color for radio-controlled airplanes, too."

"Why?"

"Get it up against the New Mexico sky, and you can't see it."

"That makes sense."

"Everybody around here seems to be stuck in the yellow-red rut. High visibility if it gets a little far away."

I didn't say anything, because my brain was kicking into high gear. The silence went on so long that eventually Buddy said, "You still there?"

"Yes. Let me ask you a question. Suppose the victim came upon the crash site of a big model airplane. What could there be about it that would be so incriminating as to prompt the kid to pick up a piece of the wreckage? And then a murder follows?"

"Where was the murder?"

"Up at the Consolidated Mine boneyard. You remember where that is?"

"Sure, but what have you got that suggests a connection between airplane and murder?"

"Not a damn thing. Except the junk was in the kid's pocket, and there was no reason for it to be there."

"One thing I'm not is a detective, Pop. But like I said, you and all your staff will figure it out. Sounds like you got it on the run. Say, keep me posted, will you?"

"You bet. And sorry about the night call. How was Spain, by the way?"

"I never saw it," my son said with a laugh. "Got

there at night, left early. What little ground I saw was brown . . . just like Posadas County."

"You home for a while now?"

"About a week, I think. Anyhow, if I think of anything else, or if Kendal does, I'll make sure we get right back to you. You want to talk to Edie?"

I heard her say, "Of course he does," in the background.

"Buddy, take care," I said, and then my effervescent daughter-in-law was on the line.

"When did you get out of ICU?" she asked, and like a fool, I told her. The lecture I got seemed to last ten minutes. There was no point in arguing. I finally mollified her by lying like a rug, promising faithfully to take all the medications as prescribed, and to visit them in Texas as soon as I could. Part of all that was true, at least. I was planning to make some visits, all right . . . but not to Texas.

24

Despite the ideas whirling around inside my head, I fell back asleep almost instantly, and woke to the telephone trying to rattle itself off the nightstand.

It was Holman, and if he didn't sound angry, he certainly wasn't his usual blabby, politic self.

"You going to be home in a few minutes?" he said without preamble.

"Yes." I looked at the glowing dial of the clock radio and saw that outside the sun already would be blistering the east side of the adobe. "Come on over. I'll put the coffee on."

Holman grunted something that I didn't catch and hung up. I lay still for a minute, then swung my feet down to the cool brick floor. I took inventory and decided I felt almost human. Holman's fist thudded on the door just as I was finishing shaving. With a towel around my neck, my bathrobe cinched up tight, and my slippers scuffing the tiles, I must have looked the part of a goddamn invalid when I opened the door and motioned him inside.

"Give me just a minute," I said. "The coffee's in the kitchen on the counter, and should be just about ready. Cups are up above on the right." When I finished dressing and entered the kitchen, I found Martin Holman sit-

193

ting at the table, a steaming coffee mug in front of him. He looked up at me, rose, and poured another cup.

"You allowed to drink this stuff?" he said, handing me the cup.

"Hell, yes," I said and grinned. Holman scowled.

"I didn't come over yesterday because I was too damn mad, Bill. Jesus H. Christ." He sat down heavily, took a sip of coffee, and grimaced. "You behaved like a damn five-year-old, you know that."

"I didn't see it that way," I snapped. I might take a lecture from my daughter-in-law, but I sure as hell wasn't about to hear it from Martin Holman.

"Yeah, well," he said, understanding the edge in my voice. "If we lose you, this whole case is going to fall apart."

"That's unlikely."

"I don't want a bunch of strangers laying this town wide open, Bill."

"That's not going to happen. Estelle Reyes is the best there is. I guarantee it."

"She's young, and you know it. And this morning she told me herself that she was just your legs, running errands, taking care of lab work." Holman saw the surprise on my face. "That's what she said. She said she didn't have the handle on this that you did."

"Bullshit. She's worth five of me," I snapped. "And the hours she puts in, we should be paying her five times what she's getting. Is that what you came over for, to chew my ass about not letting a couple doctors cut me up?"

Holman lifted an eyebrow at me over the coffee cup. "I saw Harlan Sprague late yesterday afternoon."

"So?"

"He wanted to know if he could come over and see you. I said he should call you first."

"That's thoughtful. I don't need mothering. I need to

see some son of a bitch in jail. That's all the medicine I need."

Holman took a deep breath. "I can see that asking you to lay off would be a waste of breath." I started to say something I would have probably regretted, but Holman held up a hand. "Don't get me wrong. I want this case solved as much as you do . . . as much as anyone in the department." He looked at me for a minute. "I'm not sure what sacrifices I'm willing to make to solve it tomorrow, though . . . or even next week. I think we need to understand all the angles . . . even the long-range picture."

"What are you saying, Sheriff?"

"I'm saying that there's nothing I can do to force you to relax and take care of yourself." He smiled faintly. "Short of handcuffs. Kidding aside, I'm pleading with you to use good sense."

"I am."

"Uh-huh. As far as I'm concerned, there's only one man in this department who really understands the entire picture. That's you. And you know it, damn it. I'm no lawman. I'm an executive . . . an administrator. I depend on you to make sure this department is as efficient as it can be. I don't want the county legislature to have a single excuse to say, 'Hell, let the state police run the county.' Or worse, customs. Or the DEA. I want us to do it, Bill. Us."

"I guess I should feel complimented."

"Yes," Holman said simply. "What it boils down to is that if you don't do it, nobody in this department does. And speaking of the DEA, their aircraft are working the border about twenty-five hours a day. Found nothing. State police made a decent drug bust on the interstate north of Las Cruces yesterday. They nailed two jerks who were driving a pickup truck, trying to move a couple of kilos inside a dog house they had in the back. The dog was inside the house." He chuckled, and then his face went serious. "Chief White called from Gallup. I told him we'd have something concrete by the end of the week."

"No problem."

Holman stood up and set the coffee cup in the sink. "'No problem,' he says. I wish I had your confidence. Is there anything you need?"

"No. Nothing."

"You'll keep it slow?"

"Sure."

"Then I'll get out of your hair." He gave me a long look, then said, "Thanks for the wake-up." As soon as I heard his car spitting gravel out of the driveway, I picked up the phone. It rang once.

"Sheriff's Department. Deputy Mitchel."

"Eddie, this is Gastner. I need to talk to Estelle Reyes. Where is she?"

"Just a minute." There was a second or two of voices in the background, then Mitchel said, "We'll have to telephone her, sir. You're at home?"

"Yes. But tell her not to bother calling me. I need to see her." I hung up to spare Eddie the obligation of asking how I was. Then I settled back to wait, filling the telephone pad with mindless doodles.

Thirty minutes later, Estelle Reyes arrived, and she wasn't alone. A Buick stationwagon pulled in behind her Ford. Ryan Salinger—a big, broad-shouldered, ruddy-faced man with widely spaced and deeply set eyes—and his wife and daughter followed Estelle in. Diane Salinger was trying to look composed and doing a rotten job. It was Amy I found myself looking at as they trooped in.

"Sir," Estelle Reyes said, "I got your call. I was talking with the Salingers, and they wanted to come down with me for a minute."

I extended my hand and Ryan Salinger engulfed it in his. It seemed that he made a conscious effort to keep his grip firm but gentle. "It's good to see you again," I said.

"I'm sorry to hear about your illness, Sheriff. And I apologize for not coming sooner. But . . ." He let it trail off and shrugged helplessly. "Anything we can do, we'll do."

"We appreciate that. Come on in." I ushered them inside, down the hall to the living room. They were all edgy and ill at ease.

"I've got to ask you, though," Ryan Salinger said. "I've talked to Detective Reyes now a couple times, and it's not that I don't trust her word. But I gotta ask. Is your department absolutely convinced that Scott's death was murder?"

It was hard for him to say, and hard for the others to listen to. He stood with one arm protectively around his wife's shoulders.

"Yes, I am," I said, and wasn't sure how to translate the expression on his face. "We are completely convinced it was murder."

"What do we do?" he asked. I had no advice about how to handle the grief—and how to handle the inevitable sudden release of guilt and its replacement by rage at the killers.

"Sit down," I said, and when they were all perched on the edges of their seats like patients in a dentist's office, I continued, "Be available to us anytime of day or night. Let us work without our having to worry that you're out there too, trying to track this down on your own." Salinger nodded slightly. "We've got good, solid leads," I added. "The killer made a basketful of mistakes, thank God."

"Whatever I can do," Salinger said.

"Let us work. But one question you can help us with. Did your son build model airplanes of any kind?" Ryan Salinger shook his head. "No flying models, for instance?"

"He never built models, period," Salinger said. "Detective Reyes asked me the same thing." I glanced at Estelle. She was standing by the dark cavern of the fireplace, with her elbow resting on the low mantel. I felt about a week behind. "Oh, he built a few when he was little," Salinger said, "but not anything later. He was into sports and hunting."

"That's good to hear," I said. They didn't ask me about the question. It was obvious that Ryan Salinger had the answer to the one question he cared about. I remembered how quick he had been to hie off by himself, looking for his son. I hoped he wasn't planning to go solo again. We didn't need another Fernandez case. The folks looked miserable, and so I stood up, ready to end the meeting. "I appreciate you coming by. We'll keep you posted as much as we can." They made their uncomfortable exit, and Amy took the opportunity to step close to me. Her hand squeezed my arm.

"Are you heading back to A and M?" I asked.

She shook her head. "Not yet."

"We'll do our best, Amy."

"What the hell's going on, Estelle?" I asked as soon as the Salingers had left.

"What do you mean?"

"Holman was here a bit ago. He was talking like you were some kind of mental midget. The impression was that you're just running around, doing errands for me." Estelle came close to grinning, and I added, "Hell, I just kept that scrap of junk so I'd have something to do."

"What'd you find out about it?"

"It's from a large-size model airplane. One of those radio-controlled things. With a couple questions to the right people, we can even determine what the brand name of the plastic covering is."

"And Scott Salinger never dabbled in that hobby," Estelle added.

"So his family says."

"He walked into something, then, and somehow that wood and plastic is a signal."

"You think he picked it up and put it in his pocket, maybe knowing that he wasn't going to get clear?"

Estelle nodded soberly. "That's what I think."

"Knowing that there was a chance someone would find it."

She nodded again. "It's the only explanation that makes any sense. Who are you going to ask about the brand of plastic?"

"I was thinking about Herman Tollis." Tollis was an old straight-arrow who worked for the Forest Service. He was a Boy Scoutmaster in his spare time. His Scouts had been flying airplanes for what seemed like generations. "I hesitate to just waltz into the hobby shop. You never know who might be tipped off."

"You have reason to suspect David Barrie?"

"Maybe. Maybe not. But you never know who his customers are, either." I saw something on Estelle's face. "What's the matter?"

Detective Reyes looked at her watch and frowned. "Can I use your phone?"

I nodded toward it. She pulled the slender local directory out from under the receiver and thumbed through its few pages quickly. She dialed and waited. And waited. Maybe twenty rings, and still no answer. "Who?" I asked.

She finally put the phone down. "Barrie Hobby and Crafts. You just jogged my memory. I was driving through town on my way to the Salingers'. There were three kids on the sidewalk, peering through the front door of the hobby shop. You know, leaning up and shading their eyes to see in? The place was obviously closed."

"And it still is?"

"It still is." She looked at her watch again, and then

thumbed the phone book. She dialed again, and this time it took only four rings before a female voice answered.

"Good morning," Estelle said in her best saleswoman's greeting. "I was wondering if the hobby shop would be open later today." She listened briefly. "Oh, I'm sorry. Isn't this the David Barrie residence? He said if I needed supplies I could buzz him at home." She listened again and frowned, then looked at me as she hung up the phone. "She said, quote, I don't know anything about the store. Unquote. Then she hung up."

"You had the right number?"

"She didn't deny that it was the Barrie residence. She just didn't sound like she wanted to talk."

"Go find out, Estelle. Hell, take this with you." I got her the brown envelope and handed it to her. "If you find Barrie, ask him about this stuff. If he's clean, no problems. If he spooks, you'll know. And what about the fingerprints? Anything yet?"

Reyes took the envelope and shook her head. "I should be hearing from Santa Fe this afternoon, if they have any hit. It's not as clear as I first thought." She hesitated. "You know what I figured, don't you?"

"What are you talking about?"

"The question you asked me first . . . the one I didn't answer. I made a point, when I was talking to Holman or anyone else who wouldn't know the difference, to use your name a lot. I figured I could move a little easier if attention was directed at you. And there was always the possibility that if the killer bought the story of you managing evidence, whoever it was might come out of the woodwork, trying to find out how much you knew."

"I'm bait, you mean."

"Well, it's not like I expected them to sneak in here at night and thump you on the head or anything."

"I appreciate your concern. What would you have done if they had?" I grinned with more amusement than

I felt. "According to everyone else, I'm infirm in both mind and body."

"Good point," Estelle said. "You've got a gun?"

I made a sour face and waved a hand in dismissal. "Let me know ASAP about Barrie. My gut is turning flip-flops. That's always a sign. Maybe the missus will talk to you if I'm not along. And as devious as you are, you should be able to talk her out of any information she has."

"I'm not devious," Estelle Reyes said.

"So you say."

When she left, I had the feeling my hours of relaxation at home were at an end. There's only so much rest a man can take.

25

"He's skipped," Estelle Reyes said. I held the phone tight to my ear.

"His wife is still home?"

"Sure is. Depressed as hell, obviously. She didn't know what to do at first, and didn't want to talk to me. She finally gave in. I spent half an hour listening to her sob before I could get two coherent words out of her."

"What were those?"

"David Barrie apparently left sometime the day before yesterday. She thought he was going to the store, and was a little worried about him. She said he was irritable and absentminded. She called the store mid-morning, and it was closed."

"She didn't bother to call anybody? Like her friendly sheriff's department?"

"Nope. Apparently she had a feeling that it was a skip, not something else. She isn't anxious to talk about it. Anyway, he cleaned house."

"What do you mean?"

"All the receipts he could lay his hands on. He cleaned out their joint accounts at First National. He even took a coin collection that had been in a safety-deposit box. A bunch of other stuff as well."

"And she has no idea where he went?"

"Nope."

"Is she going to file suit?"

"Another day or two to think about it, and she might. Right now, she's just sitting in her house, feeling small."

"It shouldn't be hard to find a silver Corvette. He took that, didn't he?"

"Yup. And it took about half an hour to find it. I put it on the computer this morning as a hit. The Las Cruces PD found it. They were very proud of themselves."

"Where was it?"

"Parked in the lot at Las Cruces-Crawford Airport."

"Well, son of a bitch." My pulse soared. "Get a warrant for the hobby shop, Estelle. And one for the house."

"Judge Deal said I can pick it up on my way over."

"Stop and pick me up on the way."

"Are you serious?"

"I'm serious. I feel fine."

Estelle didn't argue with me, and didn't waste any time. Ten minutes later, she pulled into my driveway, and I was ready. I yanked open the door before she even had time to shut off the engine. "Did you get the warrant?"

"Yes."

"Then let's go use it."

Mrs. Barrie seemed more than eager to cooperate—she'd had some time to think, I guess. That her husband had obviously split and left her nearly destitute except for some inventory and real estate had produced first a mix of guilt and remorse, then some healthy self-pity fired with rage.

She met us at the store, and opened the front door with a kind of grim satisfaction. "It's all yours, officers," she said.

"Mrs. Barrie, were you and your husband having difficulty before this week?"

She almost laughed, and it came out as a half-sigh. "Difficulty isn't the word. I'm fairly sure he was seeing somebody else on a regular basis."

"Another woman, you mean?"

She nodded. "He was keeping some strange hours. But I guess it didn't matter. After his daughter was killed, we really didn't have much to say to each other."

I was leaning against the doorjamb, listening with half an ear while I surveyed the store's interior layout. Her emphasis caught my attention. "His daughter?"

"Yes. Jenny was from his first marriage. She and I were so close, I felt she was mine, too, but she was really my stepdaughter."

Too bad that hadn't been true with the Fernandez kid, I thought. There was more I wanted to ask this woman. When we had first interviewed parents after the July Fourth car crash, I had talked with David Barrie. His wife had sat silently by, watching and listening to the conversation.

But now, any questions I might have found breath to ask were interrupted by the screech of tires outside. I glanced over my shoulder and saw Martin Holman's car jar to a stop behind ours. Holman got briskly out and so did his passenger—Dr. Harlan Sprague. The fact that he was blundering right into the middle of a field investigation apparently didn't occur to Holman.

I held up a hand. "No further," I said flatly. I directed it more at Sprague than Holman, since Holman was free to do pretty much what he wanted. "Dr. Sprague, did you want something in particular?"

"I thought it would be all right," Holman said lamely.

The physician blushed slightly. He didn't like being caught in the middle. "I came at Sheriff Holman's request. Dr. Perrone wouldn't come, but apparently suggested me as someone you knew and maybe trusted."

He looked at me shrewdly. "You know the risk you're taking, in your condition and away from medical care?"

"I tell you what, Doc. I appreciate your concern. If you want to wait outside in the sheriff's car, or across the street in the coffee shop, feel free. I don't want unauthorized personnel in here. I'm sorry to be so rude, but that's the way it is."

Sprague nodded with resignation. After he left, Holman took me by the elbow. Estelle was already prowling. Mrs. Barrie sat down in a chair by the cash register and waited.

"Look, Bill," the sheriff started to reason, but I cut him off. I kept my voice down to a gravelly whisper.

"Sheriff, David Barrie skipped town early yesterday. He took what money he could, and drove to Las Cruces. They found his car at the airport."

"And that has something to do with the Salinger murder?" he asked quietly.

"We think so. It'd be too much of a coincidence otherwise. Give us some time, and then I'll explain why." It didn't take much time. Estelle Reyes emerged from a back room carrying a large, brightly colored box. The top was off, tucked under.

I looked at the Japanese characters, supplemented with English and German. "Giant-scale stunter," I read aloud. Estelle had the plans for the big model airplane unrolled. "Just junk in here," I said, rummaging through the scraps of plywood, balsa, pine, and plastic. There were several almost empty squeeze bottles of glue, used straight pins, and several clothespins. "And bingo," I said. I held up the roll of plastic covering.

"And here," Estelle Reyes said. She had unrolled a sheet of full-sized plans. She pointed at a long piece of wood that formed the leading edge.

"That thing is big," Holman said in wonder. "And what are we looking at model airplanes for?"

"Says here that it's one-third scale. The wingspan is

ninety inches. And look at the size of that engine," I said ignoring the question.

"Mrs. Barrie?" Estelle Reyes showed the woman the plans. "Did this belong to your husband?" Mrs. Barrie nodded. "Do you know where it is now?" Estelle asked.

"I have no idea. All I know is that he spent months building it. He worked down here at the store. Not at home." She looked peeved. "Of what concern is a stupid model airplane? He sold them, you know. This is a hobby shop."

It seemed the right time. "Detective Reyes, would you go out to the car and get the evidence envelope?"

Estelle did so, and I pulled out the bit of plastic and spruce. There was no need to hold it up against the scraps in the box. "Mrs. Barrie, this material was found in Scott Salinger's back pocket. We have reason to believe he picked it up just before he was killed." Mrs. Barrie's face was blank. She looked at the plastic and wood, and then at the plans that Estelle still held. For emphasis, Estelle turned and picked up the partial roll of the plastic that lay in the box.

"My Lord," she breathed. She sagged into the chair.

"Now, there are other possibilities that we're checking out," I said. "There may be other explanations. It's possible that your husband was flying the airplane somewhere, and Salinger was just watching. Perhaps the plane crashed, and Salinger took a piece as a souvenir. Then, later, he stumbled into the trouble up on the hill. That's possible."

"But you don't think that's what happened," Mrs. Barrie said, so faintly I could hardly hear her.

"Mrs. Barrie," Estelle said, "I've been able to find no witnesses that your husband was flying model airplanes the last few days. There is a place out by the airport where enthusiasts fly. No one has seen your husband flying for months."

"I never realized that he was particularly interested," she said. "He told me once that he was learning to fly radio control so that he would know something about the products. Good for business, he said." She looked at me beseechingly. "You don't really think David was responsible for that boy's death, do you? I mean, he couldn't do a thing like that. Could he?"

"That's what we need to find out," Holman said when the silence stretched just a second too long. "Mrs. Barrie, I think I should take you home." The woman agreed readily. She wasn't ready to cope with the implications of her husband's sudden flight to who knew where. "Bill, I want to talk to you later today. When you're finished here."

"Right," I said, trying to sound noncommittal. "Don't forget the good doctor." I watched them go and then turned my attention back to the airplane box. I made notes, and Estelle went out to the car and got her field kit. She carefully lifted prints from several places in the store.

"What do you think?" she said finally.

"I think I want to see a print comparison. These against the one partial from the Magnum casing."

"What do you think Barrie was up to?"

"Only one thing fits . . . drugs are involved. Look at the record. His daughter killed in a car wreck. And hell, before that, she was best friends with another girl who OD'd. Scott Salinger knew Barrie's daughter was involved in drugs, but didn't know what to do about it. And then he gets himself blown away, and Barrie splits, taking all the money he can lay his hands on. And that may be plenty, if he was dealing on the side. It's the only thing that fits, Estelle. The only thing that fits."

"What are you going to do?"

"Go home and go to bed," I said, and Estelle looked surprised. I leaned back against a counter, feeling suddenly exhausted and light-headed. "I think I can stand up long enough to get to the car. That's about it. Call whoever is available, and I'll have them run me home. Then they can come back and give you a hand."

"I can run you home."

I shook my head. "I don't want you to leave here until you've combed every particle of dust. And let me know as soon as you process the prints." There was plenty more to do at the store, but Estelle would handle it far better than I. Bob Torrez's patrol car idled up to the curb a few minutes later, and I sagged into the passenger's seat wearily. On the way to the house, I called the office and made arrangements for 310 to be dropped off at my house.

The adobe was dark, cool, and welcome. I didn't bother to look at my watch . . . time had no real meaning, anyway. I undressed and made sure the telephone was carefully placed. Then I lay down and almost instantly fell asleep.

The phone had become my alarm clock. This time, I wasn't groggy. It was Estelle Reyes and my pulse jumped.

"Prints match," she said. "I'm sending off to the lab for an official verification. But it's obvious, even with the casing print being a crummy partial."

"You're one-hundred-percent sure?"

"I am."

"Then get a warrant out for David Barrie's arrest. And call the *Register*. Give them an exclusive. That'll make Leo Bailey happy."

"Yes, sir."

"Anything else?" I asked, and Estelle hesitated, as she did when she'd just done something no one else had thought of.

"Well, I drove out and talked with Jim Bergin at the airport."

"Oh?"

"There hasn't been much going on lately out there."

She paused. "The only local traffic was Harlan Sprague's plane. He came back yesterday from Albuquerque."

"So?"

I could almost hear Reyes shrug. "I wouldn't have thought anything about it, but Jim Bergin was uneasy."

"Why?"

"Well, from hearing him talk, I gather that he's a real stickler for following the book. He changed the oil on Sprague's Centurion last week. He logs all that kind of stuff . . . in the plane's engine log, and in one of his own . . . some maintenance record he keeps for regular customers."

"Again, so?"

"So, it's a two-hour flight from here to Albuquerque in Sprague's plane. A round trip would be four hours."

"Duh," I said, irritated at being led like a child.

Estelle chuckled. "Even with some sightseeing, not much more than six. The point is, the Hobbs meter in the Centurion shows almost fourteen hours."

"So somebody made a mistake."

"I don't think so. The tachometer roughly agrees. And nobody in Albuquerque refueled Mike Bravo one-seven-eight. And nobody in Mid-Valley. Or Socorro. Sprague has always paid for av-gas with a credit card. Somebody would have a record."

"Unless he paid in cash."

"Bergin says that fixed base operators would remember the plane."

"When did he leave Posadas?"

"Bergin says the day before yesterday." Estelle Reyes waited a minute and listened to me thinking. "It's about thirty minutes airtime to Las Cruces-Crawford, sir."

"That's what I was thinking."

"And if he picked up Barrie there . . ."

"Right. They could have slipped across into Mexico

as easy as can be. Jim Bergin says all you'd have to do is fly low, and it'd be a piece of cake."

"And so you think he took Barrie out of the country?"

"Well, I'd be a little slow to jump to that conclusion except for one thing. He made another long flight a few days before."

"Bergin is sure?"

"Reasonably. But you know, Sprague flies to conventions all over the place."

"What catches your eye about that particular flight, then?"

"Bergin isn't sure when Sprague left, but he knows when he returned. He landed back in Posadas late in the afternoon on the day you were in Gallup at Art Hewitt's funeral. Very late in the afternoon. Just about dusk."

"Did he have anyone with him?"

"Bergin doesn't know. Sprague put the plane away. Bergin had already gone home. It was after five."

"Then how does he know that's when Sprague came in?"

"He said he saw him. He was getting a backyard cookout ready. He saw Sprague's plane fly over. Low."

"That's the day Scott Salinger was murdered," I said, as if Estelle needed reminding.

"Yes, sir, it is."

"Do you know where he went?"

"Yes. I looked in the aircraft engine log. There's a signature from a mechanic who checked and corrected a shimmy in the front gear. The work was done at Guaymas."

"Mexico," I added.

"Right. That's three hundred miles from here."

"He goes fishing at Bahia Kino. That's about eighty miles up the coast from Guaymas."

"Right. It's just that I can't help thinking—this last

flight. Seven hours in a turbo Centurion would get you pretty deep in Mexico."

"Mazatlán. Guadalajara. Any of those, even at tree top level."

"You think there's enough cause to link him with David Barrie?"

"I can see him laying a trap for Barrie, maybe even blowing him away, if he discovered the man was a drug dealer and responsible for his daughter's death. But working with him? Hardly."

"Any ideas?" Estelle asked.

"Yeah, I got an idea. I'll ask him." I outlined what I planned to do, and Estelle hesitated. "Hey, look, Holman says I need a vacation, right?"

"Not like this."

"Sprague has offered to take me fishing in Mexico anytime. When we're up in the plane, he's a captive audience. No better time."

"I hope he doesn't ask you to step outside. At twenty thousand feet."

I laughed. "I don't think that's possible."

"You'll let me know if you do something like that?"

"Yes, mother. In the meantime, you keep nosing around. You're doing good." I rang off feeling better. Maybe it was just misplaced intuition, but I fell asleep again with the notion that Dr. Harlan Sprague would tell me things on a Mexican beach that he wouldn't in Posadas.

26

I didn't tell Holman what I was planning. I didn't want to hear the song and dance about my health. Besides, I had a few gnawing suspicions left about Martin Holman himself, among them a certain uneasiness about the paired arrival of Sprague and Holman at the hobby shop. I chalked most of Holman's actions up to being ignorant of investigation procedures, but still . . .

I gave my plan a couple more hours of thought. The most intelligent move would have been to summon all the heavy-iron help our department could find. But I followed my intuition, and that dumb feeling told me that the root of the abscess was right in Posadas and that I was perfectly capable of rooting it out. And call it pride, but I didn't want strangers proving to Holman that he was right about aging undersheriffs not being able to handle their own counties.

I made my preparations with some care, and they included a call to my son. At least in that respect, the cards were in my favor. With only ten minutes of waiting and three or four shunts, Buddy came on the line, sounding nervous. "Dad?"

"Forget what they told you, Buddy. I'm fine. I just had to tell some lies to get through to you. It's like talking to Fort Knox."

Buddy laughed, but when he heard what I had to say, he turned serious quickly. "You're not really going to do this, are you?"

"Yep," I said.

"No way I can talk you out of it?"

"Nope. But you can help. You can answer me some questions." We talked for almost twenty minutes, and when we were finished, I was pleased and he was more apprehensive than before. "Relax, Buddy. I'll call you when it's over."

"Easy for you to say. I think I'll check me out a T-thirty-eight and ride tail on you."

"You do, and I will be, as they say, most annoyed. I can take care of myself. Just hang loose."

Late that afternoon, I made another telephone call. As it turned out, Harlan Sprague couldn't resist the opportunity to catch a few fish. If what little that was left of his medical practice was an inconvenience, he didn't let it bother him. When I called, Sprague was initially startled, but then enthusiastic. He asked if my visa was in order or if I'd have to get a visitor's permit. I assured him I had the necessary papers. I didn't ask him about his own.

I added to my mental file the nagging uneasiness I felt about Sprague's sudden agreement that a trip was in order. And it was only when I parked at the airport at dawn the next day that I remembered that the good doctor hadn't made much of an issue about my precarious health, a welcome change, but unusual nevertheless. I patted myself on the back for having had the presence of mind to call my son.

The weather was still soft and cool when I met the doctor at the airport, and Sprague looked at my small duffel bag critically. "I'm glad you can travel light," he said. He loaded the airplane, taking special care that nothing rested on two heavy fishing rods. "I made these," he said as he jockeyed them into place. "Wait until you try one." He looked at the small Pan Am flight bag I carried. "You're going to keep that up front?"

I nodded, and then pointed at the Cessna. "This thing has enough room inside for a boat and motor," I said. I stowed the flight bag on the floor in front of the right-hand seat. Harlan Sprague took his time with the preflight check. I walked around with him and watched. After fingering every rivet and seam, and after the airplane had sprayed out three or four urine samples into Sprague's plastic specimen cup, the doctor seemed satisfied. We climbed in.

I've never seen an airplane engine start eagerly. This one was no exception. The prop kicked lethargically several times against the prime and then the big engine coughed, belched, and settled into a powerful rumble.

Some minutes later, the lift-off from Posadas County Airport was smooth and certain. One seven eight Mike Bravo was virtually empty—just the two of us and light baggage in a six-seat airplane, and Sprague held the Centurion in a powerful climb so steep that my ears clicked and popped. When we were well clear of surrounding mesa tops, he let the nose settle so we could see ahead.

"It's going to be a perfect day," Harlan Sprague said with relish. He scanned the sky, and then keyed the mike on the control yoke. He wore one of those nifty arrangements where the pickup is on a slender boom that curves around from the headset, ending right in front of the pilot's mouth. As I listened to him file and open his flight plan, I thought that kind of radio should be in police cars. Just push the button on the steering wheel and talk into the boom mike—nothing to pick up and fumble. According to what he was telling the FAA, we would be cruising at ten thousand feet. I thought that was on the low side for a powerful airplane that was probably capable of scrambling up to airliner coun-

214

try, but the flight was reasonably short. Maybe even semi-retired doctors felt the need to economize.

While he was talking, I reached down for my small travel bag. I found a pair of sunglasses, and while my hand was in the bag, I punched down the dual switches of the cassette recorder. I glanced at Sprague. He was still reeling out numbers to some soul on the other end. I heard him say, "That's negative," and then he turned and looked at me. "Paperwork's done. Now we can relax," he said. "We'll be flying down to Tucson first. I filed for there. Then we hop across to Nogales and clear Mexican customs there." He pointed out to my right, and I saw the silver dart and twin contrails of a commercial jet heading south ahead of us.

"What altitude is he at?"

"Probably thirty-five or forty thousand feet," Sprague said. "I don't think it's a good idea for us to fly much higher than we are, though. Not with a cardiac patient aboard." He smiled faintly. "Plus it's not far to Tucson. You comfortable?"

"Sure," I said. I was tired and my fingers and toes tingled a little, but then it was early in the day. Until my first gallon of coffee, everything was out of whack.

"So," he said, as if we had reached a point in the sky for which we had both been waiting. He was messing with his headset, turned slightly away from me. "What was it you wanted to know?"

He glanced sideways at me as he next fiddled with switches and gadgets on the dash. The plane was on autopilot, I hoped, because he relaxed with his hands off the wheel and his feet off the pedals. I could feel the gentle drift and swing as the electronic brain corrected for bumps in the road. He chuckled at the surprise on my face. "Sheriff, I don't know you terribly well, but I know you a little. The Bill Gastner I know would, obviously, check himself out of a hospital cardiac care ward at the least provocation to continue his work. He would not go off on a fishing trip to Mexico during the middle of that investigation unless everything was completely wrapped up, sealed and delivered to the district attorney's office."

He scrunched around in his seat so he could look my way without cranking his neck so much. "Maybe I just reached a point where I'm ready to admit my own limitations," I said. Sprague laughed aloud at that.

He reached out and made a small adjustment. It may have been my imagination, but it seemed that the Cessna lifted its nose a fraction of a degree. A smile kept playing at the corner of Sprague's mouth. Finally, he said, "How long is the tape?"

"Tape?" I asked, puzzled.

Nodding toward the small travel bag at my feet, he said, "The cassette in the recorder there." His eyes swung up to meet mine, and the crow's-feet at their corners deepened with an irritating smugness.

"Ninety minutes." I saw no point in trying to cover or apologize. Neither did Sprague, evidently.

"And what would you like me to say for the record?"

"Do you . . ." I started, then stopped. A small wave of nausea swept over me, and I blinked rapidly and licked my lips. "Do you have any information about the case?"

With an irritating casualness, Sprague said, "Which one?"

"Any. Do you know anything about David Barrie's disappearance?" If I looked at the clutter of instruments, I got dizzy.

The blank blue of the sky was harsh, and I realised with an odd sense of detachment that my feet and hands were nearly numb. I knew damn well what was the matter . . . and as the Centurion climbed higher into thinner air, matters would only become worse. I closed my eyes for a second or two. Sprague was feeling confident, even cocky. He could tolerate the altitude far better than I . . . Maybe he even had a supplimental oxygen bottle stashed somewhere. But I couldn't let the chance slide by. I opened my eyes and saw that Harlan Sprague was staring hard at me, his face set in a glacial, emotionless mask. The possibility of hypoxia was one I had discussed with my worried son, but now that I was caught in the trap, no brilliant options presented themselves.

"David Barrie," I repeated, working to enunciate the words.

"I know approximately where Barrie is," the doctor said quietly.

"Where?"

"Many places now, I'm sure." Sprague looked out at the sky. "When he left the seat in which you are now sitting, he was lightly drugged and suffering from rather severe hypoxia. You know what that is?" He took a nod as my answer. "I imagine . . . I sincerely hope . . . that sometime during his rapid twenty thousand foot descent to the Mexican desert below us, he regained consciousness. I would like to think that."

"You killed him." I knew it sounded stupid, but that's all I could think to say.

Sprague didn't smile. "No. Actually, I just helped him out of the plane. It's relatively easy, you know. Climb steeply to a near stall and there isn't much slipstream to lock the door closed. You notice this aircraft has no wing struts." He pointed as if he were a tour guide. "They call it a cantilever wing. Nothing for Mr. Barrie to hit on his way out. The sudden stop when he hit the desert killed him, no doubt. If not that, then the scavengers who keep the desert clean of garbage finished the job." He raised an eyebrow. "Because that's what he was, Sheriff. Garbage. He killed my daughter. And when he did that, do you remember what the good folks of Posadas did in return?"

"Tell me."

"Nothing. They did nothing. I lost my daughter, and they did nothing." His jaw set tightly and he looked away, out toward the clouds. The momentary euphoria of oxygen starvation had passed, and instead I felt miserable. I wiped my forehead. On the ground I had been fine, and I cursed my body's crumbling resistance. I looked at the instrument panel. There was that conversation with my son again, replaying through my mind. There was an altimeter there somewhere, no doubt. Who knows where. Buddy had told me to pay attention to that. I found one dial whose needle pointed left, its white bar just past the numeral 5 above a horizontal line. On the dial face it said, in small, blurry letters I could just make out, "Vertical Speed."

Buddy had said something about focus, too, I remembered. "You know your rights?" I said thickly.

"Oh, yes, Sheriff. I know them. But I'm not worried about me. Maybe about you. Not about me."

"Turn back to Posadas," I said.

"I don't think so. Not yet, anyway." He fingered the control yoke idly. "Don't you want to know the rest? Isn't that what I'm supposed to do? Tell you the rest?"

"The rest?"

"It worked well, too, until Barrie got clumsy. You see"—he settled a little like a good storyteller in front of the fire—"and I'll make this quick, because I can see your concentration is limited . . . I decided that my first priority was revenge against Barrie. But the more I thought, the more I decided that it was the entire community." He smiled at me. "I'm sure the whole world is to blame, but one must start somewhere. If it was drugs they wanted, it was drugs I would provide . . . until Barrie and all the rest knew what it was to lose, Sheriff. To lose everything. Barrie lost his daughter. That was a nice twist of fate. And justice, too. Unplanned, to be sure. His daughter stole the kilo from him. It was intended for sale up north, but she stole it. It was in the car, no doubt intended for a great party. An 'all-nighter,' as they say. I assume the boy who was driving panicked when he saw the lights of the police car in his rearview mirror. Your eager department helped considerably."

"You can't . . ." I said, but he interrupted me.

"Indeed I can. But enough of that. I would think you would be more interested in how we brought the cocaine into the country . . . since this trip is your idea, you must have some notions. I hate to admit that the idea was Barrie's. But I'll give him credit." Sprague almost sounded wistful. "It was novel. It's going to be difficult to replace him, and the others."

Sprague was right . . . it was difficult to concentrate, but a large share of the sickness I felt was revulsion at listening to this man talk about multiple murder as if he were filing fingernails. I remembered Buddy saying that I would feel happy as a clam. I didn't. Of course, Buddy had had no way of knowing what I would be hearing.

"A unique plan," he continued. "I don't know all the technical details. I just fly the big plane." He reached out and patted the panel top. "This one. Perfectly legal flight into Mexico and back. I clear customs, usually at Nogales and Tucson, where they know me. After Tucson, I head for home. Except I make a little change. I change my plan, maybe for a little airport like Cochise. Buzz the runway. If anyone is watching on radar, it looks like I landed. I fly low and hot over the border, back into Mexico. No problem. Are you still following this? And there's my contact point. Straight and level at eighty knots, fifty or sixty feet above the cactus. Up from the ground comes that magnificent little airplane, radio-controlled. My partner, flying with me, takes over from the man on the ground. They call it the 'handoff.' Just like in football. We fly in formation, Sheriff, the

219

small plane just far enough away that it's not affected by the wash from my wings. Nothing on radar, even if they could scan so low. He was good, my partner. Too bad the state police arrested him and a friend last week." Sprague shrugged. "They got careless. But they obviously didn't talk, or I wouldn't be here, would I?" He tapped a dial directly ahead of him. "Anyway, we fly across the border together. No problem. In the radio-controlled model are two, maybe three kilos of uncut cocaine. Not bad. Nothing in my plane, should someone bark at me when I land. Once across the border, the model plane is passed off to another party on the ground with a third transmitter. We use a different location for that each time. He takes the plane and lands it. I fly on to the airport. Nice, huh?"

I shook my head slowly, no longer really caring what Sprague had to say.

"Barrie decided it would be cute to use the old Consolidated Mine. The security guard there, as you no doubt already know, is something less than bright, and was thoroughly enjoying some extra income. The last flight, we came in right at dusk. That's a tricky time, as you are probably well aware. Barrie was on the ground, and took the handoff. I suppose the Salinger boy saw the radio-controlled plane, or heard it, and drove down the road to see it. For whatever reason, Barrie was not able to just ignore his audience. He caught the fence coming in and crashed the plane. Salinger, being the helpful soul that he was, rendered assistance and saw the wrong things. So Barrie shot him. You know the rest."

He looked at me and frowned. "Or at least, if you don't, it doesn't matter, does it?"

I wanted to swear at Sprague, or punch him, or something. But I was gelatin. "You're too persistent, Sheriff," Sprague said. "Reyes, I don't worry about. She jumps when you tell her to jump. And that idiot Holman

is just that. Your illness is convenient, however. I'm
sure it will be another jolt to our little town to have another funeral so soon. But believe me, the jolts haven't
even started, Sheriff. They haven't even started."

I tried several deep breaths, and even that was too
much effort. The giant vise was again constricting my
chest. Sprague's voice was soothing.

"Sixteen thousand feet, Sheriff. That's quite an ac-
complishment for a man as sick as yourself."

Sixteen thousand? A little clear space formed in my
muddled skull. I knew I had to act now. There was no
more time, no more air. And maybe I had waited too
long.

Sprague reached forward and fingered a small
switch. The airplane bumped slightly as the autopilot
disengaged. Sprague's hand was on the yoke, and he
pulled back gently. The aircraft's nose lifted a little more
until we were climbing steeply.

"There's no point in prolonging your agony, Sheriff.
It should be quite peaceful up a little higher."

The urge for self-preservation did wonders. "There
will come a time when you won't be able to lift a finger,"
my son had said. I remembered his exact words. I
turned toward the window, willing every particle of effort to my right hand. It moved, but agonizingly slowly.
The stubby-barreled Magnum was covered by the loose
tail of my sport shirt. I could hardly feel the butt, but
my fingers closed automatically and my thumb pushed
the holster snap. I drew the revolver clumsily. Sprague
watched me, and smiled.

"Incredible," he said.

"Down," I mumbled. "Take it down."

He shook his head, unperturbed. "It would be almost comical if you shot me, Sheriff. This airplane will
do almost anything, but it does require a pilot." He
grinned, and reached down to spin a big wheel low down
in the center console. My peripheral vision was long

gone, and the black walls of the tunnel grew narrow. I wondered if he had thought that all the other deaths were comical. He was looking down at the short barrel, no doubt wondering what small flick of the wrist was necessary to twist the gun from my grip with minimal danger to himself. I didn't have the strength to squeeze the trigger. But at two feet, the bull's-eye was a big one. I didn't need to squeeze. I concentrated on my right index finger, and jerked the trigger. The explosion of the .357 Magnum inside the confines of the airplane was so violent that my vision cleared for a short moment.

Harlan Sprague rose up tall in his seat, mouth wide open. His hands flew off the control yoke and fluttered wildly in the air even as his body sagged forward. His eyes were open and staring as his head slammed down, cracking against the yoke. The Cessna's nose jarred down in response to the weight on the controls. Sprague's arms hung straight down, hands almost touching the floor.

I didn't have any time to congratulate myself. My own tunnel vision narrowed, and the light at the end gradually flickered to gray.

27

Either machine guns or static on the radio jarred me to a form of agonizing consciousness and washed away the gray. My head was ready to split, with pain lancing down between my eyes so savagely my cheek-bones ached. I groaned and tried to move stiff joints. And then I remembered where I was and came fully conscious with a jerk that damn near threw my back out of joint. All the pain suddenly became a source of wonder mixed with relief.

The Centurion was thundering through the blue skies with its left wing slightly low and the nose just barely dipping below the horizon. I could breathe almost comfortably. I rubbed my face and looked over at Harlan Sprague. Blood ran from his nose and mouth. The puddle between his feet was enormous. And then I really woke up. "Son of a bitch," I said aloud. And then added, "Jesus H. Christ." I hated airplanes. I knew nothing about them. The hundred or so dials and switches on the Centurion's dashboard looked me fair in the eye and dared me.

"Shit," I said. It would have been easier to remain unconscious. "Use your head, Gastner," I said, and I leaned over toward Sprague and looked at the controls. The autopilot switch was pretty obvious, and even I

could see the "Off" and "On" designations. I unfastened
the harness that held me and then gently pulled on
Sprague. I was weak as a kitten, but I was ahead of the
rigor, and I managed to pull him back until the controls
were free. The Centurion immediately lifted its nose.

"Shit," I muttered. I yanked Sprague's shoulder harness tight across his bloody shirt and ignored the airplane until I was sure the corpse was going to stay put.
Then I pushed on the yoke, and was pleased to see the
nose drop. I knew that pilots turned the yoke to make
the wings flip-flop, and I experimented. With the plane
at what I thought was level, I snapped the autopilot
switch to "On." The wings stayed level. I released the
yoke. The nose lifted.

"Well, son of a bitch, how the hell do you keep this
thing down!" I shouted. "What the hell good is an autopilot if it doesn't work?" I sat for a minute with my hand
pushing on the yoke. With a little work, I could manage
to keep the Centurion on a mild porpoise through the
skies. My head still pounded, but it felt good to be in
one piece, if only for a little while. I searched and finally
found the little things that had to be fuel gauges. There
was plenty. The airspeed indicator was simple enough. It
told me that I was going about 150 miles an
hour . . . to where, I had no idea. The damn altimeter
was something else. It had three hands. I squinted, then
gave up. What did it matter? I could breathe, and
wasn't in any danger of hitting trees. I guessed something on the order of eight to ten thousand feet, and
what I could figure out from the altimeter agreed.

I looked down. The terrain was an even, scrub-
dotted adobe. I leaned forward and looked at the compass. The needle was pasted just off south at 176
degrees. With my luck, I would be south of the border.
If that was the case, I'd be seeing the bleak inside of a
Mexican prison for the next thousand years if I pulled
off a landing. It'd be tough explaining the corpse. The

Centurion had spiraled down from probably close to seventeen thousand feet, and I had no idea how much air space that took. "Why not north?" I said. Tentatively, I tried turning the yoke to the left. I felt resistance and remember the autopilot. My hand hesitated, but I took the plunge. I snapped off the autopilot switch. Holding my breath, I moved the yoke about a thousandth of an inch. Sure enough, the Centurion turned ever so slightly. "My kind of turn," I said, and then to Sprague's quiet form, "Too bad you can't see this, you miserable bastard." I glanced at the compass. I had 172. "More, Gastner," I said. I was too eager. As I turned the yoke, still pushing forward against the plane's tendency to climb, the left wing dropped smoothly. I overcorrected like an old lady on icy pavement. The Centurion bellowed up and to the right, and I cussed a blue streak. "Go left, you son of a bitch," I said, and wrenched the yoke. The Centurion hauled around toward the north. I fought the airplane for four or five minutes, until I was wet with sweat and my heart was banging a tattoo against my ribs. But I won. I snapped on the autopilot, tried to maintain a constant pressure against the yoke, and looked at the compass. The needle settled on a couple of clicks off north.

I sat very still, letting my system settle down. The vertical speed caught my eye. I was still climbing, and I put more pressure on the yoke. "He didn't do this," I muttered. I looked long enough and eventually saw the label that said something about trim. It was a big wheel on the left side of the center console. I looked at it for a while before I touched it. It was marked so that even an aeronautical idiot like me had a chance . . . "Up" and "Down" nose trim. "Down," I said. I turned the big wheel a little. Not much happened. I turned it some more and almost immediately felt the yoke relax away from my push. I grinned. After several minutes of fussing and experimentation, and with the cooperation of smooth, clear skies and the autopilot, I achieved level flight to the north. I figured out the altimeter and settled for the 9,500 feet that it indicated.

I had no idea where I was, but every flash of the prop had to be taking me closer to friendly skies. I decided to wait. If it ain't broke, don't fix it. I had an airplane humping along at 150 miles an hour a safe distance above the ground, under the intelligent command of diodes and transistors. There was nothing to lose by waiting. At worst, I'd end up in Montana. I knew radios, and when I called someone, I didn't want them coming back at me with frijoles and enchiladas.

I needed to listen to the radio traffic, though. It would help keep my mind off the hollow feeling just behind my breastbone and the pain that had settled into a hard ache from left shoulder to fingertips. The only headset I could see was the one on Sprague. I reached across and pulled it loose, grimacing at the blood that came with it. I wiped off the headset on the edge of the seat and slipped the unit on. There was silence. I looked at the radios. The frequency was digital, and I saw, just above the sets, a switch that said "Com-1" and "Com-2." The top radio was showing 123.6, the other 125.1. The switch said 123.6 was on the air. If that was the case, no one was saying much. I turned the volume up until I heard hissing, and then turned the squelch up to the bark and back. I set the knob at half volume and sat back to wait.

When the voice came, it startled me so badly I jumped. "Great airline pilot," I muttered, and then listened carefully. They talked on the radio with more marbles in their mouths than cops did, but at least it wasn't in Spanish.

"Piper seven niner niner kilo, winds two-five-zero at five, altimeter three-zero-point-six. Traffic is a Cub on downwind for two-six and a Bonanza ten east, inbound."

"Roger, Douglas. We're number two for two-six behind the Cub."

Douglas? The only Douglas I knew was Douglas-Bisbee. My heart skipped a beat with relief—and probably literally, too. I waited another couple of seconds, then reached over and pushed the yoke switch.

"This is Mike Bravo one-seven-eight. Who have I got?"

There was no response, and I repeated the broadcast. This time, the reply was immediate.

"Mike Bravo one-seven-eight, Douglas-Bisbee on one-twenty-three-six."

"Douglas-Bisbee, I need to know where the hell I am," I said, not adding that I needed a good deal more than just location.

"Mike Bravo one-seven-eight, are you transponder-equipped?"

"Whatever that is," I said. "Douglas-Bisbee, I'm not a pilot. The aircraft is currently on autopilot, heading just off north. About zero-one-zero. The pilot is, ah, incapacitated."

There was a stony silence. "Mike Bravo, say altitude."

"About nine thousand."

"Mike Bravo, say airspeed?" He sounded a little skeptical. Maybe it would have helped if I had babbled and screamed, but actually I felt quite proud of myself. I would have felt completely successful if Sprague had been alive and cuffed up in the back, but he had made that decision himself.

"About a hundred fifty."

"Make of aircraft, Mike Bravo."

"Cessna Centurion. I think it's a T-two ten."

"Do you know your fuel situation?"

"Three-quarters, at least."

"Mike Bravo, we need to pick you up on radar. Do you feel secure enough to make turns?"

"Negative. I chased this thing all over the sky to get my present heading. It's flying straight and level now, and that's the way I want it to stay."

This time there was a little humor in the voice. "I bet. Mike Bravo, look just below the radios on the instrument panel. There should be an instrument there with four little digit windows and a small switch on the left side that says something like 'Off-Standby-on-Test' or close thereto."

"Affirmative."

"All right, Mike Bravo, that's the transponder. Is it on?"

"Negative. Now it is."

"What frequency shows in the windows?"

"One-two-zero-zero."

"All right. The small knobs or buttons under each window set the frequency. Give me seven-seven-zero-zero."

I clicked the numbers up. "Did I win?"

"Mike Bravo, you're four-seven miles southeast of the field. We'll want you to navigate straight in. We'll clear traffic."

"Just a minute." I sat back and stared out the window. After a moment's thought, I reached into my travel bag and shook out a couple of my pills. The altimeter said nine thousand feet. I would feel better lower, but I wanted lots of spread between the plane's aluminum belly and the trees and rocks below.

Someone else came on the radio, and my friend sent him to another channel.

"Douglas, things are pretty stable. What heading would I have to fly for Posadas Municipal Airport, New Mexico?"

"Mike Bravo one-seven-eight, that's a heading of zero-six-zero. Approximately one hundred miles from your current position, but I can't recommend that. In fact, we are requesting that you follow our instructions for an emergency landing at Douglas. We can talk you down, no problem."

"That's all right. I appreciate the offer, but I'm going to take Posadas."

"Ah, Mike Bravo, we show you as originally filed out of Posadas for Tucson, and then Nogales. Pilot-in-command is listed as Harlan Sprague, Jr."

"Affirmative. Not anymore." It hadn't taken them long to double-check the aircraft number.

"Mike Bravo, if you are not a pilot, we request that you declare an emergency and use this field. We have someone here current on the Centurion who can talk you down. No problem."

I'm sure you do, I thought. "Negative, Douglas. I'm going to Posadas unless you've got missiles down there you intend to use. How long can you keep me on your radar?"

"At your altitude, most of the way."

"Then do that. And call Posadas Municipal Airport and tell the FBO there I'm inbound. The man's name is James Bergin. What frequency will I use to talk to him?"

"Mike Bravo, tune your top radio to one-twenty-one-five and monitor. Can you do that?"

"Yes. Radios, I'm good at."

"That's the emergency frequency. You'll have all the help you need. We'll be talking to you on that frequency. Tune the second radio—it's probably marked Com-two—to one-twenty-two-eight. That's Posadas, and you can go back and forth between us and them with a flick of the switch up above. Please make that frequency change now."

"Affirmative."

I fiddled with the little push buttons and the correct digits popped on the little screen.

"Mike Bravo, how do you read?"

"Loud and clear," I said.

"Mike Bravo, I would recommend that if possible, you climb and maintain ten thousand. You have some mountain peaks between you and Posadas, and we'll be able to hear you better. We have a pilot here with us who can talk you through that procedure."

"Ah, Douglas, I have a problem with climbing any more. I can't take the altitude." I knew that another thousand feet probably wouldn't make much difference, but I wasn't about to gamble again. The only reason I was still alive was that I had spent twenty years adjusting my system to mile-high climates. I didn't want to increase the point spread.

"Say again, Mike Bravo?"

"This plane is not pressurized. I don't want to go any higher." Hell, tell them, I thought. "I'm a heart patient. I've already gone through one bout of hypoxia. I don't want another."

If the controller was surprised at that, he kept it to himself. All I got was the calm, generic reply, "Roger, Mike Bravo." If I could stay as unflustered as my man on the ground, I'd have it made. Ten seconds of silence followed, and then Douglas-Bisbee said, "Ah, Mike Bravo, we have another aircraft in the area. He's familiar with your two-ten, and he's volunteered to intercept you and fly escort. He should be able to give you any assistance you need. Two-two-one Whiskey Charlie is a Beech Bonanza, and he should be off your right wingtip in another couple of minutes." Even before he finished, I turned and saw the plane a mile or so out and closing. It was single-engined and V-tailed. The pilot sidled the plane to within fifty yards, keeping pace beautifully with my autopilot . . . and just far enough away that he didn't make me nervous. He lifted a hand in salute.

"Mike Bravo, how's it going?"

"Swell," I said. "As long as I don't touch anything, this thing flies just fine."

"It's a bitch, ain't it?" The voice chuckled, and I

liked Whiskey Charlie immediately. "You sound like you have a pretty good handle on things over there."

"Until I run out of gas, I'm fine," I said.

"Well, you're to be commended for keeping your head bolted on straight. As you can see, that airplane flies itself real well. You got gas, I got gas, and we got wonderful weather. Is there any chance the pilot will be able to assist you?"

I glanced at Sprague. "Negative. He's dead."

There was silence for a few seconds. "You're all right, though?"

"Yes."

"All right. Let's get to work, then. About the change in altitude. That's not necessary as long as you don't dink with anything. I read you at about eight thousand seven hundred right now. We'll just stick with that. If you need to climb, we'll worry about that when the time comes."

"Sounds good."

"Do you know how to turn the autopilot off?"

"Affirmative."

"Look at the instrument if you would and tell me what make it is."

"It says 'Four hundred B Navomatic' on it."

"Bingo. Good deal. All right, we're going to use that little gadget to do all the flying . . . even the turn. First, look at the autopilot and see if there's a little toggle switch that says something like ALT. It should be on the right side."

"Ten-four. It's the bottom one of three switches."

"Forget the others. Don't get creative on me. Turn the ALT switch to on."

"Ten-four. It's on. Now what?"

"Now the autopilot is maintaining your altitude for you. Makes life easier. Now, just do what I tell you. And remember this. Most folks make mistakes with airplanes because they try to use brute force. Be gentle.

Do everything in tiny amounts, and smoothly. All right? If I think you really need to horse something, I'll say so, and then use some muscle. Otherwise, fingertip time. You understand me?"

"Affirmative. The old beautiful-woman trick."

"Now you got it. Tweak her gently, son. And by the way, you got any stick time at all?"

"Meaning what?"

"You ever flown? Ever grabbed the wheel?"

"Nope."

"Well, good. No bad habits, son." I glanced over at him when he said that. By God, there was more gray hair over there than on my head. The white mane was visible even at fifty yards. He talked me through the turn . . . it was no more complicated than turning a small knob and turning it back. The Centurion and my escort banked gently and the compass rotated. It wasn't much of a course correction.

"Mike Bravo . . . the hell with that. What's your name, sir?"

"Bill Gastner."

"Bill, you're talkin' to Everett Wheeler. You ever need prize-registered beef, you look me up in the Animas phone directory."

"I'll do that."

"Here's what we need to do, Bill. We need to get that white bullet slowed down. I mean, we got us two planes here that are faster'n a spotted dog caught under a red truck. You can't land at a hundred fifty."

"I knew there was a catch somewhere."

The remains of a chuckle came across when Wheeler keyed the mike. "Now, your man Bergin is going to be talkin' to you in about twenty minutes. By that time, you're going to be a pilot, Bill. And we're going to cut through all the bullshit and only talk about the good stuff. Everything working in that airplane?"

"As far as I know. Everything except the pressurization."

"Last thing we need. You're set fat as a feedlot calf. Now tell me . . . you're sitting there hands and feet off everything, right?"

"Right."

"All right. Don't do anything until I finish the entire sequence. You got that? Don't do a damn thing until I say so. What you're going to do is this. There's three pull handles dead center in the dash, under the radios. I don't remember what color they are in a Centurion, but it don't matter. We're going to get rid of two of them, and you're not going to have to worry about them again. Fair enough?"

"All right."

"The one on the right. Right, Bill. You right-handed?"

"Affirmative."

"Right. Repeat that."

"Right."

"Wave your right hand at me through the window." I did so. "Good. Right. Push that one in so you only have about the width of your index finger."

I looked at the three knobs. The one on the right was red, and beside it, in vertical letters, it said "Mixture." "You want me to push in the mixture knob," I said.

"Affirmative. By God, the boy can read."

I pushed the knob in. There was no change that I could detect. "Done."

"Big fizz, right? We're just going to work our way across. The next one, the one in the middle, is propeller pitch, but you don't need to know that. Just bang that one all the way in. You'll hear a change in engine RPM. Just ignore it."

"Now?"

"Now." I pushed in the black knob. The engine pitch

stepped up slightly. "All right. The autopilot is making any compensation that needs to be made. Just let it work. Time for the left knob. Don't touch it."

"Throttle, you mean."

"That's right. Let me tell you what we're aiming for. We want eighty when you touch down. That's a good speed. And let me tell you something else." I got the impression old Everett Wheeler was enjoying the hell out of my predicament and his chance to be the rescuing angel. "When you fly at eighty, the nose has to be a lot higher than what it is now. That make sense?"

"I'll take your word for it."

"You've seen planes land. Ever notice they got their snouts way up in the air?"

"Yes."

"Well, there's a reason for it and we don't need to go into it here. Just take my word for it and don't panic when the nose comes up. All right?"

"Ten-four."

"To see how slick that autopilot works, here's what I want you to do. Forget any damn gauge except the one for airspeed. Find that one."

"Got it."

"Now. Slowly. Slowly, did I say slowly? Slowly pull the throttle back just a mite at a time, until you got a hundred on the airspeed. Slowly, now."

I wheedled out the throttle. Eventually I heard an RPM change, and equally slowly, the nose of the airplane lifted. "This is easy," I said without keying the mike. One fifty dropped away to one forty, to one thirty, to one twenty, and finally down to approximately a hundred. I took my sweaty hand off the throttle and let the plane plow along with its nose aimed at the clouds many thousands of feet above us.

"She'll fly like that all day, Bill."

"I believe it. I can feel the controls working, though."

"Course you can. A fast airplane flies like water-logged shit at slow speeds. Not enough air going over control surfaces. Now, we can have some fun, Bill." He said that and my palms sprung more leaks. "To the left of the throttle is a funny-lookin' knob that looks like a little black tire."

"The landing-gear selector, you mean."

"Damn, I'm bein' hustled. That's the one. Push it to "Down" and tell me if you got a green light."

"Now?"

"Now."

"We're nowhere near Posadas, are we?"

"Who gives a damn. Do it anyways."

I did, and all sorts of thuds and aircraft motion ensued. "Shit," I muttered, and then the plane settled down. Out the window, I saw the right main gear hinge into place.

"You got three. By God, you do good work, Bill. Still pegged at a hundred?"

I looked at the airspeed and my heart skipped a beat. "No. Below that."

"Right. You got some drag now. And the nose is a little higher. But look at that altitude." I did so. "Right where it started, ain't it?"

"Yes."

"Right. Now let's go for the rest of the show." I didn't have time to protest. "To the right of the throttle, prop, and mixture knobs is a funny-lookin' thing that's supposed to look like the trailing edge of a wing. The flap selector."

"I see it."

"Push it down to the first notch."

I did so and Centurion humped like someone had kicked it in the belly. "Altitude ain't changed none, has it?" Everett asked, and didn't wait for an answer. "Now the nose did a little, but who the hell cares if you ain't goin' down? Right?"

"I suppose."

"One more click down. We want twenty degrees of flaps."

"One more notch?"

"Right."

"Now?"

"Now." I did, and felt out of control. "Bill, you're doin' good. You ain't dropped an inch . . . and who the hell cares what the nose is doin' if you ain't goin' down. I said that before. Now, back on that throttle. I want exactly eighty on that airspeed. Not seventy-nine. Not eight-one. Give me the big eight-zero. So do it slowly, boy."

I didn't realize I was holding my breath until around eighty-four. At that point, I had to take my hand off the throttle and relax back, sucking air. "A little more," Everett prompted, and like a chastised pupil, I went back at it. Eventually, I had eighty. I have visions of the Centurion looking like a big white duck about to splat into a pond. Its nose was high, flaps hanging down, feet groping for the ground. "Ain't she pretty?" Everett said, and I tried to relax. "Just sit back and watch," he coached. "That's what she's going to be like comin' in over the end of the runway at Posadas. When you pass over the end, what do you think you're going to do?"

"I don't think I'll be alive for that," I said, only half-kidding. "Pray a lot, if I am."

"That too. But think throttle. Just ease back on the throttle. And did you ever drive a go-cart? Something that steers with pedals?"

"Sure."

"That's how an airplane steers on the ground. Those two big pedals on the floor. And be gentle. No big movements. Now, put your feet on the rudder pedals."

"All right."

"Now, don't push the pedals. The tops of the pedals

are the brakes. Tip your toes and push the brakes. Both at the same time. Feel them? That's the tricky part. Brakin' without putting differential pressure on the steering. Just kind of bear that in mind. You don't want to see-saw the pedals. Go easy. Better to coast off the end than go cartwheelin', my boy."

"I'll remember that."

"You ready for a little test?"

"No."

"We'll do it anyway. You see the Off-On button on the autopilot?"

"Yes."

"That autopilot has the airplane all trimmed for you. I want you to put your hands on the yoke and feet on the pedals. When you're set, I want you to reach over with your left hand and snap off the autopilot. And then, try for as little control input as you can. If the nose starts to drop, gentle back. Nose up, gentle forward. Right wing drops, left, and so on. When I tell you to turn the auto on, do it. Right? Go ahead."

I looked at that Off-On switch for a while, then reached over and snapped it off. The Centurion continued as smooth as silk for about ten seconds, then the left wing began to drop. I turned the yoke and then found myself sawing back and forth. "Auto on," Everett barked in my ear. I did and the electronic brain took over.

"Good work," Everett said, but I didn't share his enthusiasm. "You didn't believe me when I said 'gentle,' did you? You got to be gentle. Let's go back up to speed. Just do things in reverse order. Flaps, gear, then throttle. Autopilot is on, so let it do all the work. Go ahead."

This isn't going to work, I thought as I went through the sequence. Soon enough, we worked back to 150, but we were also a nice, safe half mile above the ground. I thought about the rocky approach to Posadas, over the low mesa top. And then I glanced over at Harlan Sprague's corpse. "You aren't going to win," I said aloud to my silent passenger. I keyed the mike.

"Let's try it again, Everett."

28

I didn't have long to dwell on any misgivings. In what seemed like only a handful of minutes, I recognized Animas Peak ahead and to the right. Then we started down. It was as easy as punching off the "Altitude Hold" button on the autopilot and retarding the throttle. This time, as Wheeler joyfully pointed out, airspeed remained constant and altitude changed.

"Give me a car anytime," I said after we had descended to an even eight thousand feet on the altimeter.

"You just stick with me," Everett Wheeler said, and then Jim Bergin's voice interrupted us.

"Gastner, this is Posadas Unicom. How do you read?"

"Loud, clear, and nervous," I said.

"He's doin' fine," Wheeler cheered. "Two-two-one this is Whiskey Charlie on escort. We're at eight thousand, twenty-five southwest. Winds permitting, he'll be straight in for six."

"Roger, Whiskey Charlie. Winds are light and variable. Take six. There's a lot of room at the end for overrun. Make sure he doesn't come in low. The mesa edge is about one hundred yards before the runway threshold."

"Roger, Posadas. Bill, you ignore all that and just

do what I tell you. Right now, go through the procedure for slow flight. Autopilot on, altitude hold on, throttle to a hundred, gear, flaps, throttle back to eighty. Got that?"

"Ten-four."

"All right. Now, I just want you loafing along, with the autopilot doing all the work. Don't get fancy and decide to do something on your own. Go for it, son."

I ran through the procedure more quickly and expelled a loud breath as the plane once more settled at eighty and held altitude. "I need to go down and take a quick look at this airport, Bill. I'm going to buzz 'em and be right back. You all don't go anywhere, you hear?"

The Bonanza peeled off just as they do in war movies. "Bill, is there anything I can do for you?" It was Bergin.

"Get Estelle Reyes out there."

"She's already here. So is Sheriff Holman and a couple guys who look like feds. And some spectators."

"You ought to be charging admission. Put Detective Reyes on." There was a moment of silence.

"Reyes here."

"Estelle, I've got a tape that I hope caught my conversation with Harlan Sprague before our little, ah, altercation. I'm going to leave it in the machine, in my flight bag, for protection. It's right in front of my seat. Make goddamn sure that you get it if something happens during the landing."

"Ten-four. Sprague's dead, sir?"

"Affirmative."

"Do you want me to record some kind of statement?"

Optimistic gal, I thought. "I don't think that's necessary. Sprague was the end of it. The tie-in was Barrie, and the two most recent couriers were the jerks that the state police caught earlier. They were bringing in cocaine by radio-controlled airplane. Not much at a time . . . a kilo or two, maybe three. But enough to make a few souls rich and seed the ground, so to speak. Sprague was just in it to ruin some lives. The tape is important because it will clear me of a possible homicide charge. It will show that Sprague was guilty of assault with a deadly weapon."

"He pulled a gun on you in the airplane?"

"No. He pulled the airplane on me."

There was silence, and then Estelle said, "Good luck, sir."

"He don't need no luck," Everett Wheeler said, his voice loud in my ears. At the same time I caught my first glimpse of the narrow ribbon of asphalt that was Posadas County Airport, Wheeler said, "You remember how to make that autopilot turn that airplane, Bill?"

"Yeah, I remember."

"Then give me a slow one to the left until your nose is pointing right down that runway out there." That part seemed easy, because the ground was still distant and soft. "Now punch altitude hold off and pull back a little throttle so you descend to seven thousand."

Hills rose on either side of us, and I tried my best to ignore them. At seven thousand, Wheeler called for altitude hold again, plus a little throttle. "You've got a little drift to the left, Bill. Give me just a hair of a turn. That's it. Let that autopilot earn its keep. Don't let that ground upset you. You got to be close to it to walk on it, remember." My eyes were riveted to the asphalt far ahead of me. The feedlot corrals passed underneath, the mini-mall, the neighborhood where Estelle Reyes lived. "Altitude hold off, doing fine," Wheeler said crisply. "Light touch with the feet on the rudder pedals. Let auto do it." The last few thousand feet were a blur. The Centurion settled out of the sky, and it seemed to me there was a point when it turned to lead. Pavement flashed under me. "Autopilot off," Wheeler snapped, and I flipped the switch and then concentrated on not upsetting the delicate balance the autopilot had established. One wing began to dip, and I corrected too little, then too much. Wheeler said loudly, "Back hard on the yoke, throttle off. Back, hard. Hard."

The Centurion was crabbed sideways when the main wheels hit the runway well to the right of the center line, with the wing desperately low. The first touchdown was feather-light, and then, as I tried to haul back on the yoke, the full weight slammed down. The plane swung hard to the right, and I stood on the brakes. The right main gear slid off the asphalt and dug sand, increasing the slew even more. Something snapped, and the plane lunged and tore around in a wild pinwheel. One wingtip gouged the dirt and then 178 Mike Bravo slid and crunched to a stop, facing back toward Douglas-Bisbee, belly in the dirt between runway and taxi strip.

I sat motionless, eyes closed. I did remember to unlatch the door before the first vehicle and the pounding feet reached the aircraft. After that, I didn't see much point in paying attention to anything or anyone. My system's own autopilot switch tripped, and I sailed off into a smooth, gray fog of peace and quiet.

29

The week that followed was rougher than my landing in Sprague's Centurion, but it passed. Faces came and went—including one that belonged to my pilot son. I wasn't up to much talking, with all the tubes and medication. I managed a wan smile when he talked about my landing technique, and that's about all I remembered.

No doubt with relish, Dr. Perrone and his imported sidekick Robert Gonzales went to work the day after the crash. They managed a quadruple bypass, and I managed to survive it. Their prediction was that I'd feel like a man of forty after a suitable recuperation. Perrone stressed the word "suitable."

I guess they expected me to worry some, but I didn't . . . not about my health, anyway. I figured that would take care of itself. My visitors came and went frequently as time passed, including Sheriff Martin Holman. He spent a lot of time, I found out later, talking with my doctors. The portrait of an old, gray-haired, potbellied ex-cop kept nagging me. I spent some long hours trying to decide what I'd do when Holman made his announcement . . . I didn't push him for it, but I didn't figure he'd forget. And the hollow feeling continued to grow as I realized there was nowhere I wanted to go, nothing else I wanted to do. Hell, I didn't even drink much. I couldn't even look forward to being a permanently buzzed alcoholic.

Ten days after the surgery, I was up and dressed. I looked pretty good, missing about twelve pounds of belly fat and several inches of clogged coronary tubing. It was a Sunday, and I was scheduled for release the next morning, if I behaved myself. I sat by the window, reading the Sunday paper. A light rap on the door brought my head up. Martin Holman stood there, dressed to kill in his polished linen suit.

"Come on in," I said. I stood up without too much of a grunt and folded the paper.

"I understand you'll be sprung tomorrow," Holman said. I gestured at one of the hard plastic-covered chairs, and he sat down carefully.

"The big day," I said and smiled.

"Your son was pissed at you, you know that?"

"I got that impression." I shrugged. "Everything worked out.

"He mentioned that you and he discussed the possibility of hypoxia."

I looked at Holman, surprised. "He mentioned it, yes."

"But you didn't bother to take along any oxygen." Holman frowned. "I mean, if you suspected Sprague, couldn't you have snuck a little canister along or something?"

"I suppose. I didn't think about it. To tell you the truth, I didn't expect Sprague to do what he did. The notion never occurred to me." I grinned sheepishly. "My son was worried, and I told him that Sprague might pull a gun, but that I was faster. Then, my son went through this spiel about warning signs and all. But everything turned out all right. Sprague didn't leave me much choice."

Holman shook his head slowly, then took a deep

breath. "Listen, I wanted to shoot something past you. See what you thought."

"Shoot," I replied, less eager to hear it than I sounded.

"I think a more formally structured department might do us some good. There's a county meeting tomorrow, and I think now is the time to put the question to them."

"More formally structured how?"

"Well, for one thing, Estelle Reyes works her little buns off, and except for you and some uniformed assistance, she's pretty much solo. I know we're no big county, but our location helps my argument. Everyone's worried about border drug traffic. That puts us in a strategic position to join the twentieth century."

"What are you proposing?"

"How would you feel about giving Reyes sergeant rank? Assuming she passes the test and all."

"Sure. Way overdue."

"That would start it. What I want is three detectives. That way, we have one every shift, and we can double up if need be. One detective sergeant and two plainclothes officers."

"You're talking about making the department a third bigger, right off the bat."

"That's right. I have some feelers out for federal grants. Money's there, if we go for it. The publicity is on our side." He grinned. "You made sure of that with that grandstand play of yours. I say now is the time."

"Good move, Sheriff," I said.

Holman looked at me with a half-smile. "You and Estelle made us look real good, Bill. The feds are going to be talking about this for a long time."

"Well, Sprague and Barrie weren't exactly bringing in truckloads, Sheriff. They weren't big time."

"No. But the damage was being done, nevertheless. Anyway, I didn't stop by to rehash the case. I knew you'd be out tomorrow, and my guess was that you'd stop by the office. I'll be at the county meeting all morning. I wanted you to know what I was up to."

"I appreciate that."

"Just good politics, Bill. Good politics." He thumped the thin chrome arms of the chair with the heels of his hands and got up. "Well, got to go. Sergeant Reyes said she'd be up later this afternoon."

"I'll be here."

"You planning to take a little vacation before getting back in the saddle for good?"

I shrugged casually. "Ah, maybe a little later. When things slow down a little."

Holman grinned and opened the door. "Say, in about five or ten years, right?"

I laughed, more with relief than anything else, although I'm sure Martin Holman didn't know that. "That's what I was thinking," I said. "Or fifteen."

"Go for it," Sheriff Holman said, and damned if he didn't sound as if he meant it. He left, and I sat down to finish the paper, feeling good. The Travel section caught my eye. None of the vacation spots looked as welcome to me as Posadas County.